By Cecy Robson

The Shattered Past Series

Once Perfect
Once Loved
Once Pure

The O'Brien Family Novels

Once Kissed
Let Me
Crave Me
Feel Me

The Carolina Beach Novels

Inseverable
Eternal (coming soon)
Infinite (coming soon)

The Weird Girls

A Curse Awakened (novella)
The Weird Girls (novella)
Sealed with a Curse
A Cursed Embrace
Of Flame and Promise
A Cursed Moon (novella)
Cursed by Destiny
A Cursed Bloodline
A Curse Unbroken
Of Flame and Light
Of Flame and Fate (coming soon)

Feel Me

An O'Brien Family Novel

Cecy Robson

"Phenomenal - a top read of the year! From the first page of the first book this author, and this series, grabbed my attention, and my heart!" – **Nerdy Dirty & Flirty**

"I love her characters, her topics, the emotion and the romance. She always manages to snag me in with her stories..." – **Rainy Day Ramblings**

"It is with eager anticipation and excitement that I pick up every read by [Cecy] Robson...She truly is a talented writer that never ceases to amaze me with her words." – **My Guilty Obsession**

"Cecy Robson always writes such brilliant characters..." – **Feeling Fictional**

"Ms. Robson's books don't come with easy endings. It's why I love her work." – **Under the Covers Book Blog**

"Cecy Robson will once again play your emotions like a concert pianist in her latest novel in the O'Brien Family series." - **Heroes and Heartbreakers**

"Once again, a new Cecy Robson book wrecked my plans for a productive weekend. Let Me made me laugh, cry, and squirm in my seat (in a good way)–sometimes all at once."- **Teri Anne Stanley, Author of Accidentally in Love with the Biker and Drunk on You**

"Cecy Robson does it again! Super sexy MMA fighter Finn O'Brien really knows how to deliver a punch...but it's what happens outside the ring that will really knock you out! Finn and Sol will have you swooning in your ringside seat!" **-Anne Marie Walker, Author of the Chasing Fire Trilogy**

"...hands down my favorite book of [Cecy Robson's]" **-JB's Book Obsession**

DEDICATION

To R for her knowledge and her heart.

ACKNOWLEDGMENTS

This was a challenge, not simply because of the subject matter Declan and Melissa faced, but because of who they were when they faced it and who they became because of it.

To those who can relate to Declan and Melissa, this is for you. I hope I honored you and did you justice.

To Nic, who suggested I give Melissa a quirk. May shirtless pirates and studly Scots be forever in your future.

To Jamie, who always loved this story, and who showed me just how beautiful these characters could be.

To Gaele, who "really liked these two." You were right. Thank you for allowing them into your heart.

And to Kim, for all the support, hard work, and enthusiasm. I owe you a box of truffles.

CHAPTER 1

Melissa

I stare at the name plate perched on my father's desk: *District Attorney Miles Fenske*. It proclaims his position, allowing those who read it a glimpse of what he's accomplished. Yet it's only a glimpse. It's not a true representation of all he is or all he means to me. The name plate is cheap, unlike the generous soul who looks back at me with the same gentle gaze he's carried since the first moment I saw him. *What are you thinking, Melissa?* He signs to me, moving his hands in beautifully fluid motions.

We're alone in his office. He doesn't need to sign to keep our conversation private. He could whisper, and I would still be able to read his lips. But he knows I'm more comfortable communicating with my hands, probably because American Sign Language is one of the many things we learned together. As a child, I considered it our very own secret language, something he and I could share away from the hearing world.

That you're making a mistake, I sign back.

My comment earns me a smile, but I can see his concern, despite the crinkles around his eyes that deepen when he grins. "You're going to have to trust me," he says aloud.

I let out a breath. He knows I trust him. How could I not?

I was brought to the Lehigh Valley District Attorney's

office when I was about six years old, after my biological mother had attempted to sell me in exchange for drugs. My mother probably thought it was a brilliant plan. Being born with profound hearing loss, I couldn't speak or communicate, and there was much I didn't understand. I wouldn't be able to tell anyone what happened. Not that I didn't know it was wrong.

My primal instincts ordered me to run, that I was in danger, so I did—thank God I did. I kicked and fought, dodging the hands trying to grab me, scurrying out a window and onto the fire escape.

To this day, I remember the way the cold metal grating felt against my bare feet, and how I struggled to form what I thought were words as I banged on my elderly neighbor's window. Miss Lena, the lady with too many cats and twice as many grandchildren, yanked me into her apartment when she saw me. She called the police, but by the time they arrived, my mother was gone.

I never saw her again, not that I regret it.

My eyes sting as I look to my father. My mother's actions were horrific. Her callousness still haunts me. But my escape forced her from my life and led me to this wonderful man who's only ever shown me kindness.

I was placed in foster care, confused and frightened about what was happening and certain I'd eventually return "home." Instead, I was brought before the young Assistant D.A. Miles Fenske. He was supposed to handle my case, dispose of it, and move on. He was never supposed to welcome me into his heart. Yet he did.

"Melissa," he says. His words aren't clear—not as clear as they can be. My hearing aids can only do so much, but I hear enough to sense the emotion in the way he speaks my name. "Why are you so sad?"

I raise my chin. "Declan O'Brien will never be the man you are. He's not the right D.A. for this position." I shake my head. "He belongs in the Trial Unit, Arson, Fugitive, anywhere else but where you've placed him."

"I know you don't like him . . ."

I raise my brows.

". . . and that your interactions with him haven't always been positive . . ."

"That's because he was an asshole," I mumble.

He chuckles. "I assure you, he never meant to offend you and deeply regrets his actions. Declan is smart, resourceful, and kind."

I don't agree. Not completely. Is Declan intelligent? Brilliantly so, and absurdly astute in court. With short wavy blond hair and a dashing grin that lights his blue eyes, he's also gorgeous and he knows it. My problem is, he probably knows I know it, too.

As far as being kind . . . I don't know. I just don't know about him. "He'll never be the man you are," I repeat.

"I'm not asking him to be. I simply want the best person for the job, someone who will help the victims who need him most."

"That's what you claim. But he doesn't have experience handling delicate cases where offenders often inflict irreparable trauma."

"No, but as the head of Victim Services, you do," he offers with a knowing grin.

My nails dig into the wooden armrests. "If you're trying to hook us up, I'm going to be seriously mad at you."

The edges of his mouth curve. "I'm only asking you to help Declan as he transitions into his new role. This new assignment won't be easy on him."

"Because he doesn't want it. He wants to be the head of Homicide." I stand with my hands out, pleading. "Daddy, please reassign him. The Sexual Assault and Child Abuse Unit is not where someone who seeks glory belongs."

My voice trails as I catch a glimmer of his pain. "Daddy?"

At once, he grimaces, his face flushing red only to grow alarmingly pale. I race around his desk, clutching his shoulders to keep him upright.

Perspiration gathers along his receding hairline as he presses his hand to his side. It's only because he lifts his bowed head and a healthier shade of pink flushes his cheeks that I'm not screaming for help and dialing 911. "Daddy?"

He offers me a weak smile and pats my arm. "I'm all right," he says, leaning back in his chair.

"No, you're not," I say, my throat tightening. His light blue dress shirt clings with sweat along his arms and plump midsection. He's not well. My father is . . . *sick*. "What aren't you telling me?"

His hand slowly eases away from his side, his eyes scanning my face as they've done a thousand times throughout my life. "The doctors discovered new tumors along my colon," he finally says. "They're planning to resection my bowel and dispose of the affected area with the hope of avoiding chemo this time."

Very carefully, I straighten. My heartbeat slows to a dull thud, and my legs feel unsteady. I want to cry, and maybe scream, but nothing comes except that awful silence that accompanies bad news.

My father was diagnosed with colon cancer years ago and barely survived the aggressive treatment. If it's returned, now that he's older, and not as healthy . . .

"When were you going to tell me?" I ask, my fear worsening my speech impediment and causing the words to spill in shaky spurts.

He sighs. "Friday, over dinner."

To give me the weekend to absorb it, no doubt. "And your surgery? When is that?"

"A few weeks." He frowns as if debating what to say. "I'll be out of commission for a while. In my absence, Declan will lead the office as acting District Attorney." He looks at me then. "I need you to help him, Melissa. Regardless of your feelings toward him, you have to help him."

Declan

"This isn't where I fucking belong."

I'm beyond pissed, and spent the last hour typing my resignation letter. Each version I drafted ranged from a polite no thank you to a professional fuck you. I deleted each one. As much as I don't want to head the Sexual Assault and Child Abuse Unit, I'm not a quitter.

"Fuck," I mumble, pinching the bridge of my nose. "*Fuck.*"

My brother Curran crosses his arms over his chest, not caring how it creases the shirt of his Philly PD uniform. Curran doesn't care about shit like that. He would perform official duties in jeans if given the choice. "It's still a promotion, Deck," he says. "You got this D.A. spot straight out of law school and have made more of a name for yourself than most douche-bag attorneys ever will." He holds out a hand. "No offense to the douche-bag attorneys of the world."

"That's my point. After all I've accomplished, I should be leading Homicide."

I shove away from my desk and pace. When Miles gave me these new digs, I thought it was the start of all the good things coming my way. When he assigned me a county car and personal assistant, it reinforced that my hard work had paid off. I was on my way, until I wasn't.

"I spent months dismantling a mafia empire, Curran."

"I know," he says. "I was there."

"I brought down a major crime boss—and another one after that."

"Yup. Saw that, too," he agrees.

"*And* I received international attention for putting the Kensington Strangler away for twelve consecutive life terms. All that work, all that sacrifice, for what? To be shoved someplace I don't belong."

"Why don't you think you belong there?"

Out of my five brothers, Curran is probably the biggest ball-buster. Wren, our sister, is a close second. But he's not messing with me now. He's dead serious.

"Do you want to hear about babies being beaten or women dragged into alleys and raped? Day in and day out?" I ask. "These are the cases I'm going to be dealing with."

"Someone has to do it, Deck. It's the right thing."

"I'm not saying it isn't. I'm only saying I'm not the man

for this job. These low-life assholes shouldn't be allowed to breathe the same air as us."

"Is this about Finnie?" He huffs when I straighten and don't answer. "Christ," he mutters. "I suppose it's about Wren, too."

Just like that, my brother nails it on the head. For all he sometimes pisses me off, Curran isn't stupid. "Finnie didn't deserve what happened to him," I say, my anger burning down to my gut. "And neither did Wren."

"Of course they didn't," Curran snaps. "No one does. But as their brother, you owe it to them to put these pricks away."

I sit back in my chair and rub my jaw. "I don't know if I can."

Our youngest brother was sexually assaulted by a neighbor when he was ten. It screwed with his mind, and despite his jokes and his good days, those demons he buried deep came close to killing him. Yeah, we knew he was in trouble and tried to get him help. But we weren't enough, and spent too many sleepless nights waiting for that call that told us he was gone. Finnie . . . he fought his way through it like the brawler he is. We thought we were going to be okay. But after what happened to Wren, it's like all of us took a step back right into hell.

"Shit," I mutter, leaning back in my office chair.

Nothing bad was supposed to happen to Finnie. He was the baby. The one who counted on us. And Wren, as the only girl in a family with seven kids, she was supposed to be safe from harm. But she wasn't, even with six hulking brothers ready to step in if anyone tried to fuck with her.

With this new assignment—hearing stories like Finnie's on a regular basis? Talking to women who'd been abused—God damn it. Wren *and* Finnie just barely survived and the rest of us barely survived right along with them.

"I don't think I can do this," I say yet again.

"Deck, you have to, man."

A knock to the door interrupts us. I know who it is before I even ask. "Come in," I say, assuming my attorney pose because for now, I have to. For now, I'm a professional. Even if all the Philly boy in me wants to do is rage.

My boss, Miles Fenske walks in, followed by his daughter Melissa. Miles smiles warmly, nodding my way.

Mel? What can I say? She's the one person who's never been taken by my charm. Today's no different. Unlike the other women who work here, from interns to attorneys, she doesn't meet me with a grin, flash a little leg, or pretend to flirt. Her hair is brown and her eyes are almost as dark. Nothing extraordinary about her appearance, right?

Damn, I wish that were true. Her creamy skin makes her hair and eyes stand out, as if that killer hourglass figure isn't enough. And don't get me started on her lips. They look like they've been dipped in honey and soften her look further, despite her steel-hard exterior.

She walks in with her hips swinging, her bright red dress hugging her curves. With an unyielding stare she meets my eyes, giving nothing away, no matter how hard I've chipped at that armor.

Mel doesn't like me. Not that I blame her considering the way I keep wrecking each rare moment we find ourselves alone. Of course, she has to be the one woman I can't get out of my mind . . .

"How are you, Declan?" Miles asks.

I reply with a stiff nod rather than the grin I usually offer him. This is a man I admire the hell out of. Not just because of what he's accomplished in the political arena and in the judicial circuit, but because he's a good man. Not someone *trying* to be good. Just someone who is, a rare entity in the circles we frequent.

Today that smile is not going to happen. Whether he meant to or not, the old man screwed me. Yesterday, when he called me into his office, I thought it was to tell me I would head Homicide or maybe White Collar. SACU was not where I expected to land, ever.

"I'm well, Miles. And you?" I ask. Pissed or not, I won't disrespect him, especially in front of his daughter.

"Fine. Thank you," he responds. His deep voice is pleasant as always, but for some reason Melissa bristles. As her father looks to Curran and shakes his hand, my eyes trail to her.

"Mel," I say, adding a subtle tilt of my chin. It's not much of a greeting, but it's more than she's ever offered me. I don't think she's ever smiled in my presence. But it's not like I don't deserve it. Hell, I still cringe when I think about the first time we met, and every moment that followed.

"Declan," she replies. Her voice is clear enough to understand, but similar to those with significant hearing loss. Miles mentioned she learned to speak late in life, and that she articulates in the way she hears others. But her voice isn't what gives me pause.

This is the first time she hasn't addressed me by my title.

Miles laughs at something Curran says before Curran turns and lifts his hand. "Gotta run. See youz later."

"Later, Curran," I say. I keep my attention on Melissa, motioning for her and Miles to sit as I resume my professional pose.

Curran grins at Melissa. Before she can take a seat, he signs something I don't understand. Whatever it is brings out a smile I've never managed to stir. She signs in return, her reply making him laugh out loud.

I don't have to guess they're talking about me, because that's what they do. The hard stare I toss my brother's way is enough to let him know today is not the day to piss me off. He winks and grins anyway since sometimes, no matter what, Curran could give a damn.

Miles waits for Curran to shut the door behind him before speaking. "So, from what I've gathered, SACU isn't the unit you expected to lead," he begins.

"No," I agree. "Head of Homicide is the position I've always sought. You've known that since I was first sworn in." I'm all about being professional. But professional doesn't equate to pussy.

Melissa's attention cuts to her father, every speck of her gorgeous face reflecting her disappointment. She knows SACU is the last place I want to be. It's also the last place she wants me.

Miles maintains his pleasant demeanor, but he's not a pussy either. "I want the best attorneys I have to run SACU and Homicide. That's you and Zabrinski." He considers me for a moment. "It's only fair to tell you that for the time being, Zabrinski isn't stepping down as Head of Homicide."

None of this makes sense. Zabrinski's been talking about retiring for as long as I've known him. He told me last week he's putting his house on the market. As soon as it sells, he's moving to Florida where he and his wife built a house along the coast. "Why?"

"He's staying on as a favor to me," Miles explains, all traces of his smile gone. "I'm taking a leave of absence in the coming weeks. I need Zabrinski where he is and you in SACU until he steps down."

"Are you saying my assignment in SACU is temporary?" I keep my tone even, unsure where he's headed. Miles could have told me all this shit yesterday when the new assignments were given instead of letting me stew in my rage.

"It can be whatever you want it to be," Miles answers. "The choice is yours. During my absence you'll be assigned as acting D.A."

Holy shit.

"I know it's a lot to ask to head a unit you're new to, and run the office. But I know I can count on you and that you're up for the challenge."

He's not asking me if I want the promotion. He's handing it to me, believing I'll take it.

He's right.

He motions to Mel. "Melissa will work with the victims of each case you're assigned, as well as continue to run the victim services division statewide. Chief Lee will manage his detectives and any matters involving law enforcement personnel, and Shayleen will see to the non-legal staff as their duties have always required."

So business as usual minus Miles, and with me front and center. "Is the governor aware of your plans?" I ask, trying to gauge what he's giving me versus what she knows.

"She is. And if you prove yourself like I know you will,

she'll back you as D.A. when my term is up and swear you in should I step down."

Everything grounds to a halt as I latch onto those last three words he said. "Why would you step down?"

Melissa glances down at her hands when he doesn't answer right away. Now I know this offer isn't good despite the silver platter he's serving it on.

"I may be leaving the public sector earlier than I intended." He shrugs. "After a lifetime of serving, it may be time."

Before his term is up? No way. Miles Fenske is one of the hardest working men I know. He's either being asked to leave, which is impossible if he's calling the shots, or he *can't* stay.

My neck tenses in that way it always does when I know shit's going downhill fast. Without actually saying it, Miles is handing me everything I've wanted. I should be losing my damn mind. But I can't. Something's really wrong here.

Miles maintains his cool demeanor, and although Mel's trying not to give anything away, I can tell she's upset. I take a good look at her. No . . . she's not upset.

Her heart is breaking right in front of me.

"What's going on?" I ask.

The corners of his mouth tilt. "I'm giving you the chance to take over. After the years I've spent grooming you, I think you're ready."

"I meant with you." My attention skips to Melissa since Miles is holding back. As always, she adds another coat of mortar to that wall she's built around herself. But this time I see it, a crack in that protection she keeps so firmly in place. She's seconds from losing it.

I meet Miles square in the face. "Are you sick?" I ask.

His stance grows rigid. In the silence that follows he takes a moment to gather his words. He doesn't want to tell me. But I need answers and no one is leaving until I have them.

"I have cancer," Miles answers me simply. "I have to make sure this office is taken care of, no matter what happens."

CHAPTER 2

Melissa

He said it. The "C" word.

In his office, he wasn't so blunt. But Dad has always been gentle when it comes to me. With Declan he plays the role of the unflinching D.A., ready to face any problem dead on.

Like it doesn't bother him.

Like this is simply the way life is.

Like it's not killing his little girl on the inside.

Declan doesn't give anything away in his features. He doesn't have to. His silence is enough to show me he's stunned. I'll take stunned. It means he's human and not secretly celebrating the possibility of becoming the youngest D.A. in Pennsylvania's history.

I fiddle with my hands, almost wishing he'd jumped for joy. It would give me another reason not to like him. It would also prove to Dad he's not the right man for my unit.

"I'm sorry," Declan says.

He had to go and say that, the way his words slip from his mouth carrying the weight of his worry. He doesn't think Dad is coming back.

I'm not sure he is either.

The burn in my chest expands the longer Dad remains silent, filling the space with fear and more than its share of sadness. This is the part where he's supposed to assure Declan and me that he'll be fine. But he doesn't, his silence causing my next breath to release in a painful shudder.

Declan knows I'm not taking the news well and spares me by keeping his focus on Dad.

"Things often happen that can't be helped," Dad offers. "I'm trying to control those things I can. This is why I want you to take charge when the time comes." He offers a small smile. "If the time comes."

Declan steeples his fingers, his focus flitting to me. "I see," he says.

A glimpse of his concern pushes through his professional persona. It's not much, just a hint of what lurks beneath the man the staff appear to bow before, but I appreciate it more than I can explain. Kindness is something my father desperately needs and coming to terms with his diagnosis is just the start. I realize as much, just as I realize I really need it, too.

God, I'm so raw. It's taking all I have not to cry. I'm picturing what would have happened if Dad had told me at dinner like he'd planned. It would have hurt, and I would have cried those thick awful tears I hate shedding. But to witness how much pain he's enduring made this nightmare more real. As it is, I can't shake the image of his paling skin. It's like a part of him died as I held him.

"Who else knows?" Declan asks. His tone is so low, if I weren't reading his lips, I would have missed what he said.

Dad's voice remains steady. But then, he's had time to absorb the news and set a plan in motion. "The governor, the chief, and now you," he answers.

"So only those who need to know," Declan infers. At Dad's nod, he tilts his chin. "Then that's how it will stay until you choose to disclose it."

Dad nods in a way that indicates he's done talking. He stands, appearing to struggle. I hurry to help him, but think better of it. My father is a proud man. I can't let him lose face, especially now.

"I'm sorry," Declan says again, seemingly forcing himself to remain seated and not help. Like me, he recognizes Dad doesn't want to be perceived as weak.

"Don't be sorry," Dad tells him. "Just do right by me when the time comes."

I start to leave with Dad, but the look he tosses me holds me in place. "I'll leave you two to talk," he says.

In other words, stay here and play nice. "All right," I answer. I lift up on my toes to kiss his cheek, trying to keep it together and push aside the thought that our goodbyes may be numbered. "See you later. Okay?"

He smiles like always and pats my upper arm, like my world hasn't stopped spinning and he isn't as sick as he is. *Be strong*, he signs.

I'm not so sure if I can, Daddy.

I watch him leave, keeping my back to Declan until I think I'm ready to face him and not fall apart at his feet. I return to the chair directly in front of him and cross my legs, waiting for him to speak.

Maybe he's waiting for me to speak, because we end up sitting in silence longer than necessary, doing little to ease the strain that has existed between us since the first moment we met.

I start to question which victims he'd like me to reach out to first when he asks, "What did Curran say to you?"

"What?"

"Curran, my brother," he says a little louder. "What did he say to you?"

I don't mean to become defensive, but it's hard not to with Declan and his talent for saying all the wrong things to me at all the worst times. "I know who he is," I reply.

"I know. I just wasn't sure if you heard—" He grimaces as if in pain. "I don't mean because you *can't* hear—I would have asked anyone that question—anyone who said 'what' like you did." He passes his hands along his face, mumbling something under his breath that I don't catch. "Never mind."

I blink back at him with my jaw unhinged. Good Lord in

heaven, *this* is the man I'll be working with. And it's barely our first day together!

"I heard you," I say, trying to remain calm. "Your question just caught me off guard, because—" I shut my mouth. I don't want to admit that I expected him to say something about Dad because I don't want to cry, especially in front of Declan.

My hand skims across my lap and I hurry to compose myself. "He told me he liked my dress."

"Your dress?" he questions, like he doesn't believe me.

"Yes."

"The one you're wearing."

I frown and glance down at it. "Why? Don't you like it?"

"Of course, you look hot."

"*Hot*?" I ask.

He holds out a hand. "I don't mean it that way."

"And what way is that?" I ask, because no way does someone like *him* think someone like *me* is hot.

"The way that you're taking it."

I cross my arms. "And how am I taking it?"

Oh, and there's that pained look on his face again. "The way that you shouldn't," he says.

"Don't worry," I assure him. "I won't. I never have."

"Never?" he asks. "Even the day we met?"

My face heats as my eyebrows become better acquainted with my hairline. Declan and I have never spoken about the day we met. Probably because it was disastrous and humiliating. Seriously, I never wanted to nut-punch a man more.

"You really want to go there with me?" I ask.

A flush of red creeps along his neck. "Ah," he says, and not much more.

He must be joking.

I was in the process of transitioning from the state office in Harrisburg to Dad's office here in Philly. A case he was trying kept him from meeting me. I had a few hours to kill before I met with my realtor and I decided to treat myself to a late lunch.

Although my back was to the entrance of the bistro and I wasn't wearing my hearing aids, the way the light streaked across the window beside me when the door opened, drew my attention to the front of the bistro.

Declan walked in, appearing almost too flawless, sexy, and imposing to be real. His sleek suit and tie seemed to have been hand selected and tailored to demonstrate his position of power and his success. Curran trailed him, his gaze taking the room in for any visible threat.

The waitress with the ponytail noticed him right away, pausing to allow him through and admire the view. The women gathered in the corner weren't much better, nudging each other and whispering like a team of cheerleaders at the first sight of the quarterback.

I can't blame them for acting the way that they did. I was taken with him, too. It's hard not to be, given his startling good looks and magnetic charm he exudes like an aura. I just didn't expect him to look in my direction. Men like him rarely did. I turned around, returning to my lunch and the novel I was reading, certain he hadn't noticed me and never imagining he'd approach.

He rubs his jaw, watching me closely. "I didn't mean to tell you what I did," he says. "Not about you being beautiful because you are, but when I said, 'You're not deaf are you?' I only said that because I thought you were blowing me off. I never suspected that you actually were hearing impaired."

He fumbles through his last few words, but they're not ones I fixate on. "You think I'm beautiful?" I stammer.

The shade of red spreads to his cheeks and further yet. He holds up his hands. "I was only trying to prove to Curran I could get you to go out with me."

"Why?" His mouth abruptly shuts. My eyes fly open. "Was this a *bet*?"

"No!"

I simply stare.

"Not really," he admits. "I told him to pick any woman in the restaurant without a ring and that I could get her, or in this case *you*, to go out with me."

"Oh, my God," I say. I didn't think he could make the experience worse. Apparently, I was wrong. "It was a bet."

"No," he says, his voice growing softer. "It was just me being an asshole."

I shake my head, wondering how in the world we're going to survive each other. "At least we can agree on one thing," I tell him.

His admission shouldn't hurt me. Declan is nothing to me. But it does. I can't explain why. Maybe it's because he's the walking image of perfection: Strong build, brilliant mind, and absurdly good looks. And I'm . . . not.

I'm not perfect, nor do I resemble those size two models gracing the cover of fashion magazines. I'm also not like the women who look for excuses to walk into his office or laugh at the little things he says, those same women who fixate on his ass like the winning lottery numbers are scrolled across his rock hard cheeks. I'm just me, a woman who works hard, wants to do the right thing, and likes romance novels with shirtless pirates on the cover. What can I say? Long-haired men curl my toes and Fabio always knew how to rock a paperback.

I want to tell Declan as much and maybe get him to laugh just a little. But I don't. I know the kind of women he likes and is attracted to, and they are nothing like me.

He lets out a breath and leans forward, letting his hands fall to his desk. "Look, I'm sorry. About the way we met and what I just said about you and Curran. I'm trying to make things right between us."

"Okay," I say slowly, unsure whether to believe him. "But why did you ask me about Curran?"

"What?"

I tilt my head slightly. "Why do you care what he said to me? It didn't have anything to do with you."

"It didn't?" he questions.

"Not really."

He frowns as if annoyed. "It's just that when you and Curran are around each other you like to bust my balls."

Did he just say "balls"? Okay, so maybe the god-like

Declan O'Brien is human after all.

"He told me he liked my dress," I repeat. "And asked me if I wore it to celebrate your appointment to SACU."

"And what did you say?" he asks, his tone turning serious.

"I told him, no. That I bought it because I like the way my boobs look in it." I meant it as a joke then, and I mean it as a joke now, so when his eyes hone in on the girls, I'm more than a little shocked.

He catches himself a little too late, coughing into his hand. "It's a nice dress," he admits.

My jaw falls open again. Did he just check out my rack?

Another wave of pink flushes his face. He *did* just check out my rack!

I glance down again to make sure nothing is exposed. In the half second it takes me to look back up, he's reached for his pad and a pen and switched to attorney mode. "So, we're working together," he says, moving on like nothing happened.

"We are," I say, trying to keep my voice impassive. I scan his new office, feigning interest so I can force my attention off him. The bookcase, the desk, even the chairs are new. Dad really hooked him up, I guess hoping he'll stay. And now that he all but promised Declan that he'll be the next D.A., I know he's not going anywhere.

I only wish I could believe it were for the right reasons.

My hands fall to my lap. "I suppose now is a good time to tell you what I'm looking for," I say quietly.

"What *you're* looking for?" he asks.

I tilt my chin, wondering why he seems confused. "Well, yes. I have certain needs that I'm hoping you'll help me with."

His grip to his pen tightens. "Needs? For yourself?"

"For my unit," I clarify. I wish, like his brother, Declan also understood American Sign Language. Then I could sign and not give away how nervous I sometimes feel around him. I roll my ankle, trying to shake off some of my anxiety. For all he drives me crazy, he's doing a hell of a job making me feel self-conscious. That doesn't mean I'll cower or stay quiet.

"It's my understanding that the assistant D.A.s currently assigned to SACU are burnt out and requesting reassignment."

"That's right," he says, his expression sour. "Just a few hours on the job and I've already received transfer requests in writing."

"I'd like to help select their replacements."

"Excuse me?" he asks.

Okay, here we go. Boob appreciation hour is officially over. "I'm not trying to step on your toes."

"But?" he asks, leaning back against his chair.

"But nothing. I respect that the decision is ultimately yours. I'm only asking for the opportunity to provide input." He keeps his expression neutral, and I can't be sure he's listening. I force myself to continue. "There have been a few new hires, and a few D.A.s looking to be challenged. I'd like to observe them in court and see how they perform on their feet. More importantly, I want to observe how they interact with victims of the more violent crimes."

Declan appears anything but pleased. Either I've pissed him off or I've pushed him into something he's not ready for. "I'm going to lay it right out for you," he says, his tone matter-of-fact. "SACU is the unit attorneys least want. I'm surprised the A.D.A.s currently there have lasted as long as they have."

All right. I did annoy him. "They've lasted because it takes a while to become acclimated," I counter. "But once there, they realize their importance and how much the victims and their families depend on them to help them through the process."

"I'm not saying the work or the victims aren't important. What I'm saying is no one is exactly begging to work there."

"I realize SACU is the last place our attorneys want to be placed," I say, staring straight at him. "Especially those who enter this office strictly to make connections and jump start their political careers. But it's one of the most important units *because* of the sensitive subject matter and the degree of violence we see."

I don't mean to be so blunt, and maybe he doesn't either, but here we sit with our gazes locked and the tension between us escalating.

Damn it. Dad wants us to work as a team. But the more we speak, the more I'm reminded Declan doesn't want to be a part of this unit and nowhere near me.

I inadvertently trail my fingers above the collar of my dress. It's a nervous habit, much like when women tuck a strand of their hair behind their ear. But I never tuck my hair with my hearing aids in place. Any sound that brushes too close to the receiver, such as the movement of hair, putting on a hat, resting my head against a pillow, even an intimate whisper, creates back noise similar to nails on a chalkboard.

My fingertips stroke close to the swell of my right breast as I think our situation through. I freeze when I realize Declan's stare is following each subtle movement.

This is too weird. No way can Declan O'Brien be eyeing me like he wants to take a lick.

I ran into him at a restaurant a few weeks back. I was picking up takeout following a five mile run, still wearing the shorts and sports bra I ran in. Of course I had to see him. And of course he had to look good . . . and so did the blonde on his arm. She was a total stick and all legs, wearing a dress I don't think I could have shoved my left breast into. I'm so *not* his type. So then why . . .

"I'll allow the input," he says.

"I'm sorry?"

"I'll allow the input," he says, a little louder.

This time I don't correct him. I didn't hear him, too busy watching him watch me, which is absolutely ridiculous—ludicrous even—and good God, why does he have to look so good in that damn suit!

"Thank you," I say, tripping over the word.

I start to stand, but then think better of it, sensing we're not leaving on the best note. I promised my father I'd try to get along with him, so the least I can do is explain where I'm coming from. "I have a good relationship with Governor McAdams," I begin.

He frowns like I'm rubbing it in his face. "I know," he says, his features sharpening. "I've heard you're close to her and a few representatives."

The representative comment throws me off. It's just one rep—Trevor Stone—who I know, and we're not exactly friends. We slept together once following a fundraiser . . . and then again after another political event. Of course, I'm not telling Declan that.

I relax my stance, placing my hands out in front of me. "I'm not trying to drop names to impress you, Declan, nor am I trying to challenge your position in any way."

"Then what are you trying to do?" He arches a brow when I don't initially answer and adds, "Just so we're clear, I don't respond well to threats nor do I bow down to anyone because of who they know."

It's taking all I can not to slump in my seat. "That's not what I'm trying to do."

"Then you need to explain, Melissa. Because believe it or not, I'm trying here."

"I'm just letting you know where I'm coming from." I sigh when the air thickens further between us. "What I mean is I've met a lot of people doing what I do. And in fighting for victim's rights as much as I have, I've earned a great deal of attention. Some of it's not good," I admit, thinking of all the people I've pissed off. "And some of it is, like the relationship I have with Governor McAdams. But the strong relationships I've made, I've earned from trying to help those who've been hurt."

I stand, because as much as I'm trying to leave on a good note, Declan's tightening jaw is like a red flag warning me that I'm going down in flames. "Just understand I would never use who I know against you or disrespect your position. But if I need to help a victim who's been wronged, I'll do what it takes to make sure justice is served."

When he says nothing more, I turn to leave. "I'm sorry about your dad."

I pause with my hand inches from the knob. *Yeah. Me, too.*

CHAPTER 3

Declan

Melissa is slow to leave. It doesn't take a genius to know news of her father's condition is killing her. But like always, and like me, she tries not to give too much away. She wants some say in how I re-staff SACU. Fine. I'll give her a say, and maybe a little more, as long as she respects my position and remembers my legal staff answers to me.

In a way, I think I owe it to her. But I owe it to her old man more.

Miles earned my respect from the moment I met him and sat down to interview for the position of Assistant District Attorney. I expected a team of A.D.A.s to be there, maybe even the chief, too. But it was just me and him with only a desk between us.

"Tell me," he'd said. "What was your best memory from childhood?"

I wore my best suit, had a professional shave and cut that morning, and stopped by church and said a prayer to Saint Jude. I was prepared to respond to any legal scenario and reference my long list of accomplishments. I wasn't prepared for that question. Who the fuck asks a question like that?

Miles Fenske. That's who.

I considered him, my need to "wow" him making me scour through my long list of memories to find the one thing that would most impress him. I could have told him it was when I scored the winning touchdown that secured our Catholic High School as regional champs. I could have slipped in my stint as class president or when I found out I beat out Jay Takahari to become valedictorian. But that wasn't what Miles was looking for. He was looking for the man behind the attorney he was considering hiring.

"When my father died and I told my mother we were going to be all right."

Miles paused. He wasn't expecting that one. I wasn't either. I didn't know why I chose that moment, at least not right away.

"Why?" he'd asked.

"I knew we had to be," I answered without giving it much thought. "She and my younger siblings were counting on me as one of the oldest, and I wasn't going to let them down."

"And did you?"

I shook my head slowly. "No. Failure wasn't an option."

It was the truth. I didn't let them down. They needed clothes, books, fuck, even toys, we found a way. We made it right.

I watch Mel open the door, racking my brain to figure out how to make things right with her.

The opportunity Miles is offering me is one I've earned and am grateful to have. But I wasn't blowing smoke when I told Mel I wouldn't cave because of who she knows. Thing is, she won't cave either if she feels anyone has wronged a victim. But what's going to set her off? She has to know some cases are too weak to try and the best we can do is plead it out. Will she understand or should I anticipate a verbal ass kicking from the governor?

It's going to be a kind of dance between me and Mel, making sure we don't step on each other's toes. I'll avoid her feet if I can, but bottom line, I'm the one who leads.

She doesn't respond when I tell her I'm sorry about her

dad, not that I'm going to push. Instead, I watch her slowly walk out, my gaze trailing down her back until it fixes on those two round globes that make up her ass. They press against the fabric of her dress just right, like whoever designed it made it specifically for her and that eye-popping body.

I wish I didn't want to drag my hands along her gorgeous curves or taste that pouty mouth But I do. Just like I want to feel her body pressed against mine.

Shit. What the hell is wrong with me? As pissed as I was about being placed in SACU yesterday, I woke up hard this morning. Hard for Melissa. *Melissa*, who can barely stand being in the same room as me.

My eyes scrunch tight as I try to shake away the dream I had about her. We were at a black tie event, the kind where waiters walk around with silver trays packed with champagne and anyone who's anyone in politics works the room flexing their egos. I was supposed to give some kind of speech. I opted out, returning to my place with Melissa's hand tight in mine.

We had sex in my living room. I can't remember ever having a dream this graphic. She lay over my leather ottoman on her hands and knees, the skirt of her black beaded gown hiked up to her waist, my mouth buried against her. I tugged off my jacket and tie, managing to pop open the front of my shirt before I couldn't take it anymore and shoved my pants and briefs down to my ankles.

In those romance movies women like to watch, my thrusts would have been slow and sweet. But there was nothing slow or sweet about what we did. It was sexy, primal; me grunting hard and her hips circling fast. Her hair fell in messy waves around her heated face as she clamped down, turning her head enough to see me and show me the way she bites down on her bottom lip.

I wasn't a gentleman in my dream. I was the epitome of an alpha claiming what belongs to him. She loved it, calling out my name and begging me to go faster.

My problem is, I loved it too. A little too much.

I groan, thinking about how hot she made me and entertaining why she made me so hot. Melissa is different. Curvy hips, round perky ass, with what I'm guessing are some serious double-Ds. I usually date the model types, those who spend more time on their hair, shopping, and make-up and less time on anything that really matters. Why? Because they're not looking for anything serious and neither am I.

When I take a long hard look at all the political giants I know, every last one of them has a devoted wife looking adoringly back at them—standing by them, raising their children, spearheading charities, and working tirelessly on their husbands' campaigns—usually alongside the skanks their husbands are fucking when they're not around. I'm not exaggerating. It's what men of power are almost expected to do. But I swear to Christ, I'm not going to be one of them.

My mother, God love her, was one of those "devoted wives," working her fingers to the bone to support her family and raise seven children. Adoration lit her eyes whenever my father kissed her, but sadness dulled them each time he stepped foot out of the house. She knew the minute his shift ended at the post office he'd head straight to his mistress's house and into her bed. All those weekends, when he should have been coming to our games or helping around the house, he'd spend with that other woman, giving her everything my mother needed and deserved.

Do I believe in love? Not really. Despite that three of my brothers, and now my sister seem to have found it. My mother will swear on a stack of bibles, clutching a rosary that she "loved" my father and always will. But love, real love, shouldn't threaten to destroy you or abandon you with seven kids you can barely afford to feed.

Do I believe in marriage? Considering the divorce rate topples over sixty-five percent, I believe in it even less than love.

So yeah, instead of dating women who are looking for a ring on their finger, I date the ones who'd prefer a hot time in bed and not much more. They don't get attached and neither do I. We have great sex once, maybe twice, and move on.

Commitment? Yeah, of course I'm committed. Committed to being the youngest D.A. in Pennsylvania's history *and* the next in line for mayor.

I shove away from my desk and head out, needing some space from the office. This day has screwed with me in more ways than I can count. I started out pissed, thinking Miles had thrown me to the dogs, only to find out he has fucking cancer and wants to pass me his crown. I doubt he'd feel the same if he knew how bad I want his daughter.

"Hi, Declan."

In the short time it takes me to adjust my suit jacket and step into the cubicle-lined hall, Stephanie has hurried out from behind her desk. She tosses her bleached blond hair over her shoulder, giving her breasts an extra thrust forward. Her station is three rows back and to the left of my new office, but even when my office was on the other side of the building she always seemed to find me.

I'd like to say she's a nice young lady except I'm not convinced she is. Not the way she acts around me and any man she finds attractive. She's one of the newer clerical staff. I asked her what her goals were when I first met her, thinking she actually wanted to make something of herself. She answered, "Whatever you want them to be."

Not exactly what I was expecting to hear.

"Hi, Stephanie," I say, smiling.

She grins, her eyes skipping down the length of my body, flicking her incisor with the tip of her tongue when she reaches my groin. It's brief, just long enough to be sure I notice. "Congratulations on your promotion," she says. "No one deserves it more than you."

In other words, *I want you to fuck me.*

If she didn't work here, I probably would. Stephanie's legs start roughly at her neck and her straight platinum hair flows behind her every time she struts in her stilettos. The dresses she wears to show off her double zero body have forced Shayleen, the office manager, to send her home twice for violating the dress code. Stephanie is *exactly* my type. She's not really serious about anything, except satisfying her own needs. Not that I'd ever dip my pen in any company ink. Melissa, I remind myself, is *not* my type. Mel is too grounded, too driven, too . . .*committed.*

So why the hell can't I stop thinking about her?

Melissa doesn't possess the figure that typically catches my eye. That doesn't mean she's not gorgeous. Her brown eyes lure me to her, demanding I pay attention to her angelic and sexy as hell features. Too bad her body usually wins. Just like it did when we were alone in my office.

I could have kicked my own ass for practically ogling her. Around her, though, it's like that straight-laced professional I've trained myself to be leaves town and my world stops making sense. She's supposed to want me. Toss me an inviting glance before she invites me to bed. Whisper dirty thoughts to prove how bad she wants me. I'm not being arrogant. It's simply a fact. Women have been begging me to pull off their panties since I turned fifteen.

"If you need any help, I'll be available," Stephanie says, tossing her hair again.

"Thank you," I say. I lean and tap on Ellie's desk. "But I have all I need right here. Right, Ellie?"

Ellie laughs, waving me off as she blushes. "Oh, *Declan*," she says.

I walk away with the first genuine grin I've flashed since yesterday. Ellie has worked for the county longer than I've been alive. She's sweet, reliable, and ethical. Can't say the same about Stephanie. The way Stephanie flirts, I'm waiting for the day she gets caught fucking someone she shouldn't—a married attorney, an overworked detective, or a higher-up promising shit he doesn't intend to make good on. The only thing I'm sure of is she won't get caught fucking me.

It probably annoyed Stephanie that I paid Ellie more attention than I did her. Not that I care. She may think she has a shot with me, but I don't take women I work with to bed and I sure as hell keep my distance from those who are spoken for. I don't like drama and hate scandal. So if she's looking for a sugar daddy she needs to look elsewhere.

I pass a few more detectives and interns, making the

rounds and making it clear I'm staying. I'm not headed anywhere specific. In fact, I should start reviewing the list of candidates for SACU. But I've been in my office too long, and with everything that's happened, I need to move.

Without thinking, I end up in my sister-in-law's office. Tess, formerly Newart now O'Brien, top grad of U Penn Law, assistant district attorney, and married to Curran, is already knocked up with their second kid. I never expected Curran to land someone as high class as Tess. In fact, we were pretty sure he'd knock up one of those psychos he used to date, like that masseuse with the pet monkey.

I rap on the door. "Just a minute," she calls out. There's some fumbling before she says, "Come in."

I swing open the door. "Hey, Tess," I say. I roll my eyes when I realize who's here. No wonder she needed a minute.

Her light skin turns a furious red as she leans over her desk and pretends to flip through a law journal. I say "pretend," because no way would her face be this flushed if she was actually working. And no way was she working with Curran standing that close to her.

"What?" he asks, grinning as his hand strokes down her spine.

I shut the door behind me. "Curran, what the hell?"

"You have a problem with me kissing my wife?" he fires back.

"She's at work," I say, pointing out the obvious.

He walks around the desk. "I haven't seen her since I left for my shift yesterday. You act like we were fu—"

"Curran," Tess warns, her face heating more.

She pushes a blond strand that escaped her bun behind her ear as Curran takes a seat beside me. She clears her throat and lowers herself to her seat. "Declan," she says. "I would never engage in the activity your brother suggested at the office. I take my job seriously and will only behave in the professional matter you've come to expect from me."

My narrowing eyes fix on Curran. "Oh, I know *you* wouldn't engage."

Curran laughs. "You calling me unprofessional?"

"No, I'm calling you a horny bastard."

"I'll give you that," he agrees, nodding.

Tess groans. "God, it's like I married a teenager. Behave," she mumbles, arranging the files into a neat pile.

Her office is basically a closet. No windows and barely big enough to hold the three of us. But there are many reasons Tess was hired straight out of school and into this position. She's whip smart and driven. These same traits will eventually earn her a bigger office and more prestige.

"How are you?" she asks, meeting my face, the frame of her small librarian glasses drawing attention to her large eyes. "I know SACU isn't the position you were hoping for."

Curran probably told her, but like everyone else with a clue, she knew I was gunning for Homicide. "All right."

She knits her eyebrows, realizing there's more there than I'm telling her. "Really?"

"Yeah." My attention bounces to Curran. "I received some news after you left."

Curran frowns. "Good or bad?"

Both. Which is why my voice stays even. "Miles Fenske is taking a leave of absence in the next couple of weeks. While he's gone, I'll serve as acting D.A."

Tess's eyes widen in time with Curran's "Holy shit" remark.

My posture remains stiff. "If things go well, he and the governor will back me for D.A. when his term is up."

"Declan," Tess says, gasping as Curran knocks my shoulder. "That's incredible and more than you asked for."

Their excitement fades when they realize I'm not celebrating with them. "Wait. Why is Miles taking a leave?" Curran asks.

Curran is one of the best cops to ever wear the uniform, and this is the reason. Nothing slips by him. "I'm not at liberty to say," I reply.

They exchange glances, realizing it's not good news for Miles. "Damn," he says.

Tess links her fingers in front of her, appearing as bowled over as I was when Miles told me he had cancer. "So bittersweet news," she adds quietly.

"Way more bitter than sweet," I admit.

As furious as I was over Miles's initial decision, his illness is such horseshit. He's a good man who's served as the biggest mentor of my life. He guided me without imposing his will, giving me advice and making suggestions while allowing me to find my way and become the D.A. who kicks ass, who defense attorneys fucking fear. He deserves to step down on his terms, retire happily and travel the world because he goddamned earned it.

"When is he leaving?" Tess asks.

"I'm not sure," I say. My attention trails to the bookcase. Curran and Tess are my family. Two in a growing family of fourteen, and that's not even counting the baby she's carrying. Miles doesn't have family. He has Melissa. So who the hell will she have if Miles can't fight his way through this?

"So you're staying, for sure?" Curran asks.

I clasp my jaw, rubbing it hard. "Can't exactly leave now, can I?"

We grow quiet. Too quiet, an odd thing around anyone who goes by the last name "O'Brien."

I try to focus on the good that's happened these past few years. Our little brother Killian marrying his childhood sweetheart, Sofia. Curran and Tess already married a year now with their second child on the way. Finn, yeah, he found his perfect woman in Sol. Then there's Wren, who landed Evan, someone who not only puts up with her mouth, but finds that mouth and the woman behind it endearing. They're planning a small ceremony on the beach in Cape May. Yeah, with over a hundred O'Briens within an eight mile radius, good luck keeping it small. But even a jaded bastard like me can see how happy they are. Shit, how happy they all are.

I try not to react at the way Curran takes in Tess, tender and adoring, the way Ma used to watch Papa. God, I hope they make it, all of them. But as much as I recognize what they have is genuine, I can't help wondering if Papa's feelings were once genuine too, *before* he broke my mother's heart.

"What are you thinking about?" Tess asks.

"Just thinking about the day," I answer. Hell, I may not believe in love, but I want to believe it for them.

I try not to shake my head as I watch Curran stroke her hand, his touch evoking a warm smile she reserves just for him. How did these two end up together? Curran is the frat boy who never quite grew up and Tess probably spent her grade school years as class monitor, writing kids up for not having their Number Two pencils sharpened to code and studying sexism during Russia's Industrial Era for giggles. But they're good for each other and to each other. If nothing else, I can admit as much.

"If you're staying in SACU, my guess is you'll be working closely with Melissa," Tess tells me, bringing me back to the moment.

"You guessed right."

She shoots Curran a sideways glance. "Do you . . . anticipate any problems?"

With Melissa she means. Tess knows she hates me.

I shrug, trying not to give too much away. "Who knows?"

Curran chuckles. "I do. You're either going to be at each other's throats or in each other's beds."

"Curran," Tess warns, yet again.

"What?" He winks at her. "Just speaking the truth, angel face."

"What makes you think we'll end up in bed? We work together for hell's sake," I snap, pretending like I didn't have the dream that I did or fantasize about waking up next to her.

His grin widens as his attention latches onto his wife. "Been there, bro. Remember?"

Tess flips through the file closest to her, trying to ignore him as he continues. "You see, when two hot bodies spend that much time together, it doesn't take long before the sexy broad throws herself at you, so taken by your wit and ruggedly handsome face she can't see straight and begging you to please her with your super-sized masculine regions and whoop-whoop-whooping when you finally do." He holds out his hands. "What can I say? Professional or not, I am a man—a generous man who couldn't leave that sexy broad hanging, especially when she's clawing off my clothes and leaping onto my lap like a seasoned gymnast. Isn't that right, babe?"

Tess flips the page, not bothering to glance up when she answers. "I may have to beat you to death."

"Christ," I mutter.

"How long do you think it'll take you to bang her?" Curran asks, apparently ignoring everything that shot from my mouth.

"He's *not* going to sleep with her," Tess answers for me. "She's the boss's daughter."

Curran just blinks at her, appearing confused.

"Who *works here*," she reminds him.

"And?" Curran asks, still fucking confused.

"There's no 'and'," Tess insists. "There can't be. I know logic and reason often fail to make an appearance in your world—"

"Don't know what you mean, hot stuff," he tells her, grinning.

She smirks in an attempt to tame her smile, because Curran draws her smile as easily as I piss off Melissa. She clears her throat. "Think, for just a moment, how this could play out if they start having sex."

"Played out fine for us," Curran points out.

She scribbles something on her pad. "That was different. We had a history. I wasn't an employee and technically neither were you."

"So if we were both employed by the D.A.'s office, you wouldn't have thrown yourself at me like you did?" he asks innocently.

"I didn't throw myself at you, Curran," she responds, standing. "I was a consummate professional at all times who kept a respectable distance." She inches closer to where Curran is sitting, reaching for the legal binder on the shelf behind him. "And yes, if we were both employed here, I wouldn't have allowed your overt flirtation to affect me, nor would I have spent time with you outside the confines of this building."

She squeaks when Curran nabs her by the waist and hauls her onto his lap. "But baby," he says, curling her fingers to expose her huge engagement ring and the matching wedding band. "Then you would have missed out on all this. Oh, and the hot gorilla sex, too."

She purses her lips, the affection she has for my brother finding its way into her gaze regardless of the embarrassment painting her cheeks a bright pink. As much as Curran is messing around, he's crazy about her. It's obvious by the way his stare welds into hers.

I never expected him to marry so young. I never expected him to marry at all. Like me, he hated what our father did to our mother and never had a meaningful relationship prior to Tess. But here he is.

Marriage is the last thing I want and anything past a second date makes me want to turn tail. Have I ever longed for someone to spend forever with? Yeah. Once. When my sister Wren got engaged. I don't know why it affected me the way that it did. Maybe because she came damn close to losing her chance at forever.

I was there when Evan slipped that ring on her finger. But it's like as soon as she said yes, I couldn't keep watching, feeling like I was intruding on something I'm not meant to have.

"What are you thinking about, Deck?" Curran asks.

His hand drifts to Tess's knee, but both are focused on me. "That marriage isn't for me," I answer, my attention darting to the ring on Tess's hand.

I'm not trying to insult them or what they have, but considering what I said and who I said it to, I can't blame them if they're offended.

The crease along Curran's brow softens. He knows I don't mean any disrespect. Thankfully, Tess knows it, too. She smiles softly. "No one is saying you have to get married."

Curran coughs into his hand. "Bullshit."

Tess laughs. "Okay. Except maybe your mother. But once the baby is born, she'll be distracted and maybe leave you and Seamus alone for a while."

God, I hope so. For years, every time I was photographed with a woman at an event, Wren would cut out the picture in the paper and send it to Ma to bust my balls, but mainly to get Ma off her back about marriage. I could have done without the "Do you think she's the one?" phone calls. But now that Wren's engaged, Ma doesn't need any pic of me with a woman on my arm. That huge rock on Wren's hand has put more pressure on me than any photograph ever has.

It's strange. For all Papa hurt her, Happily Ever After is still something Ma wants for us.

Maybe because she was never able to have it.

I tap my fingers against the armrest. "Can I ask you something?" I ask Curran, but don't wait for his answer. "What did Mel say to you in the office?"

"When she signed?" he asks. At my nod, he grins. "I asked her if she brought that dress to celebrate your promo to SACU. She denied it, telling me she bought it to show off her boobs."

So she was telling the truth. I frown like I don't approve of the conversation. "Boobs? Did you seriously just use that word? What are you, twelve?"

"Well, technically she signed 'tits' I think. But Tess says I'm not allowed to say that word because it's vulgar and demeaning. Unless of course we're fu—"

"Curran!" she says, burying her face in her hand.

"How the hell did you end up together?" I ask, meaning it. If Tess were anyone else, I wouldn't swear. But now that she's officially family and because Curran is being his idiot self, I do. "You're going to fucking drain the class right out of her."

"I'm classy," Curran fires back.

"Of course you are, my beloved," Tess says, laughing and stroking his jaw. She leans in and presses a kiss against his cheek. "Will you do me a favor and get me a sandwich? I forgot my extra bag of food when I left this morning."

His hand skims over her growing belly. "Junior hungry?"

She smiles apologetically. "We both are. I don't think I

ate enough at lunch and it's going to be a while before I head home and have dinner."

"Okay," he says, standing when she slips off his lap. "You want anything, Deck?"

"Thanks, I'm good," I answer. I start to leave when he does, but Tess's hand sliding down my arm keeps me in place. Curran catches the motion out of the corner of his eye, clueing in that she wants to speak to me alone.

"What's up?" I ask as the door closes behind him.

"Declan, it's none of my business, but you and Melissa..."

"You don't have to worry about us," I assure her, my game face in place. "There's nothing there."

"I'm not so sure," she says.

I start to deny how I feel, but it's not me she's doubting. "I've seen the way she looks at you," Tess tells me, her tone serious despite how softly she speaks. "And it's not with the distaste she attempts to portray. She's Miles Fenske's daughter."

"Tess, I know."

"You don't," she presses gently. "He's her world, Declan. And if he's sick, her world is crumbling. She likes you. I can tell that she does. If you give in to what she's feeling and Miles doesn't pull through, she may not recover if you leave her, too."

"You're making a lot of assumptions," I tell her.

"I'm not. I'm speaking as a woman who's been too lonely for her own good and caught up in her obligations to realize it." She offers me a smile packed with sadness and an extra dose of worry. "Try to keep a professional distance, okay?"

"I will."

It's what I say. Too bad I don't think I can.

CHAPTER 4

Melissa

It takes a few days before Declan and I meet up again. I escort Rosana to his office, along with her mother, Vilma, and the interpreter who's assisting us due to Vilma's limited English.

Declan and Detective Melo stand as we walk into Declan's office, sitting only once we take our places at the conference table.

"Rosana, Vilma, this is Assistant District Attorney Declan O'Brien. He'll be handling your case in court," I say.

"Hi, Rosana," Declan says as the interpreter communicates the conversation.

I don't hear well in groups. There's too much extra sound when more than one person is speaking, which is why today will be challenging with the interpreter present. It's moments like these I count on my ability to lip read.

I settle in, hoping I don't miss anything important and smiling at Rosana encouragingly when she glances from Declan to me. We've established a rapport over the last few weeks, but it's taken a few meetings and some brief counseling sessions for her to warm up to me. Like most victims of ongoing and severe sexual assault, she's defensive and closed off.

I touch her hand lightly when she doesn't respond. "Nothing formal will happen today. Declan just wants to meet you and perhaps get a feel for how ready you are to testify."

Rosana tugs her shirt down over her belly as her attention darts back to Declan. She's a bit overweight and curvy, making her appear older than fourteen. She's self-conscious about her appearance in general, but it's more obvious today.

I'm not sure why until she leans closer to me. "Is he a model?" she asks.

I try not to grin, because the last thing Declan needs is a bigger ego. "No. He's the lawyer who'll be fighting for you in court."

"That's not what I mean," she says, keeping her attention on me. "Was he a model before this thing?"

She's mumbling, and I'm struggling to hear her. But Declan picked up on what she said without any problem. "No, I just take pretty pictures," he says with a wink. "But I'm sure your pics are prettier than mine, sweetie."

He's trying to be charming, but this isn't the right way to connect with Rosana. Her awe of Declan instantly vanishes, displaced by anger. "The only person who ever took my picture was Iker, and I didn't have any clothes on when he did it," she snaps.

Declan stops smiling, his attention shifting to Detective Melo. "Did you know about this?"

"I do now," Melo says. "Rosana, this is important. Why didn't you tell us before?"

She shrugs, her stare fixing on the carpet. "Rosana," I say gently, trying to draw her attention before she shuts down.

"You shouldn't have told him," her mother mutters. If it weren't for the interpreter doing her job, we wouldn't know what she said.

I start to defend Rosana, but Declan chimes in, cutting me off. "She did the right thing in telling us, and if we have proof, I can bring additional charges against Iker." He looks at Rosana. "It's illegal for anyone to photograph a child this way. Do you understand? He had no right doing this and I'm going to make sure he's held accountable."

Her mother tightens her jaw as the interpreter explains what Declan just said. I keep my attention on the interpreter, hoping Vilma will say more, but like Rosana, Vilma is done talking.

"Rosana, I'm here to help you," Declan says. His voice is so soft, I have to watch his lips closely while doing my best to zone out the interpreter's speech. "But if I don't know everything that happened, or if you're keeping things from me, I won't be able to defend you to the best of my ability. Is there anything else Iker has done or said that you haven't told us or the police about?"

Rosana crosses her arms, shaking her head slowly. I can't tell if she's being honest or if she's staying quiet because her mother told her to. I don't know Declan well, but if Rosana wasn't underage, Declan would be throwing her mother out to question Rosana privately.

"Tell me about the pictures he took of you," Declan says.

Again, Rosana shakes her head. Detective Melo stretches his foot out and taps mine lightly. I don't want to overwhelm Rosana, but like Detective Melo, I realize Rosana is starting to see us as the enemy. She's never going to make it through trial like this.

"Rosana," I say, "I know you don't want to talk about the pictures or what happened when he took them right now. And that's okay. We can talk about it when you're ready. But could you tell us if he took them with his phone?"

She shakes her head.

I hold up a hand when Declan stirs. "When you say, no, do you mean you don't want to talk about it, or that he didn't use his phone?"

For a long moment, Rosana sits with her arms crossed, appearing to shield herself from the world. Declan starts to say something, but I hold my hand out, hoping he trusts me enough to take the lead. One of the hardest things about working with victims who suffer severe trauma is you have to be patient. It's the only way they'll open and trust. Sometimes, it takes them an outrageous amount of time until they finally speak.

When I start thinking that today won't be the day she'll tell us, a thick tear rolls down her cheek. "He used an old camera. The one where the picture comes out of it."

Which means he wanted a hard copy and nothing we could trace on his phone.

"Did he keep the pictures?" I ask.

She nods.

"Where are they, Rosana?" I ask.

Her gaze goes blank. "There's a loose floorboard under his bed where he used to sleep. He keeps them there."

"In the apartment above yours where your uncle rented him a room?" I ask. At her nod, Declan and Detective Melo exchange glances.

"What else is in there?" I ask.

"A video camera," she says.

Shit. "Did he ever film you?" I ask.

She shrugs like she doesn't know, but I'm sure that she does.

When it becomes clear that Rosana is done talking, Declan turns to the detective. "Go see Botsko, tell him I need a search and seizure ASAP and that I want it in front of the judge within the hour."

"For just the room?" Melo asks, his eyebrow puckered slightly. He's pushing for more, but respects that Declan is the one who calls the shots.

"No," Declan replies. "I want the entire apartment searched."

"That's my brother's apartment," Vilma says, her voice shrill following the interpreter's translation. "He hasn't done anything wrong."

It takes some effort for me not to react. She's trying to protect her brother from what the search and seizure might turn up. I only wish she was that protective of her daughter.

Declan fixes her with a knowing stare and tight smile. "Then he has nothing to worry about, does he?"

Melo excuses himself. I turn to Vilma and start asking her about her hometown in Honduras. I'm trying to keep her here. If I don't, she'll warn her brother and God knows who else. Rosana confided in me that she told Vilma about the sexual assault. Vilma, an undocumented immigrant, was scared to get officials involved. Aside from telling her daughter to lock herself in their apartment, she did nothing about the incident, forcing her to interact with Iker at family functions to "keep the peace."

I don't like Vilma. Her weakness and ineffective nurturing put her daughter in harm's way. She reminds me of my birth mother in that respect and sometimes it takes a great deal for me to remain calm and not lash out at her. But Vilma is afraid, and despite her mistakes and everything she's done wrong by Rosana, I know she loves her daughter. Even though she does a shitty job of showing it.

"Can I go to the bathroom?" the interpreter says on Vilma's behalf.

"Can it wait?" Declan asks, staring right at Vilma.

"No," Vilma says.

Like I suspected, her English isn't as limited as she told us. Declan smiles. It's not a friendly smile. "Fine, one of my detectives will escort you just so you know where it is."

Vilma scowls. "I can go, too," the interpreter offers.

"I don't need an interpreter for that," Vilma says.

Ah, yes, her English is just fine.

"No problem," Declan says, keeping his smile and lifting the receiver to his phone. "Detective Hernandez speaks plenty of Spanish should you suddenly need an interpreter in the bathroom—Oh, hey, Valencia, it's Declan. Could you do me a favor? I have the guardian of one of my lead witnesses here and she needs to use the restroom. Do you mind escorting her?" He sighs. "Yeah, ordinarily I wouldn't ask, but I have this pesky search and seizure request going before the judge involving her brother's place within the hour, and I can't spare anyone." He grins. "Thanks, Valencia. I owe you."

Vilma's scowl fades and she begins speaking rapidly. "Am I under arrest?" the interpreter asks for her.

"Not at all," Declan responds. "Consider it a friendly service here at the D.A.'s office."

He barely finishes responding before Detective Valencia

Hernandez knocks on the door and pokes her head in, smiling brightly. "Hey, Declan."

"Hey, V. This is Ms. Secco. Would you mind showing her to the restroom?"

"I'd love to," she says before turning to Vilma and speaking in Spanish.

Vilma walks out in silence, but not before making it clear she doesn't want Rosana questioned outside her presence. The interpreter meets Declan with a grin. She's young, clearly impressed and already in love with him.

Declan glances over at me, pausing when he realizes that no, I'm not impressed, and that unlike with the interpreter, his performance didn't make my panties wet.

I turn to Rosana. "Did you finish your art project?" I ask. "The one with the clay?"

She shakes her head. "Not yet," she admits. Although she isn't looking at me, something shifts in her features and she smiles. "I finished the one with the spray paint. My teacher really liked that one."

"Will you show it to me sometime?" I ask.

"Yeah. But it's dark," she says. "I don't think you're going to like it."

"Is it darker than the first one you showed me?" I try not to cringe when I recall the sketch she did of a woman stabbing a man.

She laughs and finally looks at me. "You know I was just trying to scare you right, Miss Fenske?"

"Oh, and you did," I admit, laughing.

"You like art?" Declan asks.

Rosana's attention returns to the floor. "Little bit," she mumbles.

No, she actually loves it. I don't correct her, giving her a moment to connect with Declan.

"You think you can draw something for me?" he asks.

"You want me draw you a picture?" Rosana she asks, her voice challenging.

"Yeah," he says. "Why not?"

She narrows her eyes, wondering, it seems, if he's

placating her. "What do you want me to draw?"

"How about me?" he says.

"You?" she repeats.

"Sure. Draw me as you see me," he says. "Or, I don't know, on a white stallion with the sun setting behind me. Just be sure to catch my right side." He turns a little, showing his profile. "It's my best side."

It's taking all I can not to roll my eyes, especially when the interpreter starts laughing. "Oh, D.A. O'Brien, you're *so* funny!" she gushes.

Rosana shoots me a quizzical look and huffs. "This is the guy who's gonna save me?"

She laughs at my smirk. "Just be sure to catch his good side, Rosana."

CHAPTER 5

Melissa

I manage to hold onto Rosana and her mother a little longer in my office. But it's not enough time for Judge Bronson to agree to the search and seizure motion.

Declan raps on my door about an hour later. "Can I come in?"

I put my pen down on my desk, watching him as he shuts the door. "You're pissed at me, aren't you?" he asks, his expression clearly that of a man who would expect no less of me.

"I'm not angry with you, Declan," I begin.

"Didn't seem that way back in my office," he interrupts.

Wow. For someone who's accusing me of being mad, he's the one acting testy.

"I was trying to help Rosana," he says, continuing. "And I was trying to connect with her."

"By attempting to be charming?" I ask, crossing my arms.

Something in my face causes him grin. "Believe it or not, most women think I pull it off pretty damn well."

"I have no doubt. But today you didn't quite manage."

"I wasn't talking about you," he fires back. "I already

know what you think of me."

I gasp. "I wasn't talking about me either."

His face reddens, but I don't wait for him to speak. "Iker was a family friend," I begin. "He gained Rosana's trust by paying attention to her, listening intently to everything she said and making her laugh. In other words, *charming* her."

He lifts his chin, the muscles along his jaw tensing. "She's a sweet kid, who's had a really rough life," I tell him. "That doesn't make her your sweetie, like you called her. Because if you remember the last man who gave her a pet name, who paid attention to her, and who claimed to want to help her, convinced her to let him into her apartment when her mother was away and assaulted her."

"I wasn't trying to remind her of Iker," he snaps. "That wasn't my intention—"

He stops as I shake my head. "I know you didn't mean to come across this way," I say softly. "And that you were only trying to bond with her. But with a kid like Rosana, who can't even trust her own mother to help her, you have to earn her trust by being genuine and keeping some distance."

When he doesn't say anything, I'm certain that like Rosana, he'll shut me out. But then he says, "I'm sorry."

The sincerity in his features and tone is like a tangible force, holding my attention longer than it should and warming my heart in a way he's not supposed to.

I avert my gaze. "I'm sorry, too," I say. "I'm not trying to insult you or tell you how to do your job. But all those cases you've tried, however challenging, didn't involve victims like Rosana."

"I realize that now," he agrees quietly.

The silence spreads between us, but it's not uncomfortable or tense, and maybe something we both need at the moment. The mental exertion of keeping up with the conversation earlier, and the stress from the cases I handled today alone, hits me all at once. Not that it stops me from thinking matters through.

I blamed Declan for the way he came across, but had I met with him ahead of time, we could have discussed how best to approach Rosana. He's handled a plethora of cases and met with multiple witnesses and victims. But the victims in this unit are a different breed and so very fragile.

"I should have prepared you for the meeting and warned you she was defensive," I admit. I take him in from his meticulously cut wavy blond hair to shiny expensive shoes, trying not to judge this future politician standing before me. "I just never expected you to be so . . ." I shake my hand at him. "*You.*"

"You say that like it's a bad thing," he says, the corners of his mouth stretching into a way-too sexy grin that causes his blue eyes to shimmer.

For some reason, I blush. I'm not someone who blushes because she's shy or easily embarrassed—especially around someone like him who would enjoy it too much.

I shuffle the papers around my desk, trying to hide my face and not cringe when instead of walking out he edges closer. He stops directly in front of my desk, leaning forward so that his elbows rest on the smooth surface. "Are you blushing?"

"I don't blush," I assure him, gathering random sheets of paper on my desk and making more of a mess than anything.

He angles his head, trying to peer at my face. "I don't know," he says like he's giving it some thought. "I've made plenty of women blush in my life . . ."

"Oh, I'm sure you have, counselor," I say, my face growing hotter.

". . . and I'm pretty sure that's a blush you have going on. Hmm, it might be one of my best ones yet."

I slam the stack of screwed up notes against my desk and glare at him. "Is there something you need help with, Assistant District Attorney O'Brien? I'm very busy."

He straightens, cocky grin firmly in place, lean muscles flexing just enough to show he works out, and again looking way too good in a suit. Damn it, does he have to be *this* attractive?

"No, I just came in here to see if you're mad at me," he says, adding a well-rehearsed wink. "Nice to know you're not."

I push away from my desk and open my bottom drawer, reaching for my purse. "How about dinner—?"

"I don't date men I work with," I say, my grip on my purse strap way too tight.

"I wasn't asking you out," he says, his voice fading with every word.

If I wasn't blushing before, I certainly am now. For a moment, I simply freeze, my mind racing with how to respond.

My fingers clench around my purse strap hard enough to hurt. I lift my chin as he carefully straightens. The arrogance initially so vivid in his features is gone, along with any hint of flirtation.

"Look, I don't date women I work with either." He crosses his arms, appearing embarrassed for me. "We were supposed to discuss the Morris Miller case following our meeting with Rosana. With everything that went down, we never had the chance." He speaks slowly, as if trying to make sure I understand that our relationship is strictly business. No, I'm not humiliated or anything. "I know you often work late so I thought we could have something delivered and go over the case then."

He does a one shoulder shrug, trying to appear casual. With his far too rigid stance, though, he doesn't quite pull it off.

I have two choices here. Say no and all but admit that I'm too mortified to be alone with him—after wrongfully assuming he wanted to date me—or pretend to be strong and take the meeting.

"In that case, count me in," I say, beaming.

He puckers an eyebrow. "Yeah?"

"Of course. Maybe when we're done with the case, I can cover some aspects of victim trauma and discuss interview skills that may help you in the future."

"Sure," he says, eyeing me in a way that tells me he can see right through me. "Thai sound good?"

"Sounds great," I say, standing.

Oh . . . *gawd.* Why would I think he was asking me out?

I force another smile and plop my giant bag on the desk, spilling the contents across the surface when the front closure pops open.

If this were a romantic comedy, my desk would be littered with tampons, condoms, and an extra pair of panties. I wish I was that lucky. Any of those items would be welcome over the tattered paperbacks spread across the slick wood: bare-chested men with their come-hither stares firmly in place, groin muscles bulging.

Declan stills in place, his gaze traveling across each model gripping his ladylove mid-swoon. "My Lusty Highlander?" he asks, reading off the titles. "My Pirate, My Lover?" He reaches for the last before I can snatch it away from him. "The Naked Cowboy Who Deflowered Me?" He lifts his chin. "You—" He pauses, as if gathering his words. But when he swallows hard enough to bounce his Adam's apple, it's clear he's just trying not to laugh. "You like this sort of thing?"

"Of course not!" I insist.

Oh, and there's that cocky smirk I could have done without. "Then why do you have them?"

"I picked them up at used bookstore."

"They sell crotch-less panties at that bookstore?" he asks, laughing.

My face is officially on fire. "There's a woman I met at the domestic violence shelter who loves them," I say. It's true, but so do I. And no, she's not getting these bad boys.

"So you purchased them for this woman?"

"I wanted to give her a treat," I say, lying my ass off. I throw in a flirty shrug and teasing grin, trying to give the impression that I think it's *hilarious* that there are actually women who read this sort of thing, even though, I am, indeed, one of those women. "It's just the kind of gal I am."

"Uh-huh," he says, his humor fading.

My playfulness dwindles. The way he's looking at me isn't in that mocking way he was before. This look is alluring, daring me to get closer, and promising me sweet, sexy things if I do. But that can't be right. Not when he made it clear he wasn't asking me on a date.

A knock on my door breaks our eye contact. "Come in," I say. I'm thankful for the distraction until I see who it is and why she's here.

"Hi, Declan." Stephanie's dazzling smile lights up the room when she sees him. She glances briefly in my direction. "Hi," she tells me with a lot less dazzle.

She tosses her hair back in a way I'm sure she's practiced a thousand times. "Detective Melo has been looking for you," she says, focusing fully on Declan. "Something about the search and seizure. I told him I'd find you."

Declan frowns. "Where is he?"

She backs away, luring him out. "At his cubicle. He's on the phone and seems flustered."

They take off, neither glancing back.

Stephanie barely acknowledged me. Given my position, I expected her to show me a little more respect. It stings that she didn't, though I recognize that like many women who work here, Declan's mere presence has her enthralled. But the sting is still there, no matter how much I wish it wasn't.

Stephanie is pretty, stunning even. She reminds me of all the beautiful girls I went to school with, who, like her, barely glanced my way. My accomplishments never impressed those girls. Neither did my hard work. I tried to be friendly and often gathered my courage to say, "Hi."

Aside from a few obliged "hellos" back, they didn't offer much more. Instead they'd stare at my mouth, unable to get past the way I spoke. They didn't understand and they probably didn't care that I speak how words sound to me, and despite the intensive speech therapy I received, this was my normal.

I didn't know I had a speech impediment until I was told that I did. But it wasn't until I recorded my voice one day and played it back that I realized how different I spoke from the hearing world.

The experience was startling and made me self-conscious. It took my dad reminding me that even though I speak differently, it doesn't make what I say less important.

I wanted to believe him, and in a way I still struggle. Sometimes, it's really hard. Whenever I meet someone new it's like I have to prove there's more to me than just my voice.

With a sigh, I throw my purse stuffed with smutty books over my shoulder and shut my office door behind me.

"Going to court, Melissa?"

Smiling, I turn around as Detective Valencia Hernandez hurries down the hall. Her willowy frame and lovely face suggests she's more model than investigator. But most models can't throw a perp twice her size to the ground.

"Hi, Valencia," I say when she reaches me. "I need to take care of some things courtside, but then I'll be back. Is there something pressing you need?"

She smacks my arm with the file she's holding. "Of course I need something. Don't I always need something from you, girl?"

I laugh, because yes, she always does. "How can I help you?"

"It's about Betty Clemson. She can't afford counseling and is pretty damn traumatized from the armed robbery she witnessed."

I try to place the name. "Is that the case where the owner was shot at point blank range?"

"In the face? So his brains splattered the display case behind him? Yup. That's the one."

That poor man, and poor Betty, too. "Ask Debbie to call her. She can fill out a services form over the phone for her. I'll review it, fax it through to the state, and ask them to put a rush on it."

"Thanks, Melissa." She cocks her head. "You okay? You seem a little bummed."

"I'm fine. Just busy."

She gives me her all-knowing once-over. "Girl, all you do is work. Come out with us to happy hour tonight. You look like you could use a drink and a little fun."

"I can't tonight," I tell her. "I'm meeting with Declan after hours to discuss a case we're working on."

"Oh, I see," she says, laughing.

My smile fades. "It's not like that."

"Uh, huh." She gives me another smack with her folder and walks away.

I groan. Sometimes it really sucks working with investigators. They're trained to pick up on subtle changes in a person's demeanor. In a room with Detectives Hernandez, Melo—*anyone* on the law enforcement staff, I don't think I'd stand a chance. They'd see right through the confidence I try maintain and unearth every insecurity threatening to tear through me.

I hurry out the side door and down the stairwell, wishing my encounter with Declan hadn't affected me like it had. He walked away without glancing back. I know he felt rushed. If it involved the search and seizure, it was urgent, just as I know I shouldn't care. We both have work to do. But even knowing as much doesn't make the snub an easier pill to swallow. Not with Stephanie so close on his heels, and especially not with how easily she dismissed me.

My shoulder length hair sweeps behind me as I walk along the bridge connecting our building with the courthouse. With my badge firmly in place, the sheriff's officers wave me through and past the line of people waiting to clear the metal detector.

I'm supposed to observe one of the newly appointed A.D.A.s, Kirk Stevenson. He's clerked in our office for over a year now, waiting for the opportunity to prove himself. Since Declan is considering him for SACU, I'm hoping Kirk can measure up.

With a deep breath, I proceed to Judge Bronson's courtroom, increasing the speed in my stride. There are a cluster of people piled outside the double doors leading in. They speak in low murmurs, but the collection of voices is loud enough to overwhelm my hearing. I hurry forward when I catch sight of the judge's clerk walking back to chambers. "Steve," I call out.

I'm not sure he hears me until he turns around. "Oh, hey, Melissa," I watch him mouth, doing my best to tune out the extra noise. "What are you up to?"

"I'm here to observe Kirk Stevenson . . . What's wrong?" I ask when he makes a face.

He hooks my elbow and guides me down the small hall that leads to the chambers. "Look, Melissa. I'm only telling you this because my clerk assignment ends in another week." He waits as one of the deputies hurries past him before continuing. "Rumor has it Kirk just accepted a position with a firm downtown. He's biding his time here and making connections until he starts his new job."

Awesome. So much for him. I glance around, hoping I didn't waste my time by coming. "Are there any other A.D.A.s around?"

"A few." He sighs. "Including the woman who broke my heart."

I follow his stare to the corner where Tess O'Brien is standing. Oh, yes, I'd heard a few of the clerks had it bad for her.

Tess is lovely, tall and thin, except where her baby bump is showing. She doesn't notice me, too busy flipping through the file as she speaks to a defense attorney and his client. Just a few feet behind her waits her husband, Curran. He's dressed in his Philly cop uniform, watching his wife and her interaction closely.

Considering opposing council is looming over Tess and rolling his eyes as she speaks, Curran seems surprisingly calm. "Thanks, Steve," I say, walking toward them.

I frown the closer I draw. The defense attorney is being blatantly disrespectful and the client isn't much better. But honestly, what shocks me is how unaffected Curran appears. That's his pregnant wife, and for all he jokes, he's known for his tough-as-steel persona. I don't understand why he's not stepping in to throttle this jerk.

I inch closer, not wanting to leave her so vulnerable. I can't hear Tess well, but I can read her lips. "This is what you're going to do," she says. "Plead guilty to the possession and intoxication charges, and I'll drop the misconduct and indecent exposure."

Defense council huffs. "You can't be serious. He's a first time offender."

"I'm not doing that," the defendant snaps. He scowls at his attorney. "You said I wouldn't have to do any of that."

"You don't," his attorney tells him.

I stop beside Curran. He keeps his attention on Tess, but nudges me with his elbow. "Watch this," he says.

She straightens to her full height, adjusting her tiny glasses. "That's true. You don't have to plead guilty. We can set up a hearing and try this case today." She motions around. "You see all these people, all these fine and proud Philadelphians? I'm sure they're dying to hear how you got blasted out of your mind, ran across Liberty Park naked and peed on their sacred bell—no, that *you peed on American history* and the very embodiment of freedom." She turns on the attorney. "You're ready, aren't you, counselor? Because I am. In fact, I've already prepared my witnesses, including the two priests who saw your client strip off his clothes and sprint across the lawn. They're on standby and ready to go."

"I need a week," the defense attorney counters.

"To prepare for a case that's been sitting on your desk for over a month?" Tess addresses the defendant. "How much are you paying him? Never mind," she quickly adds. "Just know it's more than I make, that I received this case yesterday, and that I'm ready to try this case now. Oh, and keep in mind that not only did you basically pay him to stand here and do nothing, but that he'll be asking you for more money to try the case. Steve?" she calls out.

"Yes, Assistant District Attorney O'Brien?" Steve answers, grinning.

"Could you squeeze us in this afternoon for a quick trial?" Her eyes narrow at the defense attorney. "I assure you it won't take long."

"No problem, Tess," he replies.

My head whips back to Tess's group so I don't miss a word. The attorney starts to open his mouth, but Tess cuts him off. "Unless your client is ready to plead to the charges I recommended, I have nothing more to say to you. See you this afternoon."

She starts to leave, her pace slowing when she sees us standing there. "Hi, Melissa," she says, before turning to Curran. "What are you doing here, cop?"

"Watching you get me hot."

Her face flushes pink only to redden further when he puts his arms around her waist and pulls her close. "Curran, I'm at work," she reminds him.

"What?" he asks. "It's not like I grabbed your ass like last time."

She shakes her head, prying his hands loose when they start to wander south.

I laugh. I can't help it. It's not that I don't agree with Tess, that this is a public place and he needs to behave. But Curran is just so cute around her.

When I was first introduced to Curran, I was immediately attracted to his ruggedness and personality. Throw in the fact that he's fluent in ASL and he totally had me. I was in heaven for two solid minutes until Tess stepped forward and I realized there was something between them. But that's how my life has always been, the supposedly perfect man standing mere feet away from me only for another woman to swoop in and claim him.

"What are you doing here, Melissa?" she asks, turning back to me.

"I'm here to observe Kirk's case," I answer.

Curran stays close, keeping his arm around her. I realize his show of affection is intentional, making it clear to both the court staff and anyone passing that they're a couple.

Tess wasn't intimidated by opposing counsel, but her position in the office isn't without its dangers. Defendants often lash out, the witnesses aren't that much better. Toss in their families and friends and it's recipe for blow-ups that could end in blood. It's the reason the county employs the number of sheriff's officers they do.

Curran nods to a few officers positioned close by. They return his nod in a show of solidarity and in a silent vow to watch out for Tess in his absence.

"You're here to see Kirk?" Tess repeats. At my nod, her attention shoots to Courtroom 13. "He's been in there a while, odd considering it's a cut and dry case."

"He's probably showing off in front of his new boss," I tell them. "I just learned he accepted a position downtown."

"You're kidding," Curran says. "Dumbass was sworn in following Declan's recommendation."

"I don't think he's told anyone yet," I add.

Curran huffs. "Of course he hasn't. The asshole is trying to milk this position for all it's worth."

"Pretty much," I agree.

The defense attorney Tess was speaking with approaches her slowly and more respectfully when he catches sight of Curran.

"My client will agree to your terms," he says, muttering so low I barely make out what he says.

Tess barely blinks. "Fine. I'll tell the judge's clerk." She presses her free hand against Curran's chest. "I'll be back in a moment."

He watches her walk away. This time, it's my turn to nudge him. "I like that wife of yours."

A slow smile spreads across his face. "I do, too," he admits. "She's perfect."

I agree. Perfect for Curran and my unit.

CHAPTER 6

Melissa

"Perfect." That's how Curran described Tess. It's not true, of course. Like the rest of us, she's human and likely flawed in a way that makes her more endearing. But Curran meant it because he loves her, reinforcing my wish to one day be "perfect" for someone, too.

"How are the spring rolls?" Declan asks.

The sleeves of his dress shirt are rolled to just below his elbows and his tie is dangling on the hook beside his jacket. He's leaning so far back against his chair and appears so relaxed, I bet he'd have his feet propped up on his desk if I weren't here and if we weren't using it to eat our takeout.

I swallow and raise my tiny foil container. "Really good. Would you like one?"

I'm looking at him, but not really looking at him, since I can't. He's been gracious, but I haven't forgotten the naughty book incident, just like I'm sure he hasn't either.

He polishes off the Pad Thai and stretches across the desk, using his chopsticks to reach for a roll. "Thanks. So . . . Morris Miller, tell me about the victim. What's going on with her?"

"Tricia is a tough one," I admit. "She was in and out of

foster care—"

"Tricia Helmsley was in foster care?" he asks.

I don't blame him for being surprised, given her success. She's head of marketing at a prestigious firm and has accomplished a great deal. But like many who've been part of the foster care system, she didn't escape unscathed.

In fact, she's pretty screwed up.

"She was," I answer slowly.

Declan doesn't miss my cautious tone. He raises his thick brows. "This is why you wanted to meet with me, isn't it? There's more to her than meets the eye."

"That's one way to put it," I agree.

"She seems so normal. I should have known a somewhat stable victim was too good to be true." He looks at me. "Should I have another roll before we delve into her dirty little secrets?"

I consider what I have to tell him and place the entire container directly in front of him. "Christ," he says, reaching for it.

"Now, I'm only telling you this because it pertains to her case and it's highly probable the defense counsel will try to use it against her."

"I'm listening," he says when I hesitate.

"Tricia is a submissive at Club Hurt." For a moment, he simply freezes. "A sexual submissive," I explain.

"I understood you the first time," he says. He tosses the container on the desk and leans back in his chair, covering his eyes until every swear word I know spews from his lips. He drops his hand away. "You're serious?" When I nod, he adds, "You think she might have mentioned this sooner?"

"It's a lifestyle she doesn't want her coworkers and clients to know about, but considering Morris Miller has one of the best defense attorneys in the state with a reputation for hiring private P.I.s to dig up dirt on lead witnesses . . ." I wrinkle my nose. "I just thought you should know."

"It's going to be harder to prove Miller raped her," Declan mutters.

I'm not sure if he means for me to hear him or if he's

simply talking to himself, but I struggle to catch his words. Regardless, I need to ensure he's on Tricia's side. "But he did rape her," I say. "You believe her, don't you?"

"It's not that I don't believe her, Mel. But if this comes up—which it will, given defense counsel's pit bull approach to winning cases—it'll give the jury the wrong impression of Tricia. They'll ignore the accomplished professional standing before them, branding her a slut who asked for it. Especially if the defense spins it as consensual BSMD or whatever the fuck the acronyms are."

"BDSM," I clarify. "Bondage, domination, sadism, and masochism."

He raises his brows. "You seem to know a lot about this kind of thing."

This time, my smile comes a little easier. "And you don't seem to know enough."

He lifts one of the rolls. "Care to educate me?" he asks, a playful grin spreading across his face. "I mean, given my role here at SACU, I should know all the ins and outs, don't you think?"

He pops the roll in his mouth with his chopstick. His smirk is in place, positive he'll stir another blush out of me. Not this time, big boy.

I lean against the desk and fold my arms in front of me, my stare wistful, longing, or at least that's what I'm going for. "The pain inflicted when bound is not meant to harm or punish, Declan. It's meant to stimulate and free."

Declan stops chewing, honing in on my face. My hand drifts to my hair to play with the ends, before I lower it slowly and avert my chin as if embarrassed. "The pliable whip teases a woman's most intimate parts, enticing them to tense and strain." My gaze grows distant as if I'm remembering. "At first it's like a cool breeze you're not expecting. But in each lash there's a promise."

He swallows hard. "A promise?"

I bite down on my bottom lip. "Yeah," I whisper.

My fingertips trail along the exposed skin above my breasts. "With each lash the intensity surges, creating a light sting." I shudder. "It burns sometimes, creating a heat that reaches deep."

"How . . . deep?"

With dreamy eyes I meet his face, holding his focus like our lives depend on it. "As far as you allow it, until you're screaming with need, your body begging for that release. But it's not domination, Declan."

"It's not?" he asks, his voice low.

"No," I say, my voice more a purr. "It's freedom. Freedom to dig into a primal need women are forced to suppress." I lean forward, forcing myself not to react when he responds in turn, erasing the distance until only inches remain. "We're told to be good girls, to keep our legs closed and our fantasies to ourselves. We're taught sex is wrong, and only meant to reproduce. It's not supposed to feel good—"

"No?" he asks.

He's breathing hard. I am, too. "No, it's supposed to serve a purpose. Except there's more to sex than making babies, isn't there?" I challenge in a breathy tone. "It can feel sweet, delicious, but only once that woman in need opens herself and—"

"Hey, Declan!"

"*What*?" he snaps, whipping in the direction of the door. He catches himself a little too late, when Stephanie gapes back at him. He clears his throat. "My apologies, Stephanie. Melissa and I were discussing an important case."

"Oh, sorry," she says, not bothering to glance my way.

Wow. It's like I'm not even in the same room. Her attention is fixated on Declan. "I wanted to know if you needed anything," she says, her smile lifting. "Before I left."

"No, I'm good," he says, returning his focus to me.

"Are you sure? I don't mind staying late," she pushes. "I do it all the time."

I glance at the wall clock. It's almost six. The majority of the clerical staff leaves at four thirty. As county employees, they're paid a set salary. There's no incentive to stay unless there's a pressing matter and many have children to return to.

"It's really late," I tell Stephanie. "I'm surprised you're

still here."

For some reason, she doesn't like me questioning her. "I had work to do," she says, doing little to hide the annoyance in her voice.

I lean back, frowning. While I don't expect her to fall all over herself to please me, I'm rather baffled she's not more polite. "Is something wrong?" I ask.

She stiffens. "No. Why?"

"Because your tone and the way you're addressing Melissa suggests you don't respect her or her position here in the office," Declan answers for me. He could have kept his tone light and easy to keep her apparent awe of him going, but he didn't. While he wasn't harsh, it's clear he's not happy.

"I didn't mean to be disrespectful," she responds, to *him*.

I reach for my notes on the case. There's a lot I can say to Stephanie, but I pick my battles. If I'm going to be labeled a bitch, I'd rather it be for fighting for victims' rights, not fighting with someone who's immature, self-serving, and oblivious.

"I suppose I should apologize," she offers to Declan, trying to make amends with him.

So much for staying quiet. "Don't bother," I tell her. "Just watch what you say. We're all working for the greater good and everyone deserves respect, regardless of their title *or* physical appearance."

She presses her lips into a firm line, but doesn't bother with a retort. It doesn't matter. Her glare is telling enough.

"Have a good night," Declan tells her, tilting his head in the direction of the door.

I focus on the list I have to discuss with Declan and don't bother to watch her leave.

"What did you mean when you told her physical appearance shouldn't matter?" he asks. I glance up to find him grinning. "Are you saying she only talks to me because I'm pretty?"

I shouldn't smile. Of course I do. "You think you're pretty?"

"You don't?" he challenges.

I laugh. "Fish for compliments much?"

"I don't usually have to." He holds out a hand. "I know that shocks you."

"Nothing really shocks me about you, Declan, except for your ongoing love affair with yourself." I return to my pad of paper, adding "must kick Declan's ass" to my to-do list.

"So are you going to tell me?"

"Whether or not I think you're pretty?" I ask, underlining the ass kicking and adding a star. "You don't need me to, do you? I'm sure any one of your groupies would be more than happy to tell you between bows."

I smile and keep my voice light. I'm mostly joking, ignoring the fact that, yes, Declan has legions of ladies ready to tear their panties off at his command.

"No, whether you were referring to me and what I look like when you made the comment . . . or yourself."

This time when I look up, I meet his gaze and hold it.

"Do you think Stephanie doesn't respect you because you're hearing impaired?" His voice is steady. There's no apology behind what he's asking, but there's no malice either. "Or that she respects me because she finds me attractive?" He plays with the pen in his hand. "Your inability to hear well reflects in your speech, making the unnoticeable, noticeable. So who were you referring to, you or me?"

"Maybe both," I admit.

There's more I can say about Stephanie, but I don't want Declan to mistake my dislike of her behavior for jealousy. There's nothing of her to envy. I don't desire her looks. Insecurities aside, I'm comfortable in my skin. And if given the choice, I'll always choose kindness over gain. I'm not certain Stephanie would agree.

"All right," Declan says, his smile returning as he reaches for his bottled water. "Next question. "How do you know so much about being dominated?"

"I've spent a few nights at Club Hurt."

Water spews from his mouth, drenching the plastic takeout bag in front of him. I rush around the desk when he starts to choke, smacking his back a few times. "Are you okay?"

He swipes his mouth with a wad of napkins. "You've seriously been there?" he asks.

"I have," I say, toying with whether to come clean. My hand slips down his back and away. "Tricia asked me to go so I can understand her lifestyle. Those things I said, about being stimulated and sexually freed are more or less what she and her Doms told me."

Declan stares at me, his expression split between fascination and shock. "Just so I'm clear, you went to Club Hurt and watched Tricia get spanked?"

"Whipped," I clarify.

"*Whipped?*"

"That's her preference. But I only went because I wanted her to trust me and open up."

"By *whipping* her?" Declan asks incredulously.

I throw back my head, laughing. "I didn't whip her, Declan. And I didn't watch either. I simply met privately with Tricia and her favorite Doms. No one was in leather. In fact, one of the Doms was dressed in flannel."

"Why?"

"It was cold in the office."

He laughs. "You know what I mean. Why did you meet with her and her buddies?"

I return to my chair. "I told you. So she'd trust me. A woman in Tricia's position wants be understood, but given her history, she has some serious trust issues. She wanted me to be sympathetic to her lifestyle before she'd open up. So I went." I shrug. "The ball gag made it a little hard to breathe, but I did okay."

He laughs again, but then quiets the longer he watches me. "Do you do that a lot? Go to places outside your comfort zone to better understand victims of crime?"

"I do." I let out a breath when I start to think about it. "I'll admit, though, sometimes I've gone too far."

"How so?"

I debate whether or not to answer, mostly because I worry who it will get back to. "Will this stay between you and me?"

"Depends. Is it legal?" he asks.

It's a fair question given his role. "It is. I would just prefer my father not know."

"You, a grown woman, doesn't want her daddy to know what she did?" he asks. "I thought you were closer than that."

"We are. But what I have to say will only upset him." My voice quiets. "That's the last thing I want."

"All right," he agrees, suspicion drawing his brows tight.

"Okay. Here goes," I say, slapping my hands against my lap. "I've helped social workers search for runaways on the streets, rushed into warehouses known to house addicts to pull young girls out, and driven around in the dead of night talking with prostitutes about giving up their lifestyles."

"Shit," he says, completely caught off guard. "Any success?"

"Very little," I admit.

"Then why do it, especially when you can get hurt or killed doing shit like that? Christ, Mel, invading crack houses, driving around the worst parts of town, that's nothing short of suicide."

"At the time, all I could think about was helping those who really needed me."

"What about your dad? Don't you think he needed you, too?" He holds a hand out. "I'm not trying to be a dick. But like I said, anything could have happened to you."

He's not being judgmental. At least, that's not how I take it. If anything, he seems concerned for my welfare even though the events happened long ago. It's sweet and I do my best to reassure him. "I usually hired a bodyguard to come with me—"

"Usually?"

Okay. He went from being sweet to thinking I'm crazy, not that I blame him. But now that I opened that can, I keep going. "Sometimes even bodyguards packing big guns, big muscles, and big attitudes were hesitant to enter the places I needed to search."

"So you'd go alone?" he asks, barely able to get the

words out.

"Never alone," I say, thinking back to my more desperate cases. "But sometimes it was just me and another victim services advocate."

"Another woman?" he asks. "Mel, again, I'm not trying to be a dick, but how do two women stand a chance against dealers and pimps bent on keeping what they feel belongs to them? I love Philly. It's my home and heart. But I know firsthand how unforgiving it can be."

In his last words, I catch a flicker of bitterness and maybe pain, too. I want to hug him, knowing those he loves have been hurt despite the A.D.A. title he holds out like a shield.

I don't, of course, watching with sadness as that flicker vanishes, leaving only the shield in place.

"I know what I did was dangerous," I agree quietly. "But I was young and wanted to give these girls a chance that no else would." I smile softly, even though these memories are nothing to smile about. They were the suicide missions Declan inferred. But it's my way of assuring that despite what I saw and encountered, I'm okay on the inside.

"I don't get you," he says.

"What do you mean?" I ask, taken aback by how upset he appears.

"The odds weren't in your favor," he points out. "And like you said, your success rate was low."

"Oh, my success rate was hideous," I agree. "I think I only helped three people at most."

"*Three*?" he stresses. "After all that you only helped *three people*?"

"I know it doesn't sound like much, and it's not, given the absurd number who remained on the streets, selling themselves and wasting away. But to me, they were three people who didn't die." I shrug. "They got their chance at life."

"Do you still go out like that, into those neighborhoods and abandoned buildings?"

Because I'll officially kick your ass if you do, he doesn't add.

My stare travels to the wall behind him, struggling to admit what I do. "No. Although I'm thankful I was able to help those that I did, I stopped going when I realized exactly how much I was risking compared to what I was getting."

He lets out a breath, as if relieved. It takes me by surprise as does the kindness in his gaze. "Good," he says.

"I don't know about that," I reply slowly. "It's like so many are on this sinking ship and there aren't enough life preservers or boats to save them. Sometimes, I still want to be that person out in that ocean, pulling people into my rowboat or tossing them a life preserver. But I can't, not when I risk them pulling me under."

"Or stealing your boat?" he offers.

I laugh a little. "Yes. That, too. But if I'm struggling to reach someone or get them to trust me, like with Tricia, I attend these 'field trips' as I call them."

"Why is victim services so important to you? And don't tell me it's because it's your job." He threads his hands behind his head, scrutinizing me closely. "What's your story?"

My lips part. Declan doesn't know about me, only what he sees on the surface. I was sure Dad had mentioned at least a little about what I've been through. I guess I was wrong.

I adjust my position in my seat, that awful sense of unease I bury deep crawling uncomfortably along my skin. Maybe I shouldn't be surprised Dad didn't say anything about my past, he's always been protective. But for some reason, I am. Probably because he adores Declan.

For a moment I don't answer, wondering if I can trust this man that only days earlier, I could barely stomach. But when something softens in his features, I take a chance. "There are too many like me in the world, Declan. But most never get the help I received on that sinking ship."

He pauses, dissecting each word. "You're not talking about kids with special needs, are you?"

I shake my head. "No."

Considering I was ready to come clean about why I do what I do, I almost immediately clam up. Probably because

I'm about to add another layer of imperfection. "Did you know I was adopted?"

His eyes widen slightly. It's a subtle gesture, and if I wasn't watching him closely, I might have missed it.

This news probably wouldn't be a big deal to anyone else. But Declan is smart. He knows where I'm headed and that it's not someplace especially good. "I guess not," I answer for him.

"I never saw a family resemblance," he replies. "But I never gave it much thought, assuming you took after your mother."

"Maybe, I do. I don't remember much about her," I confess. "I could be Latina or Caucasian, maybe both or something entirely different. I really don't know or have anyone to ask."

"It doesn't say on your birth certificate?"

"There's no father listed and no mention of my mother's ethnicity," I answer. I take him in, curious about what he's thinking and maybe what he thought before now. "What did you think my childhood was like?"

"Before I realized you were adopted?"

When I nod, he stares back at me like a man who's been given a test he can't possibly pass. "It's okay," I add, smiling. "There's no wrong answer."

I'm not sure if he believes me, but he tells me anyway. "I figured Miles had a wife, your mother, and that she died when you were young."

"You assumed a lot of negative things," I say, quietly. "I'm not offended, but may I ask why you thought Dad was widower rather than a divorced man?"

"If you want to know, I'll tell you," he answers, his tone serious. "But you're not going to like what I have to say."

"Tell me anyway," I reply.

He lowers his arms so his elbows fall against the armrests. "You both always seemed a little sad, like you lost someone important to you."

I try not to react, but I'm stunned by what he says and by how easily he summed up our lives in a few simple words.

Declan is insightful and sensitive, too. In a way, it scares me. It's not a side I expected to see.

He's right, though. My father and I did lose something precious. Dad lost his opportunity to fall in love with someone and have children of his own, and I lost the opportunity to have a real mother I could cherish.

The mother I did have wasn't warm or compassionate. There were no gentle touches, no kind gestures, nothing I could recall that demonstrated any semblance of love. I knew only harshness and fear in her hands. I knew only pain.

Is it a wonder that it's so hard for me to trust, when the person who was supposed to love me most did nothing but harm me?

The pain . . . it's still raw in a way. Not just because of how I was treated, but because I've never understood how people could be so heartless. Yet as much as I'm feeling, and as deeply as it haunts me, I don't dare admit as much to Declan.

What I do reveal is the truth. "My birth mother was an addict. She tried to sell me when I was little to maintain her habit."

Declan stops moving. "What do you mean she tried to sell you? For adoption?"

It's what he asks, but the darkness shadowing his features reveals he knows better. Part of me wants to spare him, worried what he might think of me. But I take a risk and trust him a little further, even though a more vulnerable side of me warns I'm making a mistake. "Not for adoption," I admit quietly.

Disgust spreads along his handsome face and I'm certain he's stopped breathing. When he speaks, I almost expect him to change the subject. "How old were you?" he asks, instead, his tone harsh.

"Almost six, I think."

Anger overtakes his features, making it hard for me to hold his stare. "Tell me what happened," he says.

I cross my legs and place my hands over my knee, speaking carefully so he hears me and because a part of me knows there's no going back. "There was this man . . . I'm not sure if he'd seen me before and asked for me, or if my mother simply offered to get what she needed. Regardless, he came to our apartment one morning while I was watching cartoons."

"Jesus," he says, already anticipating what was coming next.

I want to stop and end the story. Somehow, I keep going. "I felt his footsteps marching toward the bedroom before my mother grabbed me and yanked me out of my clothes. I didn't know what she was doing. But I was scared by how rough she was and tried to resist. She slapped me, trying to subdue me. When I was finally naked, she shoved me into the room where the man was waiting."

"Please tell me you got away. That you weren't hurt." His breath releases in stiff motions as if in pain. "Tell me you got away."

Because his little brother didn't.

The compassion and sympathy he demonstrates threatens to release tears I thought had dried long ago. "I got away," I assure him.

He closes his eyes, long enough to release a breath and steady his breathing.

"It was summer and the window was partly open. He was drunk or high and stumbling. I was able to escape before he could hurt me." I try to smile. "Dad was the assistant D.A. in charge of my case. He told me that from the first moment he saw me, he didn't want to let me go."

Declan's gaze sweeps along my face. "I don't blame him," he tells me.

My heart stalls. He continues to take me in, like he needs to or can't stop. I think he's going to say something sweet.

"Your mother was a piece of shit," he adds.

Or perhaps not.

I glance down. "I won't argue with that."

In the heavy silence that follows, the universe disappears, leaving us gently tucked within the soothing peace enveloping us. It shouldn't feel this tranquil. My story is one of nightmares. But it is unbelievably serene, and although neither of us move, I feel Declan close in, the warmth of his body reaching out to stroke me.

We lose ourselves in each other's stare. I can't move and I barely breathe.

"Mel," he says, his blue eyes sparkling.

"Yes?" I manage.

"I . . ." He clears his throat. "I'm glad you got away."

"I am, too," I tell him gently. Our moment is gone. I know it. I reach for my notes and skim through them. "Before we get back to Tricia, I need to —"

"About your dad," he begins.

"Yes?" I ask, lowering my pad.

"He's—look, there are seven of us kids in the family. Six boys, and one girl who could kick our asses if we pissed her off enough. My mother raised us in a tiny three bedroom row home. She owned her own dry cleaning service and worked herself to exhaustion to put us through Catholic school. She'd take us to church every Sunday so God wouldn't strike us dead for all the sins we'd commit Monday through Saturday. If it wasn't for her, none of us would have made it out of the neighborhood we were raised in alive."

He reaches for his pen, appearing pissed. "We barely knew our father. When he wasn't working his part time job at the post office, he was in bed with his mistress. Those baseball games dads take their kids to? It was our mother who took us and paid for our popcorn and drinks, because that's all she could afford. Those sports we were all in, the ones fathers are supposed to attend and cheer you on at? That was my mother yelling, and my brothers and sister cheering." He looks up at me. "Ideally, we're supposed to have parents, a team that works together for their kids. But sometimes the team sucks, and only one parent steps up. That's okay. You have one good one, you can take on the fucking world. That's what your dad and my mother were to us." He starts scribbling. "Now, what did you want to ask me?"

For a moment, all I can do is gape. Declan isn't unloading to unload, he's trying to bond with me.

He glances up when all I do is sit there. "Melissa, what

else is on your agenda?"

"Your sister-in-law." It's what I say, because that area of discussion is professional, unlike my insane desire to kiss him.

"Excuse me?"

"I'd like you to consider Tess for SACU." Again it's what I say, and what's relevant. So why am I focused on his shirt, and how I'd like to ruin it by ripping it open to trace my initials on his chest with my tongue?

"No. Tess is bright, but she doesn't have enough trial experience yet." His voice cuts off when he realizes I'm blushing. "Something wrong?"

"Not at all," I answer, although something clearly is. Within a span of a few minutes and with just a handful of words, Declan has turned me into one of those ridiculous women who pant after him.

Holy heavens. I want to have sex with Declan O'Brien.

CHAPTER 7

Declan

I rest my head against my hand, hoping I don't look as nauseated as I feel. Someone knocks on my door. I'm ready to lie and yell that I'm in a meeting. But I know it's Mel and that we need to talk.

"Come in." I realize I'm muttering and that she probably can't hear me. "Come in," I call louder.

She walks in slowly, takes one good look at me, and sighs. I don't say anything, waiting for her to speak. Fuck. Me. Tricia Helmsley belongs in an institution. Marketing executive or not, the woman is bat-shit crazy.

The door clicks shut as Melissa rests her back against it. "You okay?" she asks.

When I don't answer, she takes a seat in front of me. It's only been a few weeks, but Mel already knows how to read me. She knows when I need space, and better yet when I need her. But given the amount of hours we spend together each day, trained counselor or not, I suppose she would have figured me out eventually.

I rub my face. This job sucks, though I won't complain about what it's done for me and Mel. Do we always agree on things? Hell, no. But the hostile tension between us has been replaced with a different kind of tension, one that involves her knees on either side of my head.

She's wearing a sleeveless coral dress today. It's simple, professional, and sexy as hell on her. When she walked in this morning to meet with me about the new smart phones she secured for my detectives and handed me the large cup of coffee she bought me, "just because," I couldn't stop picturing what it would be like to pull the zipper all the way down until her dress fell in a pile at her feet.

But that was before Tricia Helmsley.

"Declan," Mel pleads. "I know Tricia is a challenging witness and somewhat hard to like."

"Hard to like?" I repeat. "She asked me if I'd ever taken it up the ass when I asked her to explain what happened when Morris entered her apartment." I look up at the ceiling as I recall the ninety hellish minutes I'll never get back in my life. "You heard that, right? And when I tried to redirect her she told me how she'd have fun shaving my boys."

"She wasn't in a good place today," Mel offers.

"I don't know about that. She offered to buy me my first butt plug."

"Declan . . ."

"That was nice of her, don't you think? Oh, but the real treat was when she told me she'd get one with my birthstone on it."

"I realize—"

"My fucking birthstone, Mel. I didn't even know they bedazzled that shit. Did you?" I huff. "If that doesn't say welcome to SACU, I don't know what does."

Mel clasps her hands in front of her. "I'm going to work with her. Next time, I'm sure the prep for trial will go better."

I meet her square in the eye. "There isn't going to be a trial. I have to plead this case out."

"You can't. He assaulted her, Declan." She throws her hands out when I don't budge. "Please tell me you believe her."

"It's not that I don't believe *her*, I don't believe *in* her as a reliable witness. Look at what I'm dealing with here. She's a submissive at Club Hurt. She and Morris went out on a date. She invited him back to her place where he tied her up and assaulted her. The defense is going to build it up as foreplay and consensual sex that comes with the lifestyle she actively participates in. Did you see the witness list? One of the men on it is a Dom—or whatever the hell they're called—from that same damn club. Throw in the fact that she's unstable and attempting to sabotage her own case . . ." I swipe at my face. "You can see I don't have a lot to work with here."

"She's only acting this way because she's traumatized after what he did to her. The experience has brought up deep-seated abuse from her past."

"I hear what you're saying, Mel. But putting her on the stand is going to make everything worse for her. This case will go public no matter how quiet we try to keep it, ruining Morris's reputation sure, but also hers once the BDSM comes out. And if she can't even get through testimony with me—if she's asking me questions about my sex life, telling me what she wants to do to me because she can't handle my questions, what the hell is she going to sound like in front of the jury?"

Mel tugs her skirt over her crossed leg. She does that, fusses with her clothes when she's frustrated. I suppose it beats tearing her hair out which is what I'm ready to do. "I've been urging her to go to counseling," she says. "It's what she most needs."

"No," I bite out. "She needs shock therapy and a shit ton of meds." I stand and face the window. I'm not trying to be an insensitive asshole, but that meeting was among one of the worst of my life. Is it a wonder people burn out in SACU? You don't forget the shit you see and hear, and there's no way to undo any of it. And the victims? Christ. No matter what, they'll always have that memory. Like Finnie and Wren.

God *damn* it.

"Are you all right?" Mel asks, well aware that I'm not.

"*Fine*," I answer, making no effort to fool her.

She gives me a moment. It's what I need more than anything right now. But like I said, Mel recognizes my needs better than most.

"You hear what I'm saying, don't you?" I ask when I can finally think straight. "I know you want to help her. I do, too. But making her testify isn't the way."

I cross my arms, taking in the city I love, whose residents I'd kill to protect. At the same time I wonder how many crazies are out there. Crazies like Tricia born of predators like Morris. Damn. Seriously, damn.

My spine stiffens as I hear Mel push away from her seat. My first thought is I pissed her off and that she's leaving. With everything going on with Miles, it's the last thing I want.

For the most part, Mel keeps it together. But last week, when I arrived at the hospital following his surgery, I found her in the hall crying alone. It tore me apart to see her that way and gave me insight to how much she's holding in.

She put on a brave face when she saw me, wiping her tears and trying to smile. But I still sensed her pain. Hell, I felt it. I hated seeing her so alone and scared. My first thought was to gather her in my arms and hold her close, and I almost did. But I knew if I touched her, there was no going back. That kiss I've been fighting to give her every time we've said goodnight would have followed and maybe led to something we're not ready for.

Her bruised expression remains ingrained in my mind, and even though she's probably mad at me, I don't want her to go. Mel has a way of settling me and everyone around her. For as distant and cold I once thought she once was, she's every bit as nurturing and sweet as everyone claimed. I see that now, mostly because she's let me.

Her warmth closes in around me as I sense her approach, lifting the tension bulging the muscles along my shoulders. Damn, I want to kiss her. Me, that same guy who'd get annoyed at Curran every time he showed his wife affection. I didn't understand how he couldn't just keep his hands to himself. I get it now. There have been moments I've barely held back around Mel.

Am I still dreaming about fucking her? Yeah. Almost every damn night. But when those dreams fail to make an appearance, I make up my own fantasies. Usually they're first thing in the morning, or late at night when I'm alone and can do something about it. But sometimes, like now, when it's just me and her, my mind wanders where it shouldn't and I think about what it would be like to bust that tension between us and allow it to explode.

She touches my shoulder, luring my attention to her face and that plump, pouty mouth. "Declan, if you approach opposing counsel now, they're going to know you're doubting Tricia and her stability. They're also going to think you can't win this case."

"Not if I spin it right," I tell her. I try to keep my expression neutral, ignoring my desire to tug her bottom lip with my teeth. "I'm going to remind them of all the DNA evidence we have, including the skin cells that were scraped from Tricia's nails."

"And you think that will be enough?"

"Based on her BDSM lifestyle? Not even close," I confess. A tiny wrinkle forms on her brow when she frowns. I want to cup her face, smooth my thumb across her skin. And that's just the start. But right now, I can't go there.

"I'm going to make it clear how broken she is because of what happened between her and Morris," I continue. "And that as a result of their night together, she's attending intensive counseling. I'm also going to tell him that I'm prepared to put her counselor on the stand to verify she has PTSD and bring in an expert that will educate and spell out to the jury what victims like Tricia go through."

Mel tilts her chin. "You need me to convince her to attend counseling."

I shake my head. "No. I need her in *intensive* counseling. Minimum three times a week with a therapist that deals specifically with PTSD. Preferably a renowned psychiatrist opposing council would be fools to question." I cock a brow. "Know anyone?"

"I do," she says. "So your plan is to wait, to get her into counseling so the defense knows you're not misleading them?" I nod. "What if they still want to try the case?"

Then we're all fucked. It's what I think, but I don't say it. "If Tricia wants to go through with it, we will. But Mel, you need to talk to her about me pleading this case out. I'm serious," I add when she opens her mouth to argue. "It's not going to take much for the defense to turn her into a blubbering mess and for the members of the jury to turn against her."

The way she takes in every inch of my face, I'm sure we're seconds from going at it. Instead she answers with a small nod. "I wish you were wrong about her stability."

"Me, too," I admit. "Morris is another scumbag who needs to be put away for a long time. The problem is, Tricia doesn't have what it takes to help me make it happen. Not the way she's acting now. At the very least, Morris will have to register as a sex offender. That in itself will be a win."

She bows her head. "I just wish there was a way to give her more."

She starts to head out, but I don't want her to go. All this darkness I deal with every time I sit at my desk would be impossible to push through without Mel. In the few weeks we've worked together, she's become my salvation. It's like I can't see anything good when she's not around.

"How about dinner tonight?" I ask as she reaches the door.

Her fingers linger over the knob as she thinks about it. "That could work. I need to discuss the Winston case with you and possibly adding another detective with a grant I just had approved."

"No. No work," I say. "Just you and me, talking about anything but this place."

She pauses, as if she unsure what I'm asking. "Like friends? Going out to eat?"

I peg her with a look that cements her in place, surprising her, and me too. "Maybe not like friends," I confess, my voice gruff.

Her full lips part. She wasn't expecting this. I can't blame her, considering how bad I screwed up the first time I asked her to have dinner with me. "I thought you didn't date women you work with," she reminds me.

"I'll make the exception for you."

Warmth spreads along her cheeks. She's not blushing like she's embarrassed . . . no, not with the way those sweet brown eyes sizzle. There's a whole lot of heat that has nothing to do with being shy. I know, because I'm feeling it, too.

"I don't think that's a good idea," she says, a slight quiver to her voice.

My tone stays even. "Why?"

"We work together, Declan. My father is your boss. And—" She cuts herself off, as if she was about to say something she shouldn't. "It's not a good idea," she adds quietly, passing her hands along her skirt.

"I think you're wrong." Reason tells me to shut my mouth and move on—to end this conversation and not go there again. Except I can't. Melissa, with her killer body, sexy smile, and keen intelligence makes it hard to stop. "And I think you know it, too."

Her chest rises and falls with purpose, mimicking mine as I fight to stay in place. Ten feet. That's all that separates us. "I don't think we should," she says.

I open my mouth to say more and keep her with me. But then she throws open the door and walks out, shutting it tight behind her.

CHAPTER 8

Melissa

"I don't want to see him," Jennifer says to me. "I can't do this."

I'm an advocate for victim services, but as a director, my caseload is limited due to the severity of the cases I cover and my other obligations to the state. Jennifer's case isn't one I'm handling. *Brenda* is her advocate. But as much as Brenda means well, she's new, and Jennifer has completely consumed her time.

I'm trying to remain calm, but with the murmuring echoing from all sides and the loud voices spilling from the courtrooms, I'll admit, I'm overwhelmed. I motion Jennifer to the opposite side of the foyer, allowing the deputies escorting a row of shackled prisoners a wide berth to pass. Unfortunately, these men in their condition are the last thing Jennifer needs to see now.

"You can't make me do this," Jennifer whimpers, glancing back at them. "You can't make me do that to *him*."

I hold out my hands, keeping my voice soft. "No one is making you do anything. But your testimony can make a difference between Darren serving several years or just a few months."

"But I love him," she insists. "I don't want to see him suffer. Did you see those men?"

"This isn't about them," I say, trying to keep her focused. "It's about Darren and how he hurt you."

"But I love him," she insists, her voice cracking.

This is the hardest part of doing what I do. Some people are so broken they can't be reasoned with. Jennifer, like many women in her situation, is scared to death of her abuser. He's fractured her jaw, landed her in ICU, and placed her in debt she will never recover from. But she "loves" him. Or so she believes.

She doesn't know what real love is. Having been abused all her life, her brain has conditioned her to think those you most love should also hurt you. Kindness and compassion are elements completely foreign to her. Which is why she's in the situation she's in.

If it weren't for a police officer who witnessed the assault and pulled Darren off Jennifer, she wouldn't even be here. She didn't press charges. The police officer did. But he can only account for this incident, and Jennifer is refusing to step up for the rest.

"Do you think Darren loves you?" I ask her carefully.

Her lips press tight. "Of course he does. He says it all the time."

No. He says it *after* he beats you so you'll stay. I don't tell her this, obviously. It's the last thing any victim needs to hear. Instead, I put the blame back on Darren where it belongs. "If he truly cares about you, then why does he hurt you?"

Brenda stiffens beside me. She shies away from asking the tough questions. But the way Jennifer is reacting, this is no time to be shy.

"He gets upset. His job is really hard," she says quickly, stumbling over her words. Something shifts in her expression as her gaze sweeps over me, turning her from a cowering little mouse to vicious hell cat. "But I suppose you don't know anything about real work," she snaps. "You walk in here with your expensive clothes and your pretty hair. I bet you've never known a day of manual labor in your life. Have you, princess?"

In the span of a few seconds I went from someone who could possibly help her to her worst enemy for questioning Darren's devotion and challenging their so-called love. It's no surprise she's turned against me. It's happened to me before.

I ignore her remarks and stay calm. Nice or not, she's been hurt and needs my help. "Do you want to feel safe?"

She tightens her jaw.

"Jennifer," I say. "Do you want to feel safe?"

"What do you think?" she fires back, her voice stabbing at the air like a blade.

"If you want to feel safe, the man who hurt you needs to be placed somewhere where he can't reach you."

"No," she snaps. "He needs to be with me. He doesn't belong anywhere else. I need him. Do you understand what I'm saying? We need each other."

"You need kindness and patience, and to feel safe in your own home," I say, doing my best to help her understand. "Help us give you that opportunity."

Although I keep my hands loose at my sides, I'm prepared to block her strikes if they come. Someone as fragile and angry as Jennifer is unpredictable. She'll either completely break down or lash out. I can't presume to be safe simply because she's a victim herself.

Her expression crumbles and at once she's sobbing into her hands. I motion to Brenda. She hurries forward and places an arm around her. Thankfully, Jennifer welcomes the contact.

"I'll be over here," I mouth to Brenda, pointing to the small seating area.

She nods, but in many ways she's also in bad shape. Brenda is really smart and gentle, but I'm uncertain she'll last in SACU.

I take a seat on the bench and remove my hearing aids, trying to give myself a break from the constant assault of noise. The abrupt silence should scare me, and sometimes it's extremely jarring. Today I welcome it, taking a moment to breathe as I scan the packed area.

Tess is pleading out her first case involving a teen perpetrator. The defendant is young, about sixteen, but taller than she is and a great deal more imposing. It explains Curran's presence, as well as the deputies loitering a few feet away, eyeing her closely.

Detective Melo and Hernandez are also here, dealing with separate cases neither seem happy about.

Despite the obvious tension, Declan's arrival makes me smile. He marches toward me. I'm not sure if he's going to pass or stop and chat. I hope it's the latter. Given everything that's happened with Dad, and everything going on in the office, there's very little that makes me happy anymore.

Dad's surgery went as well as could be expected, but that isn't saying much. I lost it when the surgeon told me about the mass she discovered on his liver. If it hadn't been for Declan arriving at the hospital, I don't think I would have stopped crying that night. Like always, he appeared when I needed him most.

I sigh, thinking back to my dad. As soon as he gets stronger, he'll start chemo. The doctor hopes it will help shrink the tumor so she can remove it. But that means another surgery, and I'm unsure how much more my poor Daddy can take.

At least three times a week, I visit him after work, then spend the weekend catching up on everything I've put off to be with him.

He always meets me with a brave face, joking that I need to get a life. I don't tell him that a life without him is one I don't want to know. Goodness, there's been little to smile about.

Except around Declan.

"Hi," I say, when he lowers himself beside me.

"How's it going?" he asks. I can't hear him, but I read his lips without much effort.

"It's going," I say, struggling to keep my smile professional.

Since Declan asked me out, we've kept our talks cordial.

Well, at least I have. In truth, he's been absolutely, panty-singeing, good-God-I-want-to-kiss-him flirtatious. I've tried to dismiss it as something he does with everyone, but I'm no longer sure.

He frowns when he sees me holding my hearing aids. "Too loud?" he asks, lifting his chin so I have a view of his mouth and that face that's appeared in my dreams.

"Yes," I admit. I can hear myself speak, but not much else. It's a good thing right now, the absence of sound helping me settle.

"What are you doing here?" I ask.

He tilts his head in Tess's direction. "Watching out for my own."

I pause when I realize he's only mouthing and not speaking. Since it involves Tess, perhaps he wants to be discreet, given his role. The way he moves his full lips, though, is a bit of a turn on, and so is the way he's taking me in.

I tell myself he's only being friendly, no matter how much I'm enjoying the attention and despite that I no longer think Declan and I are just friends. We haven't acted on our feelings. But each day that passes and moments spent with him make it harder for me to keep my distance.

"It looks like she has a good handle on it," I say.

"She does," he agrees. "But this little bastard is too volatile for his own good. We're pushing for a psych eval. Tess isn't budging until she gets it." He glances over to where poor Brenda continues to try to reason with Jennifer. "How's it going over there?"

"I don't think she's going to testify," I admit.

He shakes his head. "Ramirez has been working his ass off on this case. It's not going to mean jack if she doesn't step up. Did you try talking to her?"

"I did, but I don't have a rapport with her and she shut me out."

"I wish we could make her. But labeling her a hostile witness isn't going to help."

"No," I agree. "Our side will just be taking on the role of

her abuser."

He watches her for a beat. "If she could just get away from this idiot, she could have a fresh start," he says.

"Maybe. Maybe not. Even with him in prison, someone as damaged as Jennifer is likely to find another abuser to take his place."

"Yeah. You're probably right," he says.

He lifts one of the hearing aids from my hand, holding it by the clear and flexible hook. He examines it carefully, twisting it slowly around. Most people tend to picture large clunky plastic devices when they envision hearing aids. Mine are practically invisible.

"So when are you going to have dinner with me?" he asks.

This man, who positively drove me crazy, shouldn't make me smile this easily. "I thought we decided it wasn't a good idea."

"No. *You* said it wasn't a good idea. I'm saying it is." He shrugs. "I know I'm not one of those half-naked cowboys on the cover of those naughty books you like . . ."

I bite down on my bottom lip to keep from laughing.

"Or a pirate on the seven seas, my bare chest exposed to the wicked winds." He bows his head. "And if you want the truth, I don't even own a kilt."

I cover my mouth.

"But I'm not so bad. And if it's the kind of thing that turns you on, I'm sure I can find a place that rents ass-less chaps."

If it wasn't so loud in the common area and he wasn't turned so I'm the only one who could read his lips, I doubt he'd tell me everything he is.

I like what he has to say. Declan is tall, suave, handsome, I've always known that. But this is my favorite side of him, the one who teases and plays, and proves there's more to this man than ambition.

"No need for ass-less chaps, I assure you."

The twinkle in his eyes warms me in all the right places. "What about a parrot and an eye patch? Are pointy nipple pirates more your style?"

"No," I say before I can stop myself. "I like you just the way you are."

His gaze skims over my features. "Then what's the problem? Personally, I like what I see."

If I allowed it, I'd melt right into a puddle at his feet, but I can't. "Declan, my dad's your boss. We work together. This can't possibly end well."

"You won't even give me a chance, will you?"

As our stares weld together and I realize I'm feeling more than lust, I want to give in to that desire to fall into his embrace.

"It's not a good idea," I say again. I'm already vulnerable around him. If we start to date and things don't work out . . . I can't go there with him. Not if I'm going to stay strong for my father. "I'll see you later, okay?"

"All right," he says, placing my hearing aid gently against my palm.

I stand and make my way to the elevators, passing the crowd of people waiting for their turn before the judge. As I step into the elevator and turn back to face the group, my focus falls on Declan, and that's where it stays. That's where it always wants to stay.

CHAPTER 9

Declan

Trenti is one of the most elite restaurants in town, custom tailoring their menu for each guest. The food is incredible, the service impeccable. I've been here a few times, all with big-wigs with even bigger wallets. But tonight's a little different. I'm not here to rub elbows with a bunch of suits. I'm here to show a woman what she's missing out on.

Candles flicker along each table in the dimly lit room. I march across the dark wood floors, following behind the hostess who pauses to give me a very long and appraising glance. Maybe it's the Armani suit I'm wearing, or the cologne, or lack of tie that caught her interest. Either way, I don't care. I keep my attention on the table at the far end, a smirk splaying along my lips when I catch sight of Melissa's stunned face.

As much as I want to speak to her first, I address her father, because it's been too damn long since I've seen him. "Good evening, Miles," I say, shaking his hand. "Sorry I'm late." To Melissa, I simply wink, trying not to laugh at the way her jaw practically smacks against the table.

She lowers the glass of water she's holding onto the white tablecloth. "What are you doing here?" she asks slowly.

"What do you mean?" I say, keeping my grin. "I couldn't miss your father's coming out party." I motion to his menu. "Ready for more than just mashed potatoes, Miles?"

He chuckles, placing his hand against his stomach to suppress the pain laughing causes. Seven inches of colon. That's how much they removed. Two days after the surgery, he was already calling to check up on things. "I have it covered. Just get better," I told him.

I only hope he can.

Miles confided in me that Mel visits him almost every night after work. He's worried about her. I am, too. It's like all this woman knows is SACU and her dad. It wouldn't be so bad if Miles wasn't so sick. But he is.

She keeps her chin up and I admire her for it. But if she gives me the chance, I'd like to give her more to smile about, more to enjoy in life. Except every time I ask her out, she shoots me down.

"Did they cater a menu to your needs?" I ask, pretending like I belong here as much as Melissa does, despite the way she's covering her face.

"Salmon stuffed with black beans, covered with a zesty diablo sauce over tortellini," Miles says. He makes a face. "But when Melissa informed them of my recent surgery, the chef switched it to polenta with a light mushroom sauce." He narrows his eyes at his daughter, feigning anger he doesn't quite manage. "She gets the good stuff. I get cornbread topped with mushrooms."

"I'm not surprised," I say. "That daughter of yours is too much of a rule follower for her own good."

She ignores my reference to her "thou shall not date a co-worker" commandment. "It'll be easier to digest." She points at me. "And you butt out, counselor."

"Now, Melissa," Miles says, "Is this any way to talk to our guest?"

"Dad, behave. You're already in trouble with me. Cozy dinner, my Aunt Fanny," she mumbles.

I lift my water glass and take a sip, enjoying the exchange between Melissa and her father.

"You hear how she treats me?" Miles asks. "You'd think after all those dates I gave up to take her to the movies and door to door selling those damn cookies, she'd show me a little respect."

She crinkles her nose, laughing, although she's trying to sound annoyed. "You never gave up any dates. If anything, you used your sweet little innocent daughter to get them."

"Bull *shit*," Miles says.

She turns to me, pegging me with an expression that tells me she's up to no good. "Okay, we'll let Declan be the judge."

I hold up a hand. "Oh, no. I'm only here for a delicious drama free meal."

Melissa ignores me, edging her seat closer until our knees bump. If her old man wasn't here, my hand would be finding its way on that knee. She's in a seafoam green dress with capped sleeves and she looks fucking fantastic.

"Okay," she says, motioning to her breasts. "You might have guessed I hit puberty a little young."

I try not to laugh and even harder not to look. I fail on both counts. Melissa notices, her eyes widening briefly before she averts her gaze and glances at me with lowered lashes. Aw, hell, she's sexy.

She clears her throat, edging a little further from me. "Dad was oblivious. 'You don't need those things,' he said when I asked him to take me bra shopping."

"Those things?" I ask, shifting my attention to Miles.

"Declan, I was more prepared to fly a plane around the world than I was for puberty. You'll forgive me if I wasn't exactly jumping up and down."

"He was mortified," Mel agrees. "At *first*."

"Oh, yeah?" I ask, catching the way Miles's face reddens as he chuckles.

"Mmm-hmm. And I honestly felt bad for making him take me," she admits. "But turns out, if you want to pick up women, all you have to do is take your little daughter to Victoria's Secret and tell the horde—that's right, *horde* of sales associates who rush you—*and* all the single mothers shopping there with their daughters listening in—how you don't know the first thing about lingerie. And how tough it is being a single dad and trying do right by your daughter—"

"She's exaggerating," Miles interjects, reaching for his water.

"Am I?" she asks. "How many phone numbers did you get the first time we went there?"

Miles shrugs. "Six, maybe seven."

Melissa rolls her eyes. "More like nine. His social calendar was booked for the next month." She turns to her dad. "By your third date, I no longer believed you were hanging pictures in your bedroom."

"Hanging pictures?" I ask, taking another sip of water.

Mel purses her lips. "It's how he explained all the banging coming from his bedroom."

I almost spit out my water, making Miles crack up and hang tight to his side. "How many women were you taking home?"

He sits back in his chair, blotting the perspiration forming along his brow. As much as it appears to hurt him, he seems to welcome the laughter.

It's probably been a long while since he had a good time.

"There weren't that many women." His eyes cut Mel's way. "But enough that warranted an excuse, however pathetic."

"He used to sneak them out in the morning before I'd see them." She crosses her arms. "But I knew those tramps were there."

"They weren't tramps." He pretends to think about it. "At least twenty-two to twenty-eight percent attended church on a regular basis."

"Nice, Daddy," she says, standing.

"Where are you going?" he asks.

"Ladies room. I'll be right back."

I stand with her, sitting only once she disappears. "So tell me, out of all those women, you never found the one? Someone who'd make a good wife and mother?" Seeing how devoted he is to Mel, it's shocking he never married.

Miles hangs onto his smile, but it lacks enthusiasm now that Mel's gone. "The women who kept my interest didn't hang around for long."

"Why?"

"One in particular couldn't stay. The U.S. wasn't her home. The others *wouldn't* stay because of Melissa." He swirls the water in his glass, taking a moment to gather his words and allowing what he said to sink in. His admission is an emotional slap across the face. I barely move. Miles seems to realize it, taking another moment to explain. "As with most new relationships, they expected to be the priority and for me to devote my spare time to them. But I couldn't, not when Melissa needed me more."

"Because of her special needs?"

He nods. "I always thought I'd marry and have a few kids. It's how life is, am I right? Something most people do. I never thought I'd have a child without a wife, let alone adopt one on my own. But when I met Melissa, I couldn't bring myself to walk away. I'd handled enough cases to know what would happen to her, especially given how severely delayed and malnourished she was. She was just a kid. With no chance at surviving the system. Something inside me told me not to let her go. So I didn't." He lowers his glass. "It was the best decision I've ever made."

He means it. I can tell. But it's clear how much he gave up for her. "Any regrets?"

He thinks about it. "I wish I could have found the right woman, not for me necessarily, but for her. I played the role of mother and father, and for the most part, I think I played it well. But there were times she needed more. If a boy hurt her, my first reaction was to threaten to pound the shit out of him."

"That's understandable," I say, my anger stirring just knowing she'd been hurt.

"But that's not what Melissa needed. She needed a protector, certainly. But she also needed someone who could let her cry and relate to the pain she was feeling. I couldn't do that, too caught up in wanting to knock out the boy who'd reduced my little girl to tears."

I think I should say something. But though I pride myself on being quick on my feet, nothing comes to mind. Maybe that's a good thing. Maybe Miles just wants to be heard.

"Melissa came to me the first time she had her heart broken," he says, his stare growing distant. "He was the first boy she considered a good friend and the first she developed strong feelings toward. You can imagine how crushed she was when he asked a friend of hers to the fall dance instead of her. If that wasn't bad enough, he admitted he couldn't see himself with someone like her."

"*Someone like her*?" I repeat. "What the hell is that supposed to mean?"

"I don't know," he responds. "But that's not the point. It's what he said and how she took it." He shrugs, trying to play it off as if it no longer matters, even though I think it does. "I called him an asshole and told her she was too good for him."

"It's probably the same thing I would have done," I say. In addition to stalking his ass and bashing his face in.

"Maybe," he says. "But it wasn't what she needed. She was trying to tell me she didn't feel good enough and that she never would. Instead of ripping into the little bastard and putting him down, I should have been building her up." He motions to the women at the next table. "A mother would have known that."

"I see your point," I say. "But everything I've come to know about Melissa shows me you did a damn good job."

He sighs. "Hopefully, but as a parent you always wish you could have done better, said something a little differently, tried a little harder, and opened your mind a little more. She's my greatest gift, but one I don't think I've given enough back to."

I meet him square in the eye so that he knows that I mean what I say. "Miles, Melissa couldn't have asked for a better mother or father than you."

"God, I hope so," he says, finishing off his water.

Melissa returns then, laughing when I stand. "Quit pretending to be a gentleman just because my father is here."

"Just being myself," I say, throwing in another wink.

"If you were, you'd already have that blonde's phone number listed under your contacts," she says, tilting her head to the right.

Funny, I hadn't even noticed her looking at me. But with Mel around, I have a hard time noticing other women. Her intelligence and sexiness are more than enough to hold my attention. Considering what a whore I am, it should scare the unholy shit out of me.

"It's still not too late to get laid, counselor," she tells me.

True, but it's not the blonde I want to take to bed. I don't tell her with Miles here. But I would if we were alone.

I groan, making a face like she's left me no choice but to retaliate. "You're making me pull out the big guns." She cocks her head, unsure what I mean. I ignore her and address Miles. "Care to share any embarrassing stories involving Melissa's ex-boyfriends? I'm sure her magnetic personality has lured plenty of boys home."

"*Declan*," she warns.

"I can't," Miles begins.

"Thanks, Dad," she says.

"There're too many to choose from," he continues. He ignores Melissa's gasp and begins to tell me about Rodrigo, a state senator's son who tried to serenade her beneath her bedroom window.

"He wanted to be a professional singer," Miles says, grimacing. "But the boy couldn't sing. It was like a desperate cat, trying to make his way up a chimney. And you knew the little guy wasn't going to make it."

"He's not joking," Melissa admits, pouting her sweet lips. "By the second chorus I had to remove my hearing aids so I could finish my schoolwork. He wouldn't take the hint I simply wasn't interested."

With a sigh, she reaches for her phone.

"What are you doing?" I ask, grinning. "We're just getting started."

"Don't worry, this will only take a minute," she says, returning my smile. "Hi. It's Melissa Fenske . . . No, nothing's wrong. I'm having dinner with my dad and Declan. Is Curran home?"

All traces of humor immediately dissolve from my face. "Hey, Curran. Declan is here asking my father about my ex-boyfriends. But I don't want him to feel left out, since we're only talking about me and not him. Care to share any interesting stories about his past girlfriends or hook-ups? . . . You would?" She bats my hand away when I try to reach for the phone. "Great, I'll put you on speaker."

She places the phone between her and her dad. "For shit's sake," I mutter.

Curran's loud voice immediately fills the space between us. "Her name was Wrestling Rhonda Signaterri, also known as Rhonda the Wrangler," he begins.

No . . . not . . . *Fuck*.

"What an *interesting* nickname," Melissa gushes. "I wonder how she acquired a name like that."

"Wonder no more," Curran chimes in. "So Rhonda was hot—a slutty kind of hot—but still hot. She liked to wrestle, as in, got off on it. Oh, can your dad hear me?"

"Yes," Miles answers, laughing.

"Good," Curran says. "I don't want him to miss a thing. Anyway, so Declan, of course, challenges her to a wrestling match, trying to get her worked up so maybe they can wrestle afterwards with their clothes off, if you know what I mean."

"Oh, we know," Melissa and Miles say at once, cracking up.

"Anyway, Declan wins, or so he thought. Rhonda's breathing fast and so is he. They run back to our house knowing the house is empty and our mother is at work. But me and my brothers were curious to see if Deck gets the job done, or in this case, Rhonda done.

"We sneak back to the house only to find Declan tied to Ma's bed, spread eagle wearing nothing, but a pair of tighty whities and a grin. All our shit—our T.V., our sound system, everything, is gone. Turns out while he was sleeping off the experience with Rhonda the Wrestler, her brothers Patrick the Prowler and Theodore the Thug robbed us blind."

Melissa and Miles aren't laughing. They're howling, and so is Tess in the background, because why not?

Curran continues. I don't have to see him to know the son of bitch is smiling. "I don't think we're there two minutes before our Ma walks in. Angus, our oldest brother, tries to give Declan a running start and cuts him free. Deck barely rolls off the bed before our mother snatches him off the floor by his throat. The rest of us run for our lives. *Oh*, but that's nothing. Wait till I tell you about Tina the Tramp . .."

CHAPTER 10

Melissa

Bethany's little son grins at me, showing off his bottom teeth and flapping his arms. I kneel on the floor with them and sign to Bethany. *Can I hold him?*

Of course, she motions, turning Peyton toward her. *Do you want to go to Aunt Melissa?*

Like Bethany, little Peyton was born with severe hearing loss. Already he seems to understand a great deal. He angles around to face me, offering a sweet smile and reaching for me when I hold out my arms.

"Oh, sweet boy," I say, gathering him to me.

I love babies. The way they coo and smile, and their total innocence completely melts me. Sometimes, though, I grow a little sad being around them. It's not that I've given up on marriage and family, but working where I work, and doing what I do, makes it impossible to meet a potential baby daddy.

A knock on the door has me looking up. "Hey," I say when I see Declan standing there.

Okay . . . maybe not completely impossible.

He grins back at me, reassured I've given him the smile he likes, the one that means "I haven't pissed you off today" as he puts it. Funny thing, he doesn't piss me off. We don't always see eye to eye, and sometimes we go back and forth before we reach an agreement, or at least find common ground. But . . . things are better between us. I sigh at the way his light blue dress shirt brings out his eyes. No, things are a lot better.

"I don't want to interrupt your meeting," he says, his eyes sparkling as if on cue. "But I have a meeting in another half hour, and I need you to sit in on it."

I cuddle Peyton closer, rubbing his small back. Today is a little easier to keep my smile having this sweet baby so close, regardless of where I see this conversation going. Most days, though, are harder. Declan and I have handled too many tough cases lately, all surrounding horrific circumstances, forcing us to work late. Between my Dad starting chemo and hardly any time to myself, I'm ready to snap. And if it weren't for Declan, I likely would.

Declan has completely chiseled his way into my heart. Just two months ago, I wouldn't have believed he could. I viewed him like so many politicians I interact with, an overly inflated ego stuffed into a suave suite, driven to succeed no matter who it harmed. Now, I can't find any joy until I see him.

"Does this case involve 'R'?" I ask.

Bethany is too busy looking at Declan to read my lips, but I have to keep things confidential. He gives me a stiff nod, his smile vanishing. I let out a sigh. Rosana called me crying the other day and told me her mother's pressuring her to drop all charges against Iker. I reassured her that she has our full support and counseled her on the phone until she calmed. If Declan is meeting with them this whole thing is getting ugly.

"I'll be there," I assure him.

"Thanks, Mel," he says. He nods to Bethany who can't stop gawking at him.

Who's that? Bethany signs.

I perch Peyton on my lap. *Acting District Attorney Declan O'Brien,* I sign. I'm doing my best to appear casual, but the size of my grin gives me away.

How long have you been seeing each other?

I lower my chin to kiss Peyton's head and give my face a moment to cool. *We're not dating*, I motion. *We're simply colleagues.*

Colleagues don't stare at each other like they want to take each other's clothes off, Bethany responds.

That's not how I was looking at him, I insist, even though that's pretty much how I look at him every time we're alone. But if Bethany, who doesn't know me well, can see right through me, who else knows I've fallen for Declan as hard as all those women I used to make fun of?

I think you found who you need, she signs.

I think you're reading way too much into this, I tell her.

It's what I say, but I already know she's right.

My long floral skirt bats against my legs as I swoop into Declan's office. "Hi," I say.

His suit jacket is hanging on a hook behind him and about ten case files are spread across his desk. "Hey," he says, smiling despite the hot mess in front of him.

Instead of taking a seat in front of him, I walk around to stand beside him, crossing my arms as I skim through the file names. All are particularly violent cases and require immediate attention. "You have to reassign these, don't you?"

He nods. "Curran ripped into me for giving Tess three of them, claiming she's pregnant and I shouldn't be giving her cases like this."

Curran is only watching out for Tess, but Declan and I are watching out for all these victims. "And how is Tess taking it?"

He rubs his jaw, like he does when he's troubled. "She assures me she's ready and up for the challenge." He drops his hand away. "But she's one person. I need Carmichael and Saunders to handle the rest, but they're greener than Tess."

He shakes his head. "These cases are complex and will likely go to trial if we can't agree on plea. I'm giving each two. I can't handle them all myself. And if I give them more, I don't think they'll last the remainder of the year."

"Which leaves you with three additional cases," I reason.

"That's right," he says.

Which means he'll likely try seven major cases over the next year. It would have been eight if he didn't successfully plea out Tricia's case. "I'm having lunch at the Fat Salmon with the governor on Tuesday."

He slumps in his seat. "Awesome. Order the Dragon Fly, you won't be disappointed."

I lean against the desk in a half-sitting position so I can meet his face smiling slightly. "I want you to come with me. You're doing a great job, but you're taking on too much."

His eyes skim along my body, just like they do every time we're alone. At first, he was more subtle. Now, not so much. It's like he no longer cares what I might think and wants me to know he's looking at me.

"What are you thinking?" he asks.

That I want to kiss you. I fantasize about his lips all the time. How they would taste and whether I could stop once I started. Kissing Declan wouldn't be an innocent gesture. I'd start at his mouth and keep going, down to his throat and chest and further yet.

I've never told him, but each time, it becomes harder not to at least drop a hint. I don't, of course, choosing to talk about business instead. Business is safe. Declan isn't, not when I'm feeling more than simply lust.

"The D.A. offices need more staff in SACU. I'm limited to what I can offer on the law enforcement side, but perhaps you and I can convince the governor we need more A.D.A.s in this unit statewide." I motion to the stack. "This is ridiculous, Declan. One attorney can't take on all this alone."

I grip the sides of the desk, waiting for him to argue. Declan often allows his ego to get in the way, pushing him to do more than is humanly possible. He knows how hard this job is. This time, he thankfully doesn't give me a hard time.

"All right," he says. "Thank you."

"Don't thank me yet. We still have a governor to convince."

I start to push away from the desk, but the gentle sweeps of his fingers across the back of my hand keep me in place. My breath lodges in my chest. Such a delicate touch shouldn't create such a firm hold or warm my skin the way it does, and it most certainly shouldn't send a wave of goose bumps along the length of my arms. Except, that's the power Declan seems to have over me. I love it in a way, but in another, it frightens me.

"Who was that woman in your office?" he asks.

His gaze sears into mine, making it impossible to answer right away. "Her name is Bethany. She was a victim of domestic violence. One of the local agencies helped me relocate her to Canada when the case against her ex-husband was dismissed."

His fingers stop against my knuckles. "Excuse me?"

"It's something that happens a lot," I confess. "When the victim is in danger and the system has failed."

"You're aiding and abetting a woman kidnapping her own child?"

I shake my head, hoping he'll understand. "Bethany was five months pregnant when the charges against her abuser were dropped due to lack of evidence. If she would have stayed, Tomas would have killed her. I took her to a battered woman's shelter, knowing that they'd help transport her out of the country and to safety. The only reason she returned is because Tomas is currently serving a life sentence. He met someone almost immediately after Bethany left. This woman didn't make it."

"Jesus," he mutters, dropping his hand away.

The memory surrounding the incident breaks my heart and I wish Declan hadn't pulled away. The way he stroked my hand gave me comfort I could use as I explain. "In an ideal world, the A.D.A. would have tried and won Bethany's case, justice would have been served, and Tomas would have been sentenced and held accountable for the multiple assaults he committed. That wasn't what happened. Off the record, I did the only thing I could for her."

"So, she had her baby, and now that it's safe she came back."

His voice is so quiet, I have to read his lips. Not that it stops my smile. "Not the best happily ever after," I admit. "But I'll take it."

The corner of his mouth lifts into a lopsided smile. "You looked good holding that baby," he tells me. "Happier than I've ever seen you."

I laugh, slightly embarrassed. "I adore babies and want a million."

He chuckles. "Impressive. We're Irish Catholic and I don't think we can manage that many."

I glance down. "I'd be happy with one, a healthy one."

"What do you mean by healthy?" He frowns when I don't answer. "You don't mean one who can hear, do you?"

Declan has a way of reaching me down to my core. My voice splinters, though it's not what I want. "I like who I am," I begin.

"Good," Declan says, his frown firmly in place. "Because I like who you are, too."

He's trying to be sweet. I try to make him understand without sounding like I'm feeling sorry for myself. "I like who I am," I repeat. "But as much as the great things in my life have shaped me, like my father and his kindness, there have been some awful things that have shaped me, too."

I push off the desk. "My birth mother neglected me so severely, I didn't attend school until Dad stepped in. I was significantly delayed as result. Dad fought to make sure I'd receive all the help I needed, but the process to adopt me was lengthy, limiting the services I was eligible for regardless of my needs." I shrug. "Learning ASL and to verbally speak, in addition to reading and math, took longer and was more challenging as result."

"But still you learned," he reminds me. "And not only did you catch up, you likely surpassed those your age."

"I did," I agree. "But I never felt like I belonged."

"Belonged where?" he asks, clearly confused.

"Among my peers." It's what I say, but it's only partly true. Growing up, I never felt like I belonged anywhere, except with my dad. "It was hard being different," I admit. "I wish I didn't care so much what others thought of me when I was growing up, but I did." It's hard to tell him what I do, and I almost turn away. Somehow I manage to keep my chin up and continue. "For a long time, I stopped wearing my hearing aids."

"Why?" he asks.

My mind wanders, and for a brief second, I'm there, walking the halls of my high school alma mater. My mother's actions significantly impacted me, but what occurred within the walls of that school also took their toll. "Kids would say things, mean things," I clarify. "They'd make fun of the way I spoke, that sort of nonsense."

"Is that why you'd take your hearing aids off?" he asks, anger finding its way across his features. "So you wouldn't have to hear what they said?"

I answer so quietly, I barely hear myself. "Yes."

He reaches for my hands, holding them within his. "Was that the only reason?"

I don't know if it's the kindness I sense in Declan's voice or the gentle way in which he holds me, or if maybe the memories I've suppressed for so long have found their way to the surface simply through his presence. Whatever the reason, my eyes sting in a way I wish they wouldn't. "When something brushes too close to my hearing aids, it creates a back noise, like a squeal. It's uncomfortable."

"Does it hurt?" he asks.

Wow. No one's ever asked me that. "It can. If it's loud enough." I try to relax my stance and pretend that what I say no longer affects me, even though that lump building in my throat reminds me that it does. "Girls couldn't whisper their secrets because I'd react in a way that made them uncomfortable, even though I was the only one who'd hear the squeaks and squeals." I swallow hard. "There were these boys who found out. When they'd pass me in the hall, they'd tug on my hair or flick my ear just to watch me jump."

The strong angles along his face tighten, reflecting his anger. I try to steady my emotions. I don't want him upset over things no one can change, and I don't want him to pity me. I also need him to understand that despite the traces of pain that linger, I'm all right.

"It was hard," I confess. "I pushed through and survived. But because I know what it's like to grow up and live with special needs, and because I've seen how cruel people can be, I don't want my babies to struggle." I smile, for me, and for him. "That doesn't mean that I'd love my child any less if he or she had issues. I'm only saying I wouldn't wish that kind of heartbreak on anyone."

"Neither would I," he says. "But like you said, everything you went through, good and bad, helped you become who you are." The steel hard look mixed with ardor he pegs me with knocks me on my ass. "And I think you're *fucking* amazing."

"Ah."

My face or my oh-so brilliant response causes a very slow and absurdly sexy grin to ease across Declan's face.

I'm in trouble. Serious trouble. And I must say, trouble has never looked so hot.

Declan's phone rings. He barely blinks, keeping his eyes on me as he hits the speaker icon. "O'Brien," he answers.

His secretary's voice echoes through the speaker. "Declan, Detective Melo and your witnesses are ready for you."

"Send them in please, Ellie." He stands when the phone

clicks, his playful expression daring me to follow. "You and me, have to do something about this."

I turn around as he shrugs into his jacket, my eyes scanning the pile of cases littering his desk. "Do something about what?" I ask, stacking the files as if I have no interest in straddling him.

His hand presses against the small of my back, stilling me in place. "You know what I mean," he whispers.

I start to deny it because I think I should when Detectives Melo and Hernandez burst in with Rosana in hysterics. "What happened?" Declan snaps

I hurry to Rosana. She falls into my arms as I gather her close. "My mother wants me to drop the charges," she stammers between huge gulps of air.

Detective Melo shuts the door, appearing seconds from losing what remains of his cool. I lead Rosana to the leather couch against the wall, trying to put some space between her and her mother. She sobs against my shoulder as I ease her down. She's devastated and feels betrayed. How can she not? Her own mother is siding with the man who robbed her of her innocence.

I want to shake Vilma, scream at her for failing to protect her child. But when the first of her tears stream down her face, I'm reminded that she's as broken as her daughter and likely a victim herself.

Declan turns his full attention on Vilma. "Why are you protecting the man who hurt your daughter?"

His question is blunt and his tone stern. He's not yelling, but his frustration and anger spread along the air like a mounting storm.

Valencia Hernandez sits beside Vilma, waiting for her to speak. "You need to answer my question," Declan tells her.

Vilma lowers her chin. She knows Declan won't stop pushing her until she answers. Valencia interprets as she speaks. "His family is from the same country I am. They're calling Rosana a liar. They say this is an injustice and if Iker isn't released they're going to kill my family."

Jesus.

Every emotion I feel plays along Declan's features, but the most dominant is fury. He looks at Detective Melo. "Do you still have old army buddies living in Honduras?"

Detective Melo smiles. "As a matter of fact I do." He looks to Vilma as Valencia continues to interpret. "They're missionaries now, but not exactly the kind who do God's work. I'm sure they won't mind finding Iker's family and politely requesting they stop threatening yours."

Vilma shuts her mouth, but she doesn't seem any happier. She's ready to run away screaming from this whole mess.

Declan won't let her.

"Here's the deal," he says. "I don't bend to anyone. That's not my job. My job is to put criminals behind bars and that's what I intend to do. You're not supporting your daughter. I don't like it. But legally, there's nothing I can do to make you." He leans forward. "Just so you know, she has *my* full support, and that of my office. I swear to you, I won't stop until Iker gets exactly what he deserves for hurting Rosana."

There are moments so profound and silent you can hear a pin drop. This is one.

No one moves. It's not just what Declan says, it's the force behind his words.

Rosana stops crying, lifting her head from my shoulder. She's not relieved or unafraid, far from it. She simply knows Declan believes in her.

For now, it's all she needs.

Vilma doesn't say anything, nor does anyone else when they pile out minutes later.

Except for me. I have plenty to say. "Have dinner with me."

Declan leans back in his chair, analyzing me closely. "You want to have dinner with me?" he asks, as if he can't believe I'm finally caving.

This time, I'm the one flashing a sexy smile. "Yes."

CHAPTER 11

Declan

Here's the thing. I don't date. Ever. I don't need to. I don't have to. I'm not trying to find "the one." I *attend* events with women, occasionally do dinner, or skip the formalities and head straight to bed.

It's Saturday night and I have a date with Mel at her place, where she's cooking dinner for us. I'm not sure how it happened, even though I've wanted it and instigated it, too.

Dinner at some woman's place. How did this happen, again? Oh, that's right, the hot girl I've been fantasizing about finally agreed to give me the chance I thought I never wanted.

I think the last woman who cooked me dinner was my mother, two years ago when she was visiting from Florida. I'm not too stupid to know that I should bring something. But I'm not exactly sure what that something should be.

Wine would be the simplest solution. But it almost seems too easy and not good enough for our first out of the office encounter.

Wait. Out of the office encounter? God damn it. I'm not even sure what the hell I mean.

All I know is the sexual tension between me and Mel has been off the charts. We've grown close in recent weeks. I respect her as a woman, a professional, and as a friend. A professional friendly woman I want to fuck.

But you just don't fuck a woman like Mel. Just like you don't show up to dinner with just wine.

I'm good at getting women into bed or making them think they're luring me there. But anything deeper than that is something I've never bothered with. Never had to before. With Mel . . . I'm in a whole different playing field.

I need a woman's perspective. So I make the mistake of calling my sister, Erin, better known as "Wren" or "God's cure for silence," as our mother calls her.

"Hey, what's up, Declan? Ready for the F-150 your ass needs to be driving."

"No, Wren," I say. "Wait, what the hell? You don't even sell cars anymore—"

"That doesn't mean I'm not watching out for you. And honest to shit, you've got to stop driving those metrosexual pieces of crap. I can get you a deal on a sweet ride that will have women tossing their panties against your windshield every time you drive down South Street."

"I don't need a new car," I insist. Compared to the rest of my family, I'm the most serious. I've had to be to get where I am. But I'll admit this whole thing with Mel makes me even more serious, because I don't want to screw it up.

"Look, I have something to tell you," I say, speaking slowly so she knows I'm not messing around. The problem is I'm more serious than she's used to and she takes it the wrong way.

"Holy shit," she says, her voice cracking. "Ma's dead, isn't she?"

"What? *No*, listen."

Of course, she doesn't. "Finnie!" she yells to our brother. "Ma's dead!"

"What?" Finnie shouts somewhere in the background.

"Declan says Ma's dead!"

"Christ, Wren. Ma's not dead. That's not why I'm calling!"

"Ma's not dead?" she squeaks. "You sure? Is she sick?"

"No!" I snap. "I just talked to her the other night when she came in from Bingo."

"Then why would you make me think something's wrong? Jesus Christ, you sounded like hell," she fires back. There's some shuffling. "It's okay, Finnie, calm down. Ma's not dead."

"Then why he'd make you think she was?" Finn asks, sounding confused.

"God only knows, you know how he gets," she tells him.

"You're an asshole, Declan," Finn shouts.

I am. An asshole for calling this nuthouse.

I pinch the bridge of my nose. "Look Wren, I need some advice."

She pauses. "About cars?"

"No."

"Trucks?"

"No," I say.

"How to dress like you actually have balls?" she offers.

"Just because I won't wear that damn biker jacket you bought me for Christmas doesn't mean I don't dress like I have balls."

If he wasn't covered with ink, or didn't drive a truck or muscle car, my sister didn't consider any guy a real man. *Thank God*, she upped her standards when she found Evan.

"I paid good money for that jacket," she says, getting defensive.

"Lord help me," I mumble.

"So what's up?"

I take a breath. "If you were single, what would you want a guy to bring if you invited him to your place for dinner?"

"Take out," she says, munching on what sounds like potato chips. "You know I don't cook."

"You've been on your own for like ten years and are fucking engaged, and you *still* don't know how to cook?"

"Just because I'm a woman doesn't mean I have to learn how to cook. But I have to say, Finnie's gotten pretty good at it. The other night he had us over for Shepherd's Pie. I'll be honest, despite the crust being harder than a drill sergeant's nutsack, it was pretty good."

I hang up and call Tess.

"Can I tell you something?" I ask when she answers.

"Sure," Tess says, sounding cautious.

"Mel invited me over her place for dinner. I want to bring something other than wine. I think roses will be too much and dessert will make me look like a pussy." If Tess wasn't officially family, and if I wasn't so irritated after dealing with Wren, I wouldn't be so blunt.

I wait. When she doesn't say anything, I ask, "So what do you think?"

"You're going to Melissa's for dinner?" she repeats like she can hardly believe it.

"Yeah, I—"

"I told you!" Curran barks on the other end of the line. There's some shuffling before he starts talking into the mic. "Did you fuck her already?"

"Curran!" Tess yells back at him.

"I'm serious," Curran says, ignoring the way Tess calls him a Neanderthal. "'Cause me and a few badges in your office have a pool going—off the record of course—about whether you and Melissa are banging."

"You and *my investigators* have a bet about me and Melissa?"

"It's a cop thing," Curran says, ignoring how pissed I am. "Anyway, if you've already fucked her, I've already lost. But if you can hang in there a little longer—just till Thanksgiving—"

I hang up and head to the store to buy wine.

I hop up the steps of the converted row home where Mel lives. It's nice, one apartment on each floor in one of the trendier neighborhoods in town. There's a restaurant on the corner, and a few more about two blocks down. This is the perfect place to be young and single in Philly, but I get the feeling Mel's not taking advantage of everything this area has to offer.

"Hi," she says, smiling when she answers the door.

"Hey," I say, trying to keep my eyes from bulging when I see what she's wearing.

It's cool for late August. I wore dark jeans and a T-shirt

to appear more casual, along with the damn leather jacket Wren gave me for Christmas. Mel, she's in tiny denim shorts, a tight black T-shirt that gathers around her full breasts and an open plaid shirt. Her hair is piled in a messy bun on top of her head with just a few strands dangling to frame her face.

She doesn't look pretty or even cute.

She looks beautiful.

"This is what I wear when I cook," she says, laughing and attempting to *fucking apologize* for how she's dressed. "Between the heat from the stove and oven, and how insulated the units are, it gets really hot in my kitchen."

Oh, baby, I bet it does.

She reaches for my bottle of wine and the lame-assed apple pie I bought at the bakery. "Come on in," she says, padding down the hall on her bare feet. "Just lock the door behind you."

Her ass shakes as she hurries back into the kitchen. God Almighty, how in the hell am I not going to have sex with this woman? I flip the lock. I want her, there's no doubt. But the whole drive here I've entertained everything that can go wrong if I spend the night.

She isn't just my boss's daughter, she's my *sick* boss's daughter. She's vulnerable, and easily hurt with everything going on with her dad, exactly like Tess said.

I step into the small foyer, my eyes still very much on her ass as I shrug out of my jacket. Christ, could I be more of a prick? "Where can I put this?" I ask.

She glances over her shoulder, smiling in a way that lights up her entire face and has me tripping over my own damn feet. "Closet. To your right," she says.

I open the door to hang my jacket. About three pairs of very worn running shoes line the bottom. "You run?" I ask, shutting the door.

She crinkles her nose. "Three to five miles about every other day and I hate every second of it."

"Then why do it?" I ask, crossing into the large open

living.

"Because I love to eat," she admits, laughing as she stirs something in a pot. "It's the only way I can still eat what I want and not need a fire crew to haul me out."

I chuckle because she's just that cute and sexy, and fuck me, I'm in trouble. I force my attention away from how she's bouncing along in the kitchen and scan her trendy apartment, knowing I need a moment to calm.

A gray sectional accented with navy, chocolate, and green floral throw pillows angles in front of a large flat screen, and a dark brown geometric bookshelf lines the entire right wall.

It's the bookcase that gives me pause. I grin as I catch sight of what I'm looking for. "Would you like the wine now or with dinner?" she calls out.

I make my way to the bookcase, reaching for the first of—I shit you not—at least thirty smutty paperbacks. "Whatever you want," I say, turning to the kitchen.

She removes the pie from the bakery box, placing it on the granite counter. "This smells incredible—"

The pie tin smacks against the counter when she sees where I am and what I'm holding. Even from where I stand, I can hear her jaw pop open. "Don't mind me," I tell her. "I'm just browsing through all these books you plan to donate to charity."

She hurries over, stopping abruptly, only to walk the remainder of the way very slowly, her cheeks flaming red.

"Hmm, My Scoundrel, My Lovestorm," I say, pretending to scrutinize the cover closely. "Isn't this about global warming and the negative impact on the Scottish Highlands?" I don't let her respond, replacing that book with another. "Or am I confusing it with Sunshine and Silk Fingers?"

"I know this looks bad," she begins when I crack up.

"Your vast collection, or the fact that you've probably read them at least a dozen times?"

She covers her mouth, giggling before dropping her hand

away. "We all have our guilty pleasures."

"And share of dirty literature?" I swap out the book for another. "Hey. Wasn't this the same lady who was 'deflowered' by that cowboy?" I hold the book out of her reach when she tries to snatch it from my hand. "How the hell did she end up in Tudor England?"

I catch her in my arms when she lunges, linking my arm around her waist.

We're both laughing, but as our stares lock, our smiles slowly vanish.

I've pictured her sweet body pressed against mine more times than I can count. And here I am with her firm breasts within my reach. But my gaze remains on her, searching her eyes for all her secrets and her mouth for the whispers that tell me she want me.

My body temperature rises, filling me with a need I've never had use for. This isn't lust. Lust is too damn easy. This is *different*. Who am I kidding? Everything I feel for Melissa is different, including the way I want to kiss her . . . and do a hell of a lot more.

My fingers skim down her waist to grip her hip, my muscles aching with how bad I want to keep going and strip her out of these clothes.

Shit. If this ends badly, I'll just be another asshole who came into her life and mistreated her.

But to end, it first has to begin.

My gaze burns into hers, causing her full lips to part and reveal her shock. Yeah, it's that obvious what I want to do to her.

"Declan . . ." she says, barely able to get the words out.

"Don't say anything," I tell her. "I just want to kiss you, and I really need you to let me."

CHAPTER 12

Melissa

I can't speak.

Or move.

Or breathe.

Declan is holding me, his strong body melding into mine. Is this really happening?

He leans in, tilting his chin and closing his eyes.

I should stop him in his tracks before things go where they're not meant to. I should tell him no and step away.

But I don't want to say no.

I open my mouth and allow him in.

The level of desire surging between us prepares me for the same aggression he's demonstrated in court. He's a man used to getting what he wants and will stop at nothing until it's his.

Instead, the kiss is slow, lazy, sexy, the sweeps of his tongue making me moan.

Men treat me like I'll crumble if they don't handle me with care. Declan's kiss is like a sinful invitation, tempting me into darkness. He leaves my mouth before I'm ready to stop, dragging his tongue to the hollow of my throat and finding the perfect place to nibble.

His hand slips beneath my T-shirt. "Tell me to stop," he murmurs against my skin.

"I don't want you to," I confess.

He pauses with his palm over my breast, uncertainty shimmering his blue eyes. "Are you sure?"

He circles the swell, the seductive motion tightening my nipples. "Yes," I rasp.

He doesn't believe me. He thinks I'm scared. He's right. I'm terrified.

That doesn't mean I don't want him.

My hands glide down. I reach the edge of his shirt, peeling it off him, my fingertips burning with the desire to stroke him.

Long lean muscles make up his arms and perfect ripples define his abs. I meet his face, trying to mask my awe. Clearly, I fail.

He winks. "You're welcome," he says, attacking my mouth with his.

My tongue delves deep, seeking a deeper taste as he pulls me closer. He massages my breast, taking in its entirety before withdrawing to pinch the center.

I groan as he rolls a nipple, the tantalizing aggression making me ache for more. But when his lips leave my mouth to kiss me behind the ear, that awful squeak close contact produces echoes through my hearing aid.

I jerk away, leaving his arms.

"Are you okay?" he asks.

I nod, realizing he thinks he hurt me. "Back noise," I explain.

I reach for the hearing aid behind my left ear. The moment I slip it off, half of my sound is turned off. It's an odd sensation, and one I've experienced most of my life. Yet the effect is so immediate and extreme, even now it gives me pause.

I take a breath and remove the other. The silence is

profound, cocooning me in a separate space in time and muffling my elevated breaths. It's frightening to be suddenly cut off from the world this way, to lose a vital sense so abruptly. It leaves me raw, vulnerable, in a way nothing else can.

But as I look at Declan, the way he's waiting for me and how his body longs for my touch, and remember how this amazing man found a place in my heart, I can't imagine anyone else I'd rather be vulnerable for.

I place the hearing aids on the shelf, stripping out of my plaid shirt and then my tank. My bra follows, my heavy breasts bouncing as they're set free. I keep going, until the only thing that remains are my tiny pink panties. I'm not a small gal, but I like my curves.

Based on the growing bulge pressing against his jeans, Declan likes them, too.

I smile as he takes in my large and tightening tips, passing a hand along the swell of my breast. "You're welcome, too," I say, biting on my bottom lip.

I walk backwards into my living room. Declan follows like I'm yanking him on a leash, kicking out of his shoes and socks before losing his jeans and throwing them aside.

"*Fuck*," I watch him mouth when he reaches for me, pulling me in for one hell of a kiss.

I can't keep still, not with the way he's tugging the pebbled point of my breasts and not when his fingers disappear beneath my panties. I'm shoving the waistband of his underwear down when his fingers circle and his mouth fastens around my nipple.

I clench down on my jaw, trying not to cry out with bliss. It's hard. He feels so good. Heat builds at my core, slicking me, making Declan slide his fingers faster. My lashes flutter when he pushes in deeper, his momentum increasing as I arch my spine.

The slow building arousal accelerates into full-blown passion. Declan's fingers ram faster while his teeth scrape against my dark areolas. My moaning intensifies as my orgasm builds, his touch primal, fast, taking me to my breaking point. I surrender to the ecstasy, digging my fingers into his shoulders to stay standing.

My body trembles out of control. He holds tight, prolonging the jolts of electricity spreading along my thighs until they sear through my veins and overtake my entire body. As the waves lessen, I press my hands against his chest, encouraging him to sit.

I fall to my knees and tug off his briefs. My small nails drag along his bare thighs, encouraging him to open them and make room for me. "Do we need anything?"

He shakes his head. "You tell me," I watch him say.

"No, we're safe," I tell him.

His eyes glaze with desire as I stroke. I lower my head to pull his thick erection into my mouth.

Declan jolts, his fingers gliding along my scalp. I can't hear him. I only *feel* him. The way his body shudders and how his hips rise and fall with my increasing speed. He jerks when I go deeper with each pass, his thigh muscles clenching beneath my touch.

My eyes stay closed. I'm too shy to look. But I'm not too shy to act.

I focus on what I'm doing and how much it's turning me on. I can't seem to stop, my movements quickening and my suction increasing. Declan fists my hair, I know he's watching every pull and how my lips wrap firmly around him. I think he's going to let me finish him until he yanks me up and pulls down my panties.

Declan isn't shy, he's pumped for more, remaining seated as I hover above him and he spreads my legs. His heady stare latches on mine as he grips my hips, hauling me down to his mouth.

His lips seize my delicate folds, marking his territory with each flick of his tongue. I grunt as I fall forward, my knees sinking into the cushions above his shoulders.

Declan takes his time sucking and swirling his tongue, leisurely building his speed and encouraging me to rock against him. My fingers grip the rim of the couch as my orgasm peaks. I fall forward, coming hard and shaking so badly, I barely keep from falling forward.

My heart beats out of control. He lowers me to his lap, his tongue passing over his lips. *You're on the pill, right?* I watch him mouth.

I nod, pulling the clip holding what remains of my bun.

My hair falls around my face, widening his eyes. I'm glad. I want to please him any way I can. I wait for him to start until I realize that he's waiting for me. He wants to make sure I'm ready. He doesn't realize I've never wanted anyone more.

Our lips crush together, I push up on one leg. He reaches for his erection, placing his dense head against my slick center. Our kiss breaks off and our faces scrunch as I lower myself down, his width and length stretching me slowly. It takes a long moment for our laps to connect. But once they do, I know it's time to move.

My hips slide against his thighs, my speed accelerating. His fingers thread through my messy hair, bringing me to him so I can meet his face. "I want you," he says, his skin flushed and his breath ragged. "I want you so much."

"I want you, too," I stammer.

It's the truth. Because whether Declan knows it or not, over these past two months, I've fallen in love with him.

No matter how hard I tried not to.

CHAPTER 13

Declan

"The wine is really good," Melissa says, taking another sip.

We're lying on our sides in bed. Her head is resting against her palm and there's a sheet draped over her hip. "Yeah," I agree. "It would have gone great with the fish."

Her laugh makes me broaden my smile. She'd planned this kick-ass dinner: Chilean sea bass with mango and corn relish, lobster bisque, and wild rice. She'd probably spent hours shopping and prepping for it. The bisque boiled over the sides of the pot, the fish burned in the oven along with the bread she was baking, and the rice dried to a crisp. We were too busy to care, touching and kissing until round one quickly led into round two. We would have headed into the bedroom sooner to start a third round if the damn smoke detector hadn't gone off.

We ended up ordering pizza and I could seriously give a fuck.

My hand trails across her shoulder to stroke her ear with my thumb. Her hearing aids are still on the shelf in the living room, probably between a Naughty Scott and a shirtless Duke. Again, I could care less. What I do care about is her.

I don't think it was easy for her to remove them in front of me like she did. For long few breaths, I was sure the moment between us was gone. Then I saw it, the shift in her pretty eyes that took her from fragile beauty to the strong stunning woman who's haunted my dreams.

"I'd still like to make you dinner," she says. "Would Thursday work?"

She's asking me for another date, and it's not just for sex. Here's the thing. I cut women loose pretty damn fast. It's not going to play out the same way with Melissa, not when we're working together, and not when I've been waking up wanting her for the last eight weeks.

I knew this before I kissed her, and I was willing to go for it. But now that we're talking about next time, I'm not sure I'm ready.

"I can't Thursday," I tell her.

She nods like she can already guess there's not going to be a second date. "Okay," she says.

"What about Wednesday?"

"What?"

She doesn't think I want to see her again, not in this capacity. But she's wrong. As much as I never counted on this, I don't want to discount it or her.

I place my wine glass on the bedside table, not wanting anything between us, then lean in and kiss her softly. "We're supposed to discuss the Keeley case. Why don't we do all the other shit we have pending at the office then discuss the case here?" I shrug. "Or at my place."

Her full lips curve. Yeah. She knows now I'm not about to walk away. Yet.

"I'm making dinner for my dad at his house on Wednesday so that doesn't work." She considers me. "My dad and I have this thing we do that I'd like us to do, too."

"What's that?" I ask.

She shivers when my hand grazes along her curves to massage her hip. "Work talk has to be kept to a minimum outside the office. Otherwise, we don't get a break from it."

"Good point," I say, unable to stop raking my gaze down her figure.

She reaches behind her to place her almost empty glass on the table, tilting her chin as she resumes her position in front of me. "What's it going to be like at the office?" she asks.

"Hard, now that I've seen you naked."

"I think I know what you mean," she says, pressing her hand against my chest and grazing it lightly. "As far as our coworkers are concerned, do you want them to know we were together?"

Or "are together", right? She chooses her words carefully, not wanting to presume there's something between us. I should be relieved, but there is something. Even the commitment-phobe in me can see it.

"No," I answer truthfully. "I don't want anyone to know about us."

Although she keeps her hand against my chest, I sense her pull away as that wall she keeps around herself slamming in place to protect her. I don't want her to think I've used her, but I want to be honest with her, and with me. "Mel, I don't know what's going to happen between us, or if anything will happen at all. That doesn't mean I don't want to give us a try." I wrap a strand of her hair around my finger. "I just don't want whatever happens to play out at the office."

"So keep us a secret?"

It seems like such a shit thing to do. "Yeah. We'll continue as is and take things slow."

"Slow?" she questions. "As in not have sex anymore?"

"Oh, hell no," I say.

She laughs. "Good."

"Workplace relationships can get messy. I don't want anyone questioning your position or mine because of what we are or aren't. So let's date and get to know each other in and out of bed." I watch her hair slide down my finger. "When we're at work, we'll keep it professional like it's been."

"All right," she agrees.

I pull her in for a long deep kiss. She clutches me against her, giving our contact an extra boost of heat. She feels good. But when I edge away, I still sense her apprehension.

"Any regrets?" I ask her, worried there might be.

She shakes her head. "No. What about you?"

"Only that I wish this happened sooner," I admit.

The walls come crashing down. "Me, too," she says, smiling gently.

My smile is a little wider. I didn't like her pulling away or feeling guarded around me. Not after what we've shared the past few weeks and especially these past few hours.

Her hand slides down my shoulder to rest over my heart. It's something I noticed her do during sex and once we settled into bed. I glance down at her hand and cock a brow. "You like it there?"

She laughs. "Yeah."

Her cheeks redden and she tries to pull away. I clasp her hand and keep it in place, perceiving there's more to the gesture. "What are you doing?"

She knows what I'm asking her. "Feeling you."

"There are better places to feel me." I hold out a hand. "Just saying."

Her blush turns deeper, not that it keeps her from laughing. "There are," she agrees. "But this is my favorite."

"Why? So you can push me away if I piss you off?"

"No," she says, her sweet smile in place. "Because I can feel your heart."

I don't move, losing my smile.

She scans my face, a trickle of sadness shimmering in her gaze. "Don't be embarrassed," she tells me. "It's a good heart, strong and honest, but tender when it needs to be just like its owner."

"You're giving me too much credit," I tell her. I sound annoyed though I don't mean to. Maybe I expected the type of bullshit that follows sex with most other women. Small talk, a brief thank you, followed by a quicker goodbye.

But this is Melissa. I should expect no less.

She adjusts her position, causing her heavy breast to glide along the one beneath, thankfully distracting me from a place I don't want to go.

I was never one for curvy women, but as I remember how good those curves felt in my hands I realize I've missed out.

I press another kiss against her mouth. It's only ten and we've already had sex three times. Not that it stops me from wanting more of her. I glide my hand along the sweep of her waist and carefully yank off the sheet, for a better look. Over the course of the past few hours, I've learned her body well. But I like looking at her. And I love that she lets me.

"Like what you see?" she teases.

"I do," I admit. "You're fucking beautiful."

She drops her hand, her expression riddled with disbelief. I mean what I say. The sex was hot. The best I've had, which says a lot. The intimacy we experienced, now that was something I wasn't prepared for. But it was there, making the sex raw and somehow innocent. It's a wild thought, seeing how hard we went at it.

I'm wondering if it's because I've never held a woman this vulnerable in my arms. I want to say it has nothing to do with her being hearing impaired, but I can't deny that played a part. She couldn't hear me. She couldn't hear anything. But she trusted me regardless of the fear that silence created. To have a woman give herself to me that way, I don't know. It did something to me I never expected.

"What did you think about what we did?" I ask. I almost asked what she thought about the way we "fucked." But "fuck" doesn't feel like the right word. Not with her.

Her focus lingers on my naked form. I didn't bother with the sheet. Like Melissa, I'm not shy when it comes to my body. "I liked it," she says. Her voice is husky, like she's remembering how good we made each other feel. "Did you?"

"I did." Worry finds its way into my voice. "I just want to make sure I didn't hurt you."

"Not at all," she says, her brown irises growing smoky. "You were more aggressive than the other men I've been with. But that's what made it so good."

She's giving me one hell of a compliment, basically telling me I performed better than those other dipshits she's had. It's what I should fixate on. Instead, I turn away and reach for the half-empty bottle on the nightstand behind me, taking a moment to rein in my shit.

Her hand cups my shoulder. "What's wrong?" she asks. I don't move. "Declan, please look at me."

That voice, and the concern behind it, has me turning back before I can finish pouring more wine.

"What's wrong?" she asks again, delicately sweeping her fingers along my jaw.

"I don't like hearing you talk about other men," I tell her. Christ, I want to kick my own ass for saying it, *and* for saying what follows. "Especially when you're lying in bed with me."

"I wasn't trying to rub them in your face," she says.

"I know," I answer, trying to figure out when the hell I turned into such a wimp.

"Then what—?" The frown eases away, an air of realization sparking along her features. "You're jealous?" she asks like she can hardly believe it.

"Maybe," I admit.

"*Maybe*?" she repeats.

My gaze travels down her face to her hourglass figure and back up again, taking in every sweet inch of her. She's gorgeous and experienced based on how hard she made me come. She never claimed to be a virgin or pretend to be one. But the idea of anyone else touching her makes me crazy. So yeah, maybe I am—*shit*.

What the hell is wrong with me?

"Look," I say. "Jealousy isn't something I'm familiar with."

"No?"

"Not even a little bit," I admit. "It's an emotion I've never bothered to entertain. When some asshole got ahead of me in school, turned in a better grade, or scored an extra few points playing ball, it never made me jealous. All it did was drive me to be better than him next time. I used that drive to become who I am. So me and jealousy, we don't know each other."

"Okay," she says, smiling.

"Why are you smiling?"

"Because I think it's cute that despite how you're not a jealous person, you might be when it comes to me."

All right. I am. That doesn't mean I'm proud. "You think it's cute?" I repeat.

"It really is," she says, beaming. "People see you like I think they used to see John F. Kennedy. Suave, brilliant, a born leader—someone they support and rightfully believe in. You've taken on cases that have garnered you international attention, and you're not even thirty-five yet." She sighs. "Declan, politicians and members of the city's most exclusive circles not only know your name and reputation, they consider you one of them. You must know this."

"I do," I reply. I think I should say more, but right now, she wants me to hear her. No, she needs me to.

"You met the governor once," she says, holding out a finger for emphasis. "Yet you held her attention and earned her respect from that single encounter. I don't have to tell you she's hard to get close to. Just like I don't have to tell you that you charm everyone else in the same manner. So do I think it's cute you're a little jealous of men from my past who'll never come close to the man you are? Oh, my God, yes. It's good to know you're human after all."

Her words keep me in place. This is the first time I know what she thinks of me. Despite my screw-ups in the past, I've managed to impress her. Maybe because she finally let me.

The thing is, she's impressed the hell out me, too. "Do

you ever feel jealous?" My voice is barely a murmur. If she wasn't reading my lips, no way would she know what I'm asking.

"You mean of all those perfect pretty women who turn to ogle you when we walk down the street together? Or of the ones who leap to their feet the moment they see you?" Her smile fades. "Every day."

Well, shit.

One night. We've technically only shared one night. But if I shove the sex aside and consider the way she's looking at me, the same way I'm looking at her, I know I'm wrong. Mel and I have been practically inseparable from the word go.

Yeah, we've had our share of differences. But those differences have led to a lot of talking, and those talks led to looks that had nothing to do with business and everything to do with how bad I've wanted to be with her like this. We became friends, but maybe all this time we've wanted more than friendship.

Her nails skim lightly against my arm, stimulating every nerve cell along the way. "What are you thinking?" she asks.

"That you have nothing to be jealous of because you're the hottest woman I know."

She stills. I don't think she believes me.

So I pull her to me and spend the night proving I mean what I say.

CHAPTER 14

Melissa

I hurry into my childhood home, a classic colonial located on one of the prettiest streets in Bryn Mawr. "Dad?" I call out.

Mae, the woman who used to clean our home years ago, hurries out from the kitchen wiping her hands. "Hello, love," she says, in her sweet British accent.

I hug her warmly when she pulls me into her arms. I'd reached out to Mae a few days ago to tell her Dad was sick and asked if she'd consider returning to the states to take care of him. After spending the last few years living in the small English town where she grew up, I thought I'd have to beg her to return. She didn't hesitate and hopped on the first available flight. But Mae had always been good to us.

"How is he?" I ask.

Tears fill her soft hazel eyes and she forces a smile. "He's had a rough day, love."

My hand tightens over the handle of the paper bag I'm carrying. "He seemed okay when I picked him up from chemo yesterday. Tired, but in good spirits. How did he sleep?"

She hesitates to tell me, not because she doesn't want me to know, but because she doesn't want to scare me. Mae is sweet like that. "He woke up a few hours after you left and spent the remainder of the night vomiting. I gave him some of the nausea medication the doctor prescribed. It helped settle his stomach, but he's still not well enough to eat."

"He hasn't eaten all day?" I ask. My focus travels up the wooden steps to the second floor.

"He hasn't. But he's drinking well and keeping the fluids down." She squeezes my arm. "That's a good thing."

"It is," I say, though my attention stays on the staircase.

"Have you eaten?" she asks.

I shake my head. "Not yet. I planned to eat with him. I made his favorite . . ." I swallow the lump building in my throat. It shouldn't make me so sad to describe my father's favorite foods, but it does. I hate that he's hurting and so sick. And I hate that the doctors aren't giving me more than "we'll see how he responds to the chemo."

"Melissa?"

"I'm sorry?" I ask. I'm so lost in my thoughts I didn't hear a single word she said.

Mae looks back at me with all the heartbreak I carry. "I said I can heat up the soup in the kitchen if you're hungry, but the smell might upset your father's stomach. Don't take it upstairs, all right? I don't want to risk him vomiting again."

I skipped lunch to handle a case Children and Youth had dropped the ball on, one that had Declan reeling. And I'd missed breakfast because he'd spent the night. I haven't eaten all day and I was practically drooling the entire ride here, the smell of the Irish stew I threw together wafting through every inch of my car.

But I wanted to eat with my father. Now that I know he can't eat and how poorly he's doing, I'm no longer hungry. "I'll just have some juice."

Mae lifts the paper bag from my hand. "Go up. I'll bring it to you as soon as I call in a refill for your father."

I don't want to take advantage of her kindness and think I should just get my own damn juice. But God, I'm so tired, I'll take any help that I can.

"Thank you, Mae." I say, starting up the steps.

She's such a gift. I wish her time with us hadn't been so brief. She was only with us a year, but it was such a good year. I broke down when I picked her up at the airport, knowing she'd take care of Dad in my absence.

I reach his door and knock gently. "Dad?"

I poke my head in when he doesn't answer. He's lying in bed on an angle, a stack of pillows strategically placed along his back to keep him comfortable. He has a nurse that comes in four times a week, but today is her day off. This was all Mae.

He's wearing his light blue pajamas that I bought him for his birthday. The thought of him not seeing his next birthday crosses my mind, but I quickly shove away the thought.

The T.V. is on, but his eyes are closed. "Daddy? Are you awake?" I whisper.

"Of course I am. It's seven o'clock at night." He frowns with his eyes closed. "Are you calling me old?"

I laugh because he wants me to, not because I feel like laughing. The chemo has turned his once fair skin a horrible shade of gray. I slip beside him. "Mae says you're not eating."

He shrugs. "I need to lose weight anyway."

My eyes skim over his belly. The bulge once so prominent is now almost gone. He hasn't been the same since the surgery. I didn't expect an immediate recovery. But this chemo seems to be slowly killing him.

I shrug out of my coat and place it on the end of his four-poster bed, removing one of my hearing aids so I can cuddle against him and lay my head on his shoulder. "When you're up for it, there's Irish stew downstairs," I tell him.

"Sounds good."

"You're lying."

"You're right, it sounds awful," he grumbles. "Damn nausea."

I smile against him, mostly because I've always liked

feeling close to him. My smile falters when I inhale and smell the pungent odor of medicine. There's nothing left of his familiar aroma that hints of home and comfort. All that's there is the reminder of the cancer he's battling.

A battle I'm not certain he'll win.

I kick off my heels and curl closer, shaking off the negative thoughts. Instead I focus on all the good things that make my father who he is and everything that makes lying against him so special. He feels as warm as always, and I fit as perfectly against him as I did the first time I allowed him to hold me.

"Do you remember the first night we became a family?"

"Of course," he says. "I still have the scars to prove it."

I laugh, this time meaning it. "Sorry I bit you."

"Yeah. It shows." He laughs now, because I'm not the frightened child he attempted to welcome into his home.

When we met, I was so taken by his soft brown eyes and how safe he made me feel, even though I couldn't understand him. But when the social worker dropped me off at his house, I thought she was shoving me into the arms of a man who planned to hurt me, exactly as my mother had. I kicked and screamed, and yes, also bit him.

Dad, bless his heart, backed away, holding his bleeding hands out and mouthing words I couldn't understand. I curled into a ball, sobbing in the corner of the living room. Even after all these years, the memory is vivid.

I was in hysterics and cried myself into exhaustion. When I woke, I had a warm blanket around me. Dad was sleeping a few feet away on the floor, wearing the suit he'd worn to work.

He fed me Cheerios that morning. To this day I always smile every time I see a box in the store.

"I'm surprised you didn't send me right back into foster care," I confess. That first night with him was one of many nights I'd freaked out on him.

"Oh, believe me, I thought about it more than once," he

admits.

"Daddy!"

He laughs, stroking my arm. "It's not that I didn't love you right away."

"It's that you didn't *like* me," I finish for him.

He pauses. "Yeah, you kind of sucked."

I throw back my head, laughing. He laughs right along with me, kissing my head. "Melissa, I knew I couldn't let you go from the moment I saw you. But I was in way over my head and doubted whether I was the best parent for you. All the men I knew told me I was crazy, and all the women regarded me like a creep who belonged on some list."

I giggle, that much I knew. "Except for Grandma and Grandpa."

"Yes, God rest their souls." He angles his body so he can look at me. "Every night I came home, I begged your Grandma to stay, knowing you were more trusting of her than you were of me. But every night she left me and told me to get to know my daughter." He winks. "I'm glad that I did."

"I'm glad you did, too," I say, remembering how it took several months before I'd allow him to hold me. "When did you know we were going to be okay?" I ask.

He thinks about it for so long, I start to wonder if he fell asleep. I glance up almost at the same moment he begins to speak. "You'd been letting me tuck you into bed for a while." He shifts beneath me. "Do you remember? I'd sign to you that it was bedtime. Like a good little girl, you'd stop coloring, or whatever you were doing, and follow me upstairs. I'd watch you brush your teeth—by the way you kind of sucked at the teeth brushing thing, too."

"Oh, the truth finally comes out," I interrupt.

"And your taste in clothing was only so-so."

"Dad, I was six."

He chuckles. "Anyway, I'd wait for you to get into bed and lightly place the blankets around you. But I wouldn't get too close and avoided direct contact. One night, I took a chance. I signed, 'Goodnight, I love you' like always, but this time I kissed your head. Your eyes widened like you were scared. I walked out, thinking I made a big mistake and probably set us back." He pauses for a moment. "But in the morning when I woke, you were lying asleep beside me. That's when I knew we would be okay."

My eyes burn as I recall that memory. "It's because I didn't know what love was."

"What?" he asks.

"I didn't understand love. I knew the word by signing it, because it was one of the first words you asked the ASL teacher to teach you. But I didn't know what it meant until you showed me."

"Oh."

It's such a simple word he says. But I feel the tears behind it, just like I feel the ones filling my eyes.

Mae walks in, carrying my juice. She takes one look at us, places the juice on the table, and runs away sobbing.

"Nice. Way to make Mae cry," he says like it's my fault.

I wipe the tears that manage to escape, although by now I'm laughing. "You started it."

"No. You did," he says, coughing as he chuckles.

I push up and sit beside him, worried he's not as comfortable with me so close to him. "What's new at the office?" he asks.

"The usual: violent cases, a rotating door for repeat offenders, and the staff cracking inappropriate jokes to get through it."

He waits before asking, "How's Declan handling it?"

I think about everything Declan has taken on, and how he makes running the office and juggling his caseload appear effortless. The staff, as much as they were hesitant to approach him as acting D.A., as if somehow afraid that they were betraying Dad, all but run to Declan now. He's earned their respect by working hard and supporting his team. It's only when we're alone that I see the toll the responsibilities have taken on him. But I don't tell my father as much, keeping my response brief. "He's doing really well."

"Good," he says. "I knew he would."

"And we're sleeping together."

Oh, and there's that dramatic pause I was expecting.

"That's great, honey," he says slowly.

"Dad . . ."

"No, really, it's what every father wants to hear."

"*Daddy*." He reaches for the remote and flips the channel. "Are you seriously going to watch ESPN now?"

"Yup," he answers, turning up the volume.

It's the same thing he did when I told him I lost my virginity to Samuel Hudson. "You wanted this," I point out. He turns back to me, raising his brows. "Okay, maybe not all the sex."

"*All* the sex?" he asks, making a face. "How long has this been going on?"

"A few weeks." Actually, several times a night over the past few weeks, but Dad is already looking ill enough. No need to share the dirty details. Although . . . if he weren't so sick, I might have told him how Declan showed up at my door dressed as a hot pirate the other night.

"Argh," he'd said, right before I pounced.

"Are things serious between you?" Dad asks.

They're serious for me, but that's definitely *not* what my father needs to hear. "I'm not sure. We spend a lot of time together, inside and outside of work, but . . ." I shrug. "No one at the office knows. We're keeping it quiet—"

"Mae and I have been having sex for years," he blurts out.

I can actually feel my jaw unhinge.

"The first time was when you were fourteen. You were away at camp. I came home early and found her on her hands and knees scrubbing the bathroom floor. One thing led to another and—"

"*You had sex with Mae on the bathroom floor!*" I cover

my mouth when I realize how loud I'm being.

He bats his hands, shushing me. "It's just one of those things that sort of happened," he says.

For as green as he appears, there's no squelching that twinkle in his eye. "'*Sort of* happened?'" I gasp.

"Yes." He gives it some thought. "The next few times were in the cabana, and a couple of times in the pool. Oh, the kitchen was another favorite."

"You were busy that week I was at camp," I say, trying really hard not envision all the places they defiled in my absence.

He shakes his hand out. "Oh, no, those moments came later that summer. We'd take advantage of the times you were out with friends or fishing with your grandpa. But yes, your week away made for some interesting adventures."

"'Interesting adventures?' You *tramp*," I say, cracking up.

He sighs. "She always looked good in that apron."

I slump back against the headboard. "Golly gee and wow, Dad, how many times did you and Mae hike up Smut Mountain?"

"I told you, years," he says like I'm not paying attention.

"Years?" I repeat. "But she was only with us the one year." My voice trails when I realize what happened. "Oh, my God. Your trips to Europe, when I was at college, they were to see Mae, weren't they?"

"They were," he admits, his voice growing distant.

"Why didn't you ever do anything about it?"

He tries to smile, though this time it doesn't quite reach his eyes. "Because her home was in England, and mine was here with you."

My heart stalls as I work up the courage to ask him what I already know. "If I weren't around, would you have followed her to England?"

"I don't know," he answers.

It's what he says, but I don't believe him.

Mae walks in, pretending as if she hasn't spent the last few minutes bawling her eyes out. I thought she cried for me and Dad. And maybe she did. But I realize now that maybe she cried for them, too.

"Miles," she says. "It's time for your medicine, dear."

He sits up as she hurries to his side of the bed. He smiles at her as she fills a medicine cup with a thick brown liquid. I catch a fondness between them I've never noticed. But I see it now. It's probably always been there.

Despite everything we talked about, it's their interaction that causes me to lose my composure on the drive home.

My father gave up so much.

Including his happiness in exchange for mine.

CHAPTER 15

Declan

The Eagle's defensive tackle tears down the field and we lose our damn minds. "Go, go, go—*oh*!"

And the Giant's Number 25 takes him down five yards from the field goal. Game over. We pile away from Killian's giant flat screen, except for our oldest brother Angus who's flipping the screen off with two giant middle fingers. "Fuck you!"

This is what Sundays are all about: football, family, and stuffing myself with food guaranteed to give me the big one before my time.

Instead, I'm wondering if Mel is still at her dad's, how well she's holding up, and counting the hours until I see her again.

When exactly did I surrender my balls?

Banging from the kitchen has me looking across Kill's large family room. "We're out of wings," Finn yells. "Sofe said she made lots of wings. Where the hell are the wings?"

"Fuck *you*!" Angus yells again as the replay flashes across the screen.

"In that bottomless crater you call a stomach," Killian

yells back at Finn. He reaches for another chip. "They were gone by half time. It's my fucking house and I only had one."

I shake my head, laughing. "How does Sofia put up with him? Hell, with any of us?" I'm not kidding. Every time we come over, Sofia makes a ton of food and doesn't stick around to enjoy it.

"She likes taking care of us. It's kind of her thing," Killian says. He finishes swallowing, the corner of his lips tugging into a smile. "She wants to start trying for a baby."

"No shit," Curran says, taking a pull of his beer.

"*Fuck you!*" Angus hollers yet again.

"Angus," I yell. "Get over it, man. We'll get them next time." I turn back to Kill. "You think you're ready?" Christ, he and Sofe are so young.

"We've known each other forever. I think it's time." He grins in that way he always does when he talks about Sofia, exactly like he has since they were kids playing on the street. "When I picture us years from now, it's always with a houseful of kids running around. I want it, you know? I told her we could, but first I want to go to a few places we've never been—the islands, Ireland, Italy, countries we won't necessarily be able to see if we have babies right away." He shrugs. "I want to spoil her some. God knows she deserves it," he says, motioning to the mess in front of us and what remains of the food she prepared.

"You're so fucking whipped," Seamus says, digging through the dip like he's afraid Sofe will be insulted if he doesn't finish every last morsel.

"Nah," Curran says. "He just knows he has it good."

This is what I struggle with. I know that Kill and Curran mean it when they say they love their women. Finn, too. That doesn't mean I believe in love.

At least for me.

Maybe.

Fuck. How did I fall into a relationship?

It's not a good time to ask, not with Seamus whoring

around with every single woman in Philly, and Angus who only wishes he could whore around. Angus has been engaged for twenty non-fucking years and he's a miserable bastard.

Christ. I'm not sure what I'm feeling with Mel is real or something I think I'm *supposed* to feel. Either it's too soon, or it can't possibly be normal. Davies from Arson was flirting with her the other day in the hall. She politely declined his offer to dinner as I approached, her eyes widening when she caught my less-than-thrilled expression. Can anyone blame me? The way he leaned into her, how he couldn't keep his eyes off her ass when she walked away, it took all I had not to shove the Sexual Harassment policy in his face and yell at him to get back to work.

Ever since we started sleeping together it's like every single guy—and even some of the married staff—want more than her professional advice. It's not like I've never noticed men watch her bounce down the hall or stare a little longer than necessary, but lately it's like these horny bastards can't get enough of her.

"So you and Sofia are good?" I ask Killian, ignoring the tension claiming my shoulders.

"Real good." He cocks his head. "Why?"

I should let it go because I don't want to piss him off or disrespect his marriage, but this jealousy shit isn't like me. At least, it never used to be. But here it is, eating at me. It has to get better over time, and who better to ask than Kill and Curran who are sitting right in front of me.

"No big deal," I say, turning it around on him. "I just know for a while there were a few guys at the gym checking her out." I shrug. "Just wondering if that changed when you got married."

I normally don't probe my brothers for bullshit like this. Kill, who's pretty laid back, except when it comes to Sofia, lowers his deep voice in time with his darkening expression.

"If you want to know the truth, my ring around her finger hasn't done a damn thing."

Seamus polishes off the dip. "You serious?"

"Yeah, I'm serious. All those idiots working out—the same idiots swearing up and down that they want to be the next MMA champion—still stop what they're doing when she walks by. Oh, and those stupid marketing reps, I'm ready to break them in half. They're always like, 'Hey. Where's your girl, Sofia? I need to talk to her about our new product.'"

"What's so bad about that?" I ask.

Finn sits down with a plateful of ribs he found in the fridge. "It's their way of telling him they want to fuck her—Hey, you going eat that hot dog?"

I pass Finn my plate without even looking at him. "You can't be serious." At Kill's stiff nod I ask, "How the hell do you put up with that?"

"I don't. I threw the last three assholes out of my gym. Sofia called each one back—get this—*apologizing* on my behalf for overreacting."

"Oh, hell," I say.

"It's all good," Finn says through a mouthful of food. "She got us a sweet deal on a bunch of merchandise for the gym. But yeah, they still want to fuck her." He does a double-take when Kill glares at him. "What? I'm just speaking the truth. It's the same damn reason I don't let Sol come to the gym. If anyone puts the moves on her with me standing there, someone's leaving in an ambulance and it's not going to be me."

"Christ," I say, shaking my head.

Curran huffs, pointing at Killian. "Finnie has a point. You should have ripped those bastards in half. Get this, me and Tess went to her OB the other day. She's been going alone because I'm usually working or with the baby. But this last time I had the day off and wanted to go, seeing how I've been missing out and because I never missed one when she was pregnant with Fiona. So I show up with her and in walks this dude."

Seamus leans in. "Her doctor's a man?" Curran nods.

"And you didn't know?"

"The moron's name is Dr. Rosey. *Rosey*. Would you think that name belongs to a man?"

"No," we all grumble.

"So at first I'm just in shock," Curran says, continuing. "So I shake his hand like a dumbass. But then he pulls out these stirrups—"

"Pants?" Finnie asks, sounding as confused as the rest of us appear.

"No. *Worse*," Curran says. "They're these things at the end of the examination table used to spread a woman's legs open."

"Jesus *Christ*," we all groan. Finnie and Seamus are so grossed out they push their plates of food aside.

"I know, on the table my woman is laying on!" His face reddens, he's still pissed. "I'm standing there watching her put her legs in these things. But it's when good ol' Dr. Rosey slaps on the rubber gloves that I completely lost my shit."

"Did you tell him to get away from her?" I ask.

"Of course I did. Do you think I was going let some man feel up my wife—my *pregnant* wife—in front me?" He throws his hands in the air. "Tess was all mad, saying I embarrassed her and blew things out of proportion." He points at me. "But you know what? Now she has a new doctor and this time I made damn sure she's a woman."

My brothers all nod in agreement. "You did the right thing," Angus says.

"I know I did," Curran agrees. He looks at me. "You're fucking Melissa, aren't you?"

Sometimes, I really hate Curran. "No," I say, waiting too long to answer.

"Liar," Seamus says, regaining his appetite and stealing Finnie's hot dog.

"You don't even know who we're talking about," I snap.

Seamus laughs. "Maybe not, but we know whoever she is, you're fucking her."

"Watch your mouth," I growl.

Finn smirks. "I saw that coming a mile away."

"You didn't see shit," I tell him.

He ignores me, calling to Curran. "Didn't I tell you it was only a matter of time?"

"I'm the one who told you, asshole," Curran fires back.

I dig my hands into my hair. "Will both of you shut the fuck up?"

Killian frowns. He's been quiet, but it's more like him to sit back and observe. "You like her, don't you?"

I reach for a beer, but then think better of it. "She's nice."

"Nice?" Killian repeats.

"Yeah." It's all I can think to say. I'm having a real hard time pretending Melissa isn't more than a nice woman I work with. Every waking thought is about her. The way she smiles when she sees me, or how she settles me with her presence, even when the cases I'm juggling seem like more than any one man can handle.

"Damn," Curran says. "Tess was right."

This time, it's my turn to frown. "What do you mean Tess was right?"

I expect to find Curran smirking like always, and maybe having a laugh at my expense. But he's not doing either. His tone is as serious as his expression. "She said she knew you were going to fall for Melissa. That anytime she was around you, it was like she was intruding on something personal."

"She said that?" I ask. Curran can be full of it. But he's not joking now.

"Those were her exact words," he says, polishing off his beer. "Guess she knew what she was talking about."

Guess she did. I rub my eyes. *God, kill me.*

"You're in trouble aren't you?" Curran asks, like he knows exactly where I'm coming from.

Hell, maybe he does. "In more ways than I can count," I admit.

"Did you knock her up?" Angus asks.

"No, Angus," I groan.

"So run, man," Angus insists. "Run while you can before you're engaged to a woman who hates your guts . . ."

"Molly doesn't hate your guts," I counter.

". . . And you stop having sex for years," he continues. "I'm in hell, Declan. Every day I wake up in hell."

"Angus, why are you and Molly still together if you don't even like each other?" Seamus asks, throwing out a hand. "You've been engaged for like, two decades now. Cut her loose and walk away."

"She wants to have five kids, *five*," he says, ignoring Seamus. "I told her that unless it's immaculate conception that shit's not going to happen."

I stand and head into the kitchen to dump my trash when I realize what time it is, and because I don't want to hear Angus bitch about Molly. This thing between him and Molly is exactly what I don't want. They're with each other because they think they should be, stuck in a place neither wants to be, holding each other back from what they could have and accomplish.

Son of a bitch.

"Thanks, Kill," I tell him, trying to shake off what I'm feeling. "And tell Sofia I said thanks for having us."

We exchange goodbyes like brothers do. I expect to make a quick exit, kicking myself for bringing anything up. I should have just sucked up what I'm feeling and dealt with it. Now, my head is spinning with a slew of garbage I could have done without.

It's like all the good Kill, Curran, and Finn have doesn't make up for all the shit Angus deals with. Maybe because I think Angus is more the norm—two people together because they think they have to be. That's not love. That's not real. It's exactly what my parents had and the same thing I've spent my life avoiding.

I'm almost to my car when Curran jogs down the steps. "Hey, Deck, wait up."

"Curran, I have to go."

He ignores me. Wow. There's a shock. "Why are you being a moody bastard?" he says when he catches up.

"I'm not," I practically snarl.

He leans back on his heels. "Yeah. It shows."

I'm ready to get out of here, walk away and not look back. But I'm headed to Mel's and straight into everything I can't come to terms with.

Curran makes it clear that he's not going anywhere. I take a chance, since it's obvious I'm not dealing well with this thing on my own. "Look, I might be in over my head with Melissa." I sigh. "I like her. With the exception of a couple of nights, we've spent every night together."

"Since when?"

I give it some thought, wondering where the time's gone. "A few weeks."

"That's a good thing, isn't it?" He motions to the house. "Better than the shit Angus is putting up with by staying with Molly."

"I don't know if it's any different," I say.

"What the hell's that supposed to mean?" he asks.

"That I'm not sure if what we have is genuine or if it will even last."

Anyone else would tell me to dump her and walk away, like Angus did. But Curran knows me and because he does, he sees right through me, asking me the one question I've tried to avoid. "Do you love her?"

I don't answer because no matter what's happened between me and Mel, how much we've shared, and how deep we've shared it, I'm still the man who thinks love is temporary and mostly bullshit. "We're exclusive," I say instead. "But I'm at a crossroad."

"A crossroad?" he repeats.

"I've never been with a woman this long," I remind him. "We're keeping it quiet at work and having a good time alone. But I think we're at a point where I either have to move forward, or not and break her heart."

"Seeing how worked up you are, it sounds to me like you don't want to hurt her."

"I don't," I answer truthfully. Jesus, when I think about how good she is to me, and how much we rely on each other? It's the last thing I want.

"Good," Curran says, frowning. "It would be a douchebag thing to do, especially with everything going on with her dad."

I huff. "Tell me about it."

"So are you going to do it? Move forward, I mean?"

"I don't know. The next step is huge." I zip up my jacket when the breeze picks up.

Curran huddles into his sweatshirt, smirking when he realizes where I'm going with this. "Thanksgiving?" he questions.

"It's two weeks away. I have to decide whether or not to ask her." I pause when I realize he's laughing. "You think this is funny?"

"It's not a death warrant, Deck. It's a relationship. Either it works or it doesn't, and you move on."

"The problem is, I think I should move on," I admit.

"Why?" he asks. "I thought you liked her?"

I lean against my car, put off by how much I'm telling him. "I wasn't ready for this. Things got serious between us fast. I never expected to feel this way and I almost can't."

"Why?"

"I still have a lot to do. I wasn't just blowing smoke when I told you I wanted to become the next mayor."

Curran shrugs. "So become the next mayor. Mel isn't stopping you. If anything, she can help. Look at how she talked the governor into hiring extra staff for SACU and how she puts out fires and takes care of shit when you're ready to lose it. She's good to you and is good for you."

"Are you saying I should invite her to Thanksgiving?"

"Yes, Declan." His brows furrow. "Why are you making

this harder than it is? You sound like a goddamn coward."

"I'm not trying to sound like a coward," I snap, my voice so sharp it takes Curran by surprise. I tone it down when I realize I'm yelling. "Believe it or not, I'm trying to do the right thing and I'm not so sure that I am. She's not like the others. You hear what I'm telling you?"

"I know," he says. "If she was, you would have dumped her by now and fucked at least five other women after her."

"It's more than that," I admit. I scan the area, taking in the brick homes and big back yards. This is the kind of neighborhood where you can raise a houseful of kids, have barbecues, and make memories. Exactly what Kill and Sofia will do, and Curran and Tess, and Finnie and Sol. It's something they've probably always wanted. But I never have. Before Melissa I never entertained the thought of that home with the white picket fence or who'd be waiting for me inside.

And now . . . aw, hell. What did I get myself into?

"I wanted to be the next D.A.," I tell Curran, staring past him. "And now I'm doing it. Mayor is my next step, and probably governor after that. How can I accomplish everything I want and still be there for Melissa? I can't. So I turn my back on her, leaving her with no one but her sick father. The last time I saw Miles, I was sure he was living on borrowed time."

"So in inviting her to Thanksgiving, you think you're offering her more than you're ready to give? Leaving her with the impression there's more down the line?"

"It's not just dinner, Curran. It's her meeting the family and . . ." I shake my head. "Christmas is next, then everything else. I want to share this time with her, I do. But not if it means putting us in a position neither of us ever wanted."

"You mean a position *you've* never wanted, right?"

Curran doesn't mess around, not when it's real. "That's right," I admit through my teeth.

"Hell, Deck. Man up," he tells me. "Melissa is a good girl, but she's not stupid. You start acting like you don't want her around, you won't have to worry about leaving her. She'll dump your ass and you'll fucking deserve it."

I watch him jog back into the house, cursing under my breath when I realize he's right.

CHAPTER 16

Melissa

I'm at my desk in the spare bedroom I use as my office, trying to pull together a proposal for a child advocacy center, but I can't keep my mind on work. Dad's stomach is so sensitive, all he can tolerate are those awful shakes. Every time I think he may be getting a little better, he gets a little worse. My eyes dart to the picture of us at the governor's ball. This is the first year we likely won't attend together. I only hope last year wasn't the last.

My phone buzzes, vibrating against my desk and giving me an excuse to turn away from the picture. "Melissa Fenske," I say.

"Hey, Melissa Fenske," Declan says on the other line. "May I come in?"

A tear sweeps over my cheek as I grin. What would I do without Declan to make me smile? I push away from my chair. "Hi, babe," I say. "I'll be right there."

Declan has the code to get into my building, but he can't get into my apartment without a key. I've been thinking about asking him if he'd like my spare, but no matter how good things are between us, I still feel him holding back. I'm not,

not anymore, which makes the distance he keeps between us hard to take.

My heels click across the floor. I usually take off my shoes the minute I step inside my home. But I was in a rush to finish an email, and then I started working on the proposal . . . only for me to sit and worry about my dad.

I'm scared it's only a matter of time before I lose him.

I open the door, smiling the moment I see Declan, my mood instantly lifting. "I'm sorry. I didn't hear you knock."

"It's all right," he says, bending to kiss me. His lips brush sweetly against mine, although they don't linger as long as I'd like. It doesn't bother me, we have all night, but it does make me wonder if something's on his mind.

He walks beside me as we make our way in, shrugging out of his jacket. He didn't shave today. The rugged look, though, works for him.

I reach up and stroke the stubble along his jaw. "Are you hungry?"

He makes a face. "I think it's safe to say I'm never eating again."

"Sofia hooked you up again?"

"A little too well," he says. He plops on the couch, reaching for me. "Hey, where are you going?" he asks when I edge away.

"I have something for you." I bounce into the kitchen and snag the large envelope from the granite counter, my pace slowing as I sit beside him. I hold up a hand when he frowns. "I swear it's not more work. It's from Rosana."

"Rosana?" he questions. He reaches in, his eyes widening when he pulls out a large piece of paper. "Holy shit."

"What is it?" I ask, lowering myself beside him. My eyes round as I take in the charcoal drawing. Rosana didn't simply sketch flowers, an animal, or something I'd expect from someone her age.

She drew a perfect likeness of Declan.

"Oh my God," I say, leaning in close. I'd seen Rosana's

passion for art first hand. But this is far advanced for someone her age, especially given her limited training. "Declan, it's amazing."

Rosana meticulously sketched Declan sitting behind his desk, his tie loose, his sleeves rolled up his arms, and his stare intense as he leans forward. The details are incredible and the shadowing so perfect, it more resembles a photo that's been digitally altered than something created by hand.

He steals a glance my way. "You didn't see it before?"

"No. When I met with her on Friday, she seemed a little off. More quiet and shy than she has been. When she gave me the envelope she told me it was for you and made me promise I wouldn't open it." I shake my head. "We were both busy with meetings, and I had so many files to carry out, I forgot it in the office. I stopped by on my way home from seeing Dad when I remembered."

He nods like he's listening, but doesn't say anything, his eyes appearing to take in every detail of the work.

I wrap my arms loosely around his and place my chin on his shoulder. "That's the day you did a practice run of all the questions you'll be asking her on the stand."

"I know," he says. "She was so quiet, I wasn't sure if she was listening or if I was even getting through."

"It looks like you more than broke through, Declan. You touched her heart." I smile softly. "Look at the way she captured you. She probably spent the entire meeting studying your face."

"Maybe . . . man, this kid has talent. If she's not thinking about being an artist, she should be." He rubs his jaw, but it's in that way he does when something's bothering him.

"What's wrong?"

"Nothing's wrong. It's just . . . ." His attention returns to the picture. "This was really sweet of her, but I'm not sure why she did it. I swear to Christ, every time I have to tell her something about this damn case, it's like I'm pushing her away and closer to her breaking point."

"She's fragile," I agree. "And she's been through too much in her life. But that has nothing to do with you." I kiss his cheek. "If anything, she sees you as one of the few good men left in her world." I smile fondly. Rosana not only drew a perfect likeness of Declan, she captured the strength he emanates and flawlessly replicated the larger than life hero everyone sees. All he needs is a cape waving in a makeshift breeze. "You earned her trust," I whisper.

She's not alone. I've surrendered my heart to Declan, although I'm not certain he wants it. I don't mean to sound negative. It's just that as intimate as we've been, there's a part of him he keeps tucked away from me. I feel it every time we're alone. It's the reason I haven't told him I love him.

He scrutinizes the picture, growing distant. "I don't know how."

"You gave her a voice," I say. I'm trying to keep him with me, but he seems to drift further away. It makes me sad.

Today has been exceptionally rough, so I focus on the good things between us and how he's sitting beside me. "You made her feel like she mattered—"

"She does matter," he interrupts, as if afraid I doubt him.

"I know, Declan." It's something we both believe down to our souls. "But she likely hasn't always felt that way. You listened to her and proved you'll stand by her, even when her own mother wouldn't. People like Rosana, who are hurt by those who should most love them, don't easily let down their guards. But she did so with you."

I realize I'm counting myself among those people, likely because my encounter with Dad has left me so raw.

"I'm just doing the job," he says.

His modesty is sweet. When I first met him, I couldn't get over how arrogant he seemed and couldn't stand him because of it. As I started seeing him in action, I realized his arrogance was rightfully earned, not that it made me like him better. But the more time we spent, the more I saw that he's simply confident, a man who prides himself on his work and steels himself with an endless source of strength. Declan *is* the next big thing. I just didn't realize it right away.

"You're not just doing your job," I say gently. "You're proving to Rosana that you genuinely care about what happens to her. That's the hardest part about working in SACU. You end up giving your heart, even when you're trying not to." I pause to take in the man who's become my world. "I'm so proud of you, Declan."

He lowers the picture onto the table, keeping his full attention on it. But then something shifts in his eyes, making me think his thoughts aren't solely on Rosana or the gift she gave him.

I skim my fingertip over his temple where his hair is too short to curl. "Are you all right, love?"

He winces when I refer to him as "love." It's clear that's not a word he's ready for.

"I need to talk to you about something," he says, his voice so low I struggle to make out the words.

Fear trickles down my spine, I'm not sure what he's going to say. "What is it?" I ask.

He bows his head as if giving a great deal of thought to what follows. I'm certain he's ready to move on until he angles his chin to face me. "Would you like to spend Thanksgiving with me?"

My hands fall away from his arm. His question catches me off guard. Not because of the holiday, I realize it's coming up, but because of his demeanor. He doesn't seem happy.

"It's okay if you don't want to," he adds. "I just don't see myself spending it without you."

I know what he means, but with my father so sick, I wasn't planning on doing much. "I'd have to see how Dad's doing," I say. "It's only been us for the holidays since my grandparents passed away."

He lifts my hand and kisses it. "I'd like him to come as well. We're having it at Curran and Tess's house this year. Their house and Wren's are the only ones big enough to hold us."

"Your family will be there?" I ask carefully. "All of them?" He nods, his demeanor uncharacteristically solemn. But I suppose this is a big deal. "Will your mother be there as well?"

"Yes," he says.

Whoa. Okay.

Declan has been very careful when it comes to our relationship. He holds back in public, but I do as well. We both have a lot on the line holding the positions we do. It's bad enough everyone thinks my title was handed to me because of my father. The last thing I want is for people to think I'm sleeping with the acting D.A. to hold onto my job.

I assumed he'd eventually tell Curran about us, but . . .

I take in his somber features. Asking me to meet his family is a lot for him. Perhaps he doesn't realize it's a lot for me, too. My dad is my family. I have other relatives, sure, but they live outside of Pittsburgh and we're not close. The last time I saw them was at a cousin's wedding when I was very young.

My hand passes over my long skirt as I think about the last young man I brought home. It happened my senior year of college. Dad didn't like him, and after he cheated on me with one of my sorority sisters, I didn't like him either.

"What are you thinking?" he says when I don't answer.

"That you're sweet for inviting us," I answer truthfully.

Thanksgiving with Declan and the entire O'Brien clan. I don't dare ask what it means, not when I'm certain he may not be ready, and mostly because I know that I am.

I need him. I only wish he needed me, too.

"If Dad's up to it, we'll come. I wish I could give you a definite answer, but we're taking things day by day." I try to smile, because despite all the doubts and uncertainties racing through my head, I am happy he asked. "Thank you for the invitation and for thinking of us."

He doesn't seem happy. If anything, worry shrouds his

face like a blanket. "What if your dad's not up to it? What will you do that day?"

I don't want to think about my father getting worse, but it's unavoidable. "We can meet up afterward if you're available. But if you can't, don't worry. I don't want to take you away from your family." It's hard to keep my voice steady when I mention his family. Declan is lucky to have an army of loved ones who adore him. If Dad goes, I'll be alone.

I blink back the tears that want to fall, but I don't turn away soon enough. "Hey," he says, cupping my face to wipe my eyes. "What's wrong, beautiful?"

The way Declan regards me, his face so full of compassion and kindness, is more than I can take, triggering the misery I've been beating back all day.

I lean in and kiss him, wanting to feel something else besides sadness. But when I deepen my kiss and crawl on his lap he pulls back, holding me carefully. "You're not okay, are you?" he asks.

No, but I want to be.

I reinforce that dam I've built so it doesn't break and unleash everything I fear. "Today was tough day," I admit. My hands slide over his hard chest, smoothing over his shoulders. "That's not how I want it to end. I want to feel good. Will you help me?"

His gaze warms. He knows what I need, and he doesn't deny me.

He lifts me from his lap, slowly dragging my figure down his hard form as he straightens and pulls off my dress, his eyes never leaving mine.

His hands, so large and strong, carefully reach for my hearing aids, removing one at a time in that same leisurely manner he peeled off my dress. They're devices, electronics, really. But the way he slips them from my body is as intimate as the way he unclasps my bra and frees me of my panties.

I reach for his belt buckle. He clasps my wrist, lifting my hands to kiss each one. "Let's make this all about you," he says. "I can't give you much, but let me give you this."

I'm not certain I know what he means, but what I think he means causes a tear to drip down my cheek. "Don't," he says, his hands gliding along my jaw. "Just let me make you feel good."

His hands were gentle against my face, but his touch becomes more daring as they feel their way down my curves. The moment his fingers graze over my backside, this man who can be so gentle turns primordial.

Exactly what I need him to be.

His lips crash against mine, his mouth ravaging me as his hands travel to my breasts to explore, tease, tug. I whimper when he rolls both nipples before his tongue drags down my throat. I can't hear him, not this far away from my ears. But I can feel his breath against my skin, whispering those dirty words he knows drive me wild.

My spine bows backward when his teeth fasten onto the tip of my breast. He holds tight to my waist with his arm while his other hand slips between my legs. I watch him work me, no longer shy like I used to be.

I'm still wearing the garter stockings and my heels, but that's how he wants me. He spreads my legs and falls to his knees. My breath catches as he lifts my right foot and places it on the coffee table. I grunt when he buries his face between my legs, clasping his shoulders to keep from falling.

"Declan," I gasp, his mouth pulling in my delicate skin, suckling hard and encouraging me to rock. "*Declan.*"

The force of my orgasm has me toppling over. He catches me, lowering me to the couch as he shoves down his pants. In one smooth motion he enters me, his face fixed on mine as he pumps his hips and he kneads my breasts. I kick out when he pushes deeper, my legs flailing and my nails digging into the fabric of the couch as my passion escalates out of control.

"Touch yourself for me," he says, his gaze traveling briefly to watch. "Yeah. Just like that," he says, his eyelids heavy with lust.

This kind of sex, so freeing and ardent, is more than I've experienced with another man. It awakens me, making me feel desired, as if only the two of us can make each other feel this good.

We both finish, his hips slowing as he curls forward. He swears as he watches me, tightening his jaw in agonizing bliss. I know he's not done, but neither am I.

It doesn't take long for him to catch his breath and harden again. His appetite for me is insatiable and our emotions are so riled there's no room to think, only feel.

He hauls me into his arms and carries me down the hall, stopping outside my bedroom. "I'm glad you're flexible," he says. "Because I really want to make you come this way."

He lifts my right leg and throws it over his shoulder as he pushes inside me. My head slides against the wall as Declan thrusts hard, my body shaking with how fast his body beats against mine and how much I want him.

This is so what I need.

No. *He's* what I need.

This moment takes longer and the orgasms come harder. Almost the moment he finishes, his cautious demeanor returns. My hand slips to where his heart beats out of control and his chest rises and falls in quick succession. I can *feel* how much he wants me and how much he cares, and I can feel all the strength lying deep within. But everything I feel doesn't seem like enough.

I never planned on loving Declan. But I do.

Even though I know he's not ready to love me in return.

CHAPTER 17

Melissa

Declan warned me he had a huge and loud family, but clearly I had no idea what huge and loud meant. We arrive at Curran and Tess's home just as the sun sets. Even from the bottom of the porch steps and with the door closed, I can hear the T.V. blasting and what sounds like an angry mob screaming at each other.

I trail Declan as he guides Dad up the steps, the voices growing more boisterous and heated. I clasp Declan's arm as he reaches for the doorknob.

"Did we come at a bad time?" I ask.

He smirks, reaching for me. "No, they always sound like that."

He throws open the door. The cacophony of sound has me toppling back. If not for Declan's firm grip, I'm not sure I would have kept my feet. He motions Dad forward and into the foyer, keeping his other arm around my waist.

Everyone is yelling. *Everyone*. My senses are on overload. Yet it's when the mob of people taking up every inch of space in the large family room abruptly quiets that I almost fall over.

All eyes are on us. Dad, ever calm and composed, glances back at me like we're about to be eaten.

Declan barely blinks. "This is Melissa and her father, Miles," he announces. "Show some class for once in your lives and be nice to them."

An array of "fuck yous" "I have goddamn class" and other such colorful references overpower my hello.

Tess appears (thank God!), lifting the pan of stuffed shrimp from my hands. She kisses my cheek. "Don't worry. You'll be fine," she tells me, before disappearing into the advancing crowd.

The moment Declan helps me out of my coat, arms, lots and lots of arms, pull me into bodies ranging from extra-large to extremely tiny. Kisses greet me from all sides. I'm inundated with affection, struggling to make out what people are saying between the loud voices surrounding me and the back noise. Everyone speaks at once, causing my head to jerk in all directions. I fail miserably at catching everyone's names. But it's what I do pick up that eases some of my distress.

"Thank Christ you're not another skank," his sister Wren tells me, smiling brightly.

"Look, and she actually has an ass," his older brother Angus adds, pointing.

I should be embarrassed, but all I can do is smile. They're . . . *lovely*.

"Where's Ma?" Declan asks Wren.

She takes a swig of her beer. "Out in the garage."

Declan frowns. "What is she doing out there?"

"Pouring more whisky into her cup." She holds out her hand. "I'm sorry, pouring more 'iced tea' into her cup," she replies with finger quotes. "You think we'd be talking this way if she was in here?"

"Okay. I'll check on her in a minute," he says. "Come on, Miles, let's watch the game." He touches my arm so I'm sure to read his lips as someone blasts the volume. "Are you okay?"

I nod, trying to keep from reacting to the increasing volume. Declan notices anyway, veering back to yell at one of his three hundred brothers. "Hey, Seamus. Turn it down —"

"It's okay," I say, squeezing his arm.

He doesn't think it is, and mostly it's not. But I don't want to make a fuss, especially when everyone is being so welcoming.

Declan considers me for a beat. "I'm okay," I insist. "Really."

Although he doesn't seem to believe me, he nods once and leads my Dad into the family room. No sooner do they sit in front of the mother of all flat screens than someone slaps a beer in each of their hands. I'm not sure Dad should drink, but I don't want to baby him, nor do I want to keep him from having fun.

I watch him settle, wishing Mae could have come, not just for me, but mostly for Dad. She used the short week to return to England and settle some affairs so she can commit to staying long term with dad. "I don't want to have to leave him again," she told me. By the way her voice trembled, she meant, "I don't want him to leave me."

Wren says something. I don't realize she's talking to me, until she touches my arm.

"I'm so sorry," I say. "Can you repeat that?"

She grins. "I asked if you want to go into the kitchen and see if Tess needs help, seeing how she looks ready to pop."

"Of course," I say.

I follow her, glancing back at Dad and Declan. One of the brothers says something that makes them chuckle. Dad wasn't feeling well earlier and Declan seemed tense on the ride over. I want them to have a good time. Now that they're getting comfortable, maybe they will.

We're only halfway across the family room when Tess rushes out with a tray packed with appetizers only to be intercepted by Finn. "What are those?" he asks, motioning with a jerk of his chin.

"Vegan egg rolls," she answers.

"*Vegan*?" he says, like it's a dirty word. "What the hell?" He calls to those around him. "Hey! Tess fucked up Thanksgiving—"

She rams the egg roll into his mouth and keeps walking. Finn grimaces, chewing like a puppy would on a lemon, his scowl relaxing with every bite. "Hmm. These are pretty good," he says through a mouthful of food. He chases after her. "Can I have another one?"

Wren throws her arm around me, laughing. "You'll get used to us," she tells me.

We round the corner and step into the kitchen. Relief floods me as the noise cuts down by half. I let out a sigh, closing my eyes briefly.

Wren drops her hand away. "You okay?" she asks. "You seem inundated. I know we're an obnoxious bunch, but it's all in good fun."

I squeeze her hand. "I'm sorry," I say. "It was a little bit of sensory overload in there with the T.V. on and everyone speaking at once. Sometimes, despite my hearing aids, it's hard to distinguish where sound is coming from and with so many people, it's hard to lip read."

"Gotcha," she says. "I used to date a guy who was hearing impaired. Biggest, *hairiest* balls I've ever seen." She takes a big gulp of her beer, shaking out her hand. "I'm not sure how he could even walk straight and was convinced he was fathered by Bigfoot. He tried to deny it, but that shit wasn't natural, you hear what I'm saying?"

I cover my mouth, laughing when Curran marches in with Tess and Declan. "Would you like some wine?" Declan asks.

He barely looks my way. I'm not certain he's talking to me.

"Melissa?" he asks, handing me a glass.

"Um. Sure," I say. "Anything is fine."

I start to ask what Tess needs help with when Curran taps my shoulder. *Hey, Melissa. Glad you could come*, he motions. *I hear you and Declan are going at it like gorillas in the fucking mist. Good for you.*

My eyes fly open as I slowly look back at Declan, torn between laughing and curling beneath the nearest cabinet. He glances up as he tops off my wine. "What's wrong?" he asks.

I don't answer, because I *can't*, especially when this tiny older woman steps in from the garage. I straighten, unsure how to respond knowing she's Declan's mother.

Curran answers for me. "I just told her that I'm glad you're doing it like gorillas. Oh, and that she could spend Thanksgiving with us."

"Curran!" Tess screams, but it's the little old lady's slap upside his head that reddens his face.

"Get back in the family room before your mother kills you," Tess says, shoving him in front of her and leading him out of the kitchen.

"Sorry, Ma," Curran calls over his shoulder, even though it's clear that he's not.

Wren motions to her mother's drink. "You enjoying your iced tea there, Ma?" she asks, winking my way.

"I would be, me darlin'," she tells her in a very sweet and thick Irish accent. "If my only daughter would give me the grandchildren I deserve."

"Ma, Evan and I are engaged. What more do you want?"

"Grandchildren," she says, as if Wren didn't hear her the first time.

"Christ," Wren grumbles, making a quick exit out of the kitchen.

On my best day, I don't I think I'd be prepared to meet Declan's mother. And this for certain isn't my best day. She's tiny, perhaps five feet tall and maybe ninety pounds, at best. Yet the strength she carries in her blue eyes reminds me of Declan's, and so does her smile. Despite her kindly disposition, however, I don't doubt this woman could take me to the ground.

"Hi, Mama," Declan says. He bends practically in half to kiss her cheek. "I'd like you to meet Melissa."

I try to step forward, but stop, given that Declan isn't exactly motioning me forward. He seems far away despite the mere feet separating us.

I do my best to smile and offer her my hand. "It's a pleasure to meet you, Mrs. O'Brien," I say.

She returns my smile, nodding in way that I think means she approves of me. "Please call me Mama."

I swear it's like I can feel my heart fill. I place my hand over my chest. "Thank you. I'd like that."

My smile dissolves when I realize Declan isn't smiling. He lowers his head, his expression tight.

"Her father is in the next room," he says quietly "I'll introduce you, Ma."

He presses his hand against her small back, leading her in the direction of the family room. She cocks her head as if confused by his actions. I am, too, unsure what's bothering him. He glances back at me. The motion is brief and not reassuring, even though I need it to be.

I should follow them and use the opportunity to become better acquainted with her. After all, it is my father she's meeting. But Declan's response makes me feel like he needs a moment.

The timer goes off over the stove, giving me an excuse to turn away. I open the oven door. Tiny quiches line a cooking sheet, the edges already browning and close to burning. I reach for a towel placed on the counter and lift them out of the oven.

I'm searching for a plate to serve them on when Tess, Sofia, Wren, and Molly return to the kitchen. "Oh, crap," Tess says. "I forgot all about these. Thank you, Melissa."

"Of course," I say.

I force a smile, making small talk with the women as I try to dismiss Declan's behavior. I suppose he's nervous, but I was rather taken aback by how he acted. He seems so different lately, especially today, and very unlike the man who I've slept beside these past two months.

He's just nervous, I reason yet again. I don't want to believe there's more going on. We depend on each other so much, and we've grown close. Or so I thought . . .

"Where's Evan?" I ask Wren, realizing she appears as alone as I am.

The women look back at her, appearing sad. Wren smiles, although she seems sad enough for all of them. "On a business trip, meeting with some big shots in Europe." She laughs. "They don't celebrate Thanksgiving, so this was another week for them and another great opportunity for Evan." She shrugs as her good humor fades. "He told me he'd do his best to make it back today, but everyone else is trying to make it back, too."

"I'm sorry," I say.

"Yeah. Me, too," she replies. "But he promised me this is the last Thanksgiving I'll spend without him." She grins, and points at me with her bottle. "I'm holding him to that."

I don't know Evan. But something in her voice assures me he'll keep that promise.

I busy myself peeling potatoes and helping Wren set the table, because, and I quote, "I don't fucking cook."

We spend our time running in and out of the kitchen with plates of appetizers. But as we finish lining the table with casserole dishes, I find myself with nothing to do.

I turn to Tess as she walks in with her little daughter perched on her hip. "What's left?" I ask.

"Nothing," she says, sounding relieved. "Just to carve the turkey, but Curran has another twenty minutes before it's time."

The noise level grows with the escalating action of the football game. My attention wanders to Declan only to squint when everyone yells at once. "All right, I'll be outside if you need me."

"Would you mind taking Fiona?" she asks.

"Do you think she'll let me?"

The mini-version of Tess in ponytails lifts her head from her shoulder and kicks out her feet, excitedly. Tess laughs. "She loves being on the porch at night. Curran and I will sit with her outside for hours sometime. It helps us all settle."

"I'd love to," I say, reaching for her.

Fiona falls against me. "Aw, sweet girl," I say, cuddling her close.

Tess wraps her a large blanket around us. "Let me get you your coat."

"I'll be all right," I say.

Tess adjusts the blanket around my shoulders, her focus skipping to where Declan is sitting with my father and his mother. "Melissa, about how Declan is behaving—"

"You mean acting like an asshole," Wren clarifies.

"Wren," Tess says quietly, like she doesn't want me to hear, or for Wren to acknowledge how distant he appears.

She huffs. "Come on, Tess, he hasn't even checked in on her. If they hadn't shown up together, I wouldn't even know they were a thing."

She's right, but I don't want to admit something that will embarrass us both. "He's distracted," I tell them. "There's a lot going on at the office he has to sort through."

"That doesn't make it okay to ignore you," Wren says.

Sofia passes us on her way to the kitchen, shooting me a worried glance. Wonderful, she's noticed too.

My face warms. "This is all new to him," I say. I try to act unaffected, but the hurt remains. I adjust my hold around Fiona and motion toward the front of the house. "I'll be outside if you need me, okay?"

"Of course," Tess says. "Thank you for looking after the baby."

"It's my pleasure," I assure her.

I skitter around the family room as another touchdown is scored and the O'Briens lose their minds. Sofia steps into the family room and places more food on coffee table. Killian pulls her onto his lap when she tries to walk away. Declan watches them as she settles comfortably against him, his face absent of any emotion that might tell me what he's feeling. But when he looks up at me, and he sees me holding the baby, I catch something I've never seen in him.

He looks . . . *defeated*. I'm not sure what's happening. I want to talk to him about it, but as he bows his head and rubs his hands, I realize it's not the right time.

I step out onto the porch, shutting the door behind me. There's no breeze, but the cold settles around me, chilling my cheeks while little Fiona keeps the rest of me warm.

"Hey, Melissa," Finn yells, startling me.

He laughs when Fiona grins at him. The light on the porch doesn't extend to where he's sitting, swathing him in darkness. "Sorry, I didn't mean to scare you," he says.

Finn is not someone people would call shy. He's seemingly just as loud and personable as the rest of his family, but every now and then, he needs a moment alone. If I hadn't had the opportunity to get to know him, this is a side of him that I wouldn't have imagined.

I move closer to where he's sitting on a couch and ease down.

"Too loud for you in there?" he asks, stretching out his fingers.

Fiona instantly grips them in her small hand, shaking them.

"It's a little overwhelming," I admit.

He strokes Fiona's head as she settles against me. "Yeah, I think I've heard that about us once or twice." He puts his bottle of water on the floor. "You should have been there when we met Tess—or better yet, when Evan met *us*. I'm surprised they didn't run away screaming."

"Was it that bad?" I ask, rubbing Fiona's back.

"Worse," he says. "Evan wasn't even dressed."

"Oh," I say, grimacing.

"Yeah," he says, laughing. "Poor bastard."

He trains his gaze ahead and away from me. I start to think that maybe he needs this time alone. But I can't return inside just yet. I sink into the cushions. They're cold, but it feels good against my back after all the running around we did in the kitchen.

I quiet, closing my eyes and taking a moment to rest my battered senses. Fiona tucks her little body closer. I think she's falling asleep, but I can't be sure.

"Are you on call today?" Finn asks, his breath visible in the frigid air.

"No," I tell him. "I have someone else covering for me."

"Good," he says. "You probably need a break from it all."

The way he responds makes me think he's talking about himself as much as me. "How are you doing?" I ask.

He offers a small smile. "Better. A lot better."

"I'm glad," I tell him. "I haven't seen you in a while and you haven't called."

"Sorry," he says.

"Don't be," I assure him. "You don't need me as much. That's a good thing. But I'm always here if you do."

"Does Declan know about all those times we talked?"

I shake my head. "Only if you told him."

"Nah. I haven't said shit. When everything that happened, happened, I needed them to know I was okay." He huffs. "Even though I wasn't, I needed them to believe I'd still get there."

"And you did," I agree, smoothing my hand along Fiona's back.

"I had help." He nudges me. "Lots of it. Don't know where I'd be without it."

God, he looks so much like Declan, only younger. Instead of blond hair, ginger curls top his head.

"How are you and Sol?"

His big smile is enough of an answer. "She's the best,"

he tells me. His smile fades. "She's visiting her mom and says she'll be here. But it's hard on Sol when she goes and sometimes she needs a little time to recover."

His voice trails as he looks out to the large expanse of Curran and Tess's front lawn. I don't see or hear anything, but I can tell Finn picked up on something. He rises, moving fast and toward the front door.

The noise inside explodes like grenade when he throws the door open. "Hey, Wren, *Wren*! Evan's here."

I stand with Fiona as Finn backs away and Wren races through the threshold. "I swear to Christ, Finnie, if you're messing with me, I'm going to beat your ass."

Her words cut off as a tall man with dark wavy hair about Declan's age steps near the bottom of the steps and into the light, smiling. He releases the handle of his suitcase and drops the heavy briefcase at his feet. "Hello, love," he tells her in a British accent.

Wren launches herself forward. The force she uses to straddle him should knock him to the ground. He hangs tight, welcoming her embrace and one hell of a kiss.

"What are you doing here?" she asks, pulling only slightly away.

He carries her up the stairs as if she's nothing, yet smiles like she's everything. "I didn't want to miss our first Thanksgiving together." He eases her down slowly, clasping Finn's hand when he hurries up with his bags. "Thank you, Finn," he tells him, keeping his other arm secure around Wren.

"Hey, thanks for showing," Finn replies. He tosses the bags just inside the foyer. "This is Melissa, Deck's woman," he says, motioning to me.

Ordinarily the introduction as Declan's "woman" would make me happy. Not today. "Hello, Evan," I politely say.

"Pleasure," he says, shaking my hand. He's pleasant, but it's as if he can't wait to return to Wren.

"How's your evening?" he asks her.

"Awesome," she says. "Ma's already asking when I'm popping out our first kid."

He grins, guiding her inside. "Perhaps we should assure her we can't wait to start."

"Don't tell her that," she says, laughing. "I swear she thinks my ovaries will turn to stone or some shit."

Finn turns around. "Evan wants a ton of kids," he nudges me. "Wanna bet they give Curran and Tess a run for their money?"

His good humor dwindles as a pang of hurt fills my chest. Declan and I are never this affectionate in public. He'll hold my hand, certainly, and open the car door for me. Occasionally, he'll even kiss my cheek. But he's never this open and free. Wren and Evan can't seem to keep their hands off each other. And here, Declan hasn't even spoken to me since he left the kitchen.

"You all right?" Finn asks.

I'm ready to lie and assure him that I am when Declan steps out. His stare locks on me, and how I'm holding Fiona. "Dinner's ready," he says.

Finn frowns at him, placing his arm around me when I don't move right away. "Come on, Melissa. The food's not going to eat itself."

Declan steps in front of Finn. "Do you mind?" he asks, fixated on the way his arm rests on my shoulders.

"What the fuck, Deck?" Finn counters, his arms slipping from my shoulders.

"Finn?"

A small voice has us turning in the direction of the walkway. A young woman edges forward. She's beautiful, although it's clear she's been crying. "Is everything okay?"

Finn jets down the steps, gathering her to him. She falls into his embrace, clutching him. "I'm sorry I'm late," she stammers.

He whispers something I don't quite here. "That's Sol. His fiancée," Declan says. "Let's give them a moment."

He's speaking to me, but looking at them as if his heart is splintering. I step forward, pulling his attention away. "Declan, what's wrong?" I ask him.

"Nothing," he says, averting his gaze.

"I don't believe you." I adjust my hold on Fiona to stroke his arm. "What's wrong, love?"

The way he withdraws tells me I couldn't have picked a worse choice of words. "Let's just get inside," he says, refusing to meet my gaze. "It's like the damn Arctic out here."

For a moment I can't even move, stunned by how upset he seems. But he's not moving either. He waits for me to step forward, placing his hand on my back so carefully, I almost don't feel him. I think in touching me, he's trying to close the distance prying us apart. Yet the moment we're greeted by the warmth from the foyer, he drops his hand and he pulls further away.

I pause in the foyer as Curran hurries forward, offering his thanks when he lifts Fiona from my arms. I barely hear him, too distracted by the noise and by the way Declan stands stiffly beside me.

I don't know what's happening, or why he's keeping me at arm's length.

I only know that it's killing me.

CHAPTER 18

Melissa

Declan stays unusually quiet through most of dinner, barely saying anything to anyone. I wish I can say that the O'Briens don't notice, but even though they maintain their animated chatter, I don't miss the looks tossed my way. Even Sol, who seemed so upset when she arrived, tosses a worried glance in my direction. She nestles against Finn, who seems scared to let her go, whereas Declan I'm sure already has.

When Killian and Sofia say their goodnights to have dessert with her family, I use it as an excuse to leave, too.

"Dad's tired," I say. "Could you take us home?"

Declan nods. "Of course."

We walk my father into his house in silence and settle him in despite his insistence that he's fine. My hope is that Declan will tell me what's troubling him when we're alone. But that hope is quickly crushed.

He's barely speaking to me. "We're staying at your place?" I ask when he passes the road that leads to my apartment. It's not a ridiculous question. By now, I'm not even sure he wants me in the same car as him.

"That's what we planned," he says, keeping his focus on

the road.

This is the part where most women would start screaming, and maybe I should. But I'm so hurt right now the best I can do is not cry. My overnight bag and keys are at his place. I don't want to fight with him. That doesn't mean I'm spending the night, since he's spent most of this one ignoring me.

We drive to his place in silence. When he parks in front of his apartment building, I don't wait to see if he'll come to the door and open it for me like he always does. Mostly because I'm certain he won't.

He slows his pace when he sees that I don't wait for him and slip out of the car. I walk past him, standing in front of the double doors leading into the building, my focus burning a hole through the clear glass.

He doesn't say anything, and I keep my attention ahead as he hits the security code into his building. I stiffen when he places his arm around my waist and leads me forward. It's something he does whenever we arrive at his place after dinner out or when I follow him home after work, those other times he *didn't* disregard me.

This time, the way he holds me is different. I can feel it just as I can no longer excuse it. Not after everything I've risked for him.

Instead of allowing the contact and leaning into him, I step away and ahead.

"Mel?" he says.

I hit the button to the elevator. A few tenants he knows hurry in from the cold and rush into the lobby as I idly watch the numbers along the screen count down the floors, sparing me from having to formulate some kind of response. The large group piles into the elevator with us, two of them stepping off on the same floor as us.

The tension pushes us further apart. The moment he unlocks the door to his apartment and throws it open, I hurry in and into the bedroom, my eyes burning as I gather my toiletries from the bathroom.

Declan steps into the bedroom still wearing his coat, pausing when he sees what I'm doing. "You're leaving?" he asks, his deep voice curt.

I don't answer. Instead I carry out my small bag and shove it into my travel suitcase, my heels tapping against the wood floor as I storm out.

Heavy footsteps sound behind me. I'm almost to the kitchen when Declan grabs the handle, keeping me in place. "What are you doing?" he asks.

It's a standoff, me staring at the wall, his eyes fixed on me, and neither one budging from our spots. "Don't go," he bites out.

I whirl around. "Why did you invite me to Thanksgiving?" There are lots of questions I could ask, lots of things I can say, but this is the one I need to know.

He doesn't answer, slipping his fingers from the handle of my suitcase just as I release it. It falls with a thump against the wood floor, causing something within it to break, not that I care.

The weight of what I'm feeling makes it hard to face him. I hate being so weak and vulnerable, but I'm not so weak that I'll let him get off this easy. "*I* didn't have to be there," I say. "But I did it for you and for us, and all you did was embarrass me."

He lifts his chin. "I didn't mean to embarrass you."

"But you did," I remind him. "The way you ignored me, it's as if you were trying to warn your family not to get too close, that you didn't plan on keeping me around."

He doesn't deny it, and right now, that hurts more than anything he could have said. Tears roll down my cheeks. "If you don't want me, just tell me. But don't you *dare* stay with me because you think my father is dying, or because you feel sorry for me. I deserve better than that."

I swipe my suitcase off the floor. There's more to pack, but I don't bother. He can keep it around for the next girl he brings to his bed. I hurry away, snagging my keys off the counter.

Declan tears down the hall. "Mel—*Melissa*."

My heart sinks at the sound of his voice. I don't stop, tears blurring the view of the front door. He slams it shut with his palm when I try to open it, his chest pressing hard against my back. "I'm sorry," he says.

His breaths are ragged with what I can only determine is anger. I ram my eyes shut, trying to hold in the disappointment that's been fighting its way out all night. He releases the door, his hand sliding down my arm and to my waist.

He bends to kiss my shoulder. "I'm sorry I hurt you," he says.

For a moment I don't move. I hate to cry. It only shows those who hurt me exactly how deep my wounds go.

I gather my strength so I don't break down sobbing. "Why did you?" I ask. He doesn't answer. I turn around, needing to see his face. "I don't understand what I did wrong."

As much as his tone and words suggested his apology is sincere, his features are severe, *angry*. "You didn't do anything wrong," he tells me. "If you want the truth, you've done everything right."

My brow knits tight. I have no idea what he means. "I wanted to give us a try," he continues. "I couldn't stop thinking about you, or wondering what it would be like to kiss you, to touch you. So I did. I just never expected to feel this way."

"And what do you feel?" I ask, even though I'm afraid to know.

"That I might be in love with you."

I don't swoon, go weak in the knees, or fall all over him like I'm supposed to. Not when he whispers these words like they're a bad thing and not when he stands so rigid against me.

I simply wait, unmoving, wishing he'd make sense so I know whether I need to walk away or wrap my arms around him like I very much want to.

"I didn't expect things to get serious this fast," he admits. "You met my mother tonight, Mel. The last girl she met was on prom night my senior year of high school."

"I only met her because you asked me to be there," I remind him. My gaze searches his face for any sign that can tell me what he's thinking. "But it's like you're punishing me for agreeing to go with you. Did you want me to say no? Is that what you were hoping?"

"No. I wanted you with me," he says.

His stare is so intense I can barely find my words. "Then why are you making me feel like I've forced you into a corner or somehow manipulated you?" I speak slowly, struggling to understand what he's doing. "You didn't have to introduce me to your family. No one needed to know we were together. You did this, Declan. *You.* I never put any pressure on you, so don't stand here acting like I did."

"That's not what I'm saying" he says, his voice rising. "But I need you to be honest with me. Did you expect us to be where we are? We've been together, what? Just over two months and we've barely known a night apart."

"No," I confess. "I never expected this."

"Neither did I," he repeats. "I wasn't ready for any of it."

My chest tightens. I'm so emotionally battered, all I want to do is lie down. But I can't. Not yet.

"Do you think this was a good time for me to fall in love?" My eyes well when he turns his head away in pain. "It's not," I choke, my tears falling. "My dad isn't getting better, Declan. In another few months, I'm probably going to walk away from a career that I love to take care of him in his final days."

"Mel," he begins.

I shake my head, cutting him off. "You came and made everything better by being with me, and I'm grateful to you because of it. No matter how scared I was that I was in over my head, I loved every moment of it. Until *tonight*."

I reach for my suitcase. Declan sweeps me into his arms before I can grip the handle and presses me against the wall.

His kiss is deep, branding me with everything he's feeling. At first I try to pull away, but his insistence and the way his hands drag along my body reignites the tenderness I experience every time his bare flesh touches mine.

"Don't go," he says between breaths. "Please . . . don't leave me."

My arms link around his neck as he lifts me and carries me to the couch. As our passion surges, I expect him to peel away my clothes and for his hand to disappear between my legs. Instead he sits, keeping me on his lap and holding me close.

"I don't believe in love," he says, breaking away. "And I've never wanted to settle down."

Despite how I told him I wasn't asking him for anything, his words sting. I lower my chin. He says he doesn't want to hurt me, but he's doing one hell of a job.

"But with you," he says, appearing torn. "It's like I have to."

"I don't understand," I tell him truthfully.

He doesn't seem to either, but tries to explain. "When we arrived and my family came up to you, it's like right away, you belonged. With the exception of Sofia, who she's known since she was a little girl, Tess who's an ivy league grad and the mother of her grandchildren, and Sol who brought Finn back from edge, my mother never considered anyone good enough for her sons—and don't get me started on Wren. Evan's company makes billions, but it's what he did for Wren that proved his worth."

"She asked you to call her Mama," he points out. "She immediately knew what I've known all along, that you're the best thing to ever walk into my life."

I wipe my eyes, his words like daggers to my heart.

"Sofia sits on Killian's lap and all I think is, Melissa should be sitting on my lap. You swept in and out of the kitchen making food, smiling and engaging with my family like you've been a part of it forever. But when I saw you holding the baby, it's like I saw the future I wasn't supposed to have."

I can't move, tears drenching my cheeks, but none that fall are happy tears. Declan isn't happy sharing what he does. It hurts him to say it.

"You're always there to tell me when I'm out of line. You cook for me, you take care of me. You listen to me—when I just need to be heard or ranting because I'm ready to punch someone's face in. You came into my life because you were forced to, but stayed when I needed you most. You're the one, Mel, there's no doubt in my mind."

"But you're not ready to have me," I finish for him.

"No," he admits, his voice softening. "I've *never* been ready to have you."

This all goes back to his cheating father, who betrayed his mother and their children. I should understand, and I do. But knowing and understanding doesn't make his words easier to take.

Sitting on his lap the way I am, and hurting this much, I'm not the unbiased counselor I trained to be. I'm the woman who doesn't want to lose him. Even though I think I already have.

"I wasn't supposed to feel this way," he says, stroking my cheek until I meet his gaze. "And I'm not sure I want to."

"Why?" I ask, barely getting the word out.

"Because I don't believe in happily ever after. I only believe in the drive that's taking me to the top, the hard work that's brought me where I am, and the goals I still need to accomplish. I don't believe in love," he repeats, his voice splintering. "But if I did, it would be what I feel for you."

He waits for me to speak. When I finally do, it shatters my resolve. "Based on my past, and too many friends and lovers who have hurt me, I didn't believe in trust. It's not something that comes easy for me. But I took a chance and I trusted you." My voice is shaky and I can't stop trembling. "You didn't want to love me, but you're forgetting that I didn't want to trust you."

I slip off his lap. He doesn't stop me. "My father, the man who does love me is dying. He wasn't supposed to develop cancer. He was supposed to walk me down the aisle when I found someone who could promise me forever, and I was supposed to give him grandchildren to keep him young when he was old and feeble. My dad is probably not going to walk me anywhere, and he'll likely never hold his grandchildren here on earth. But at least he was brave enough to love and value my trust."

Darkness shadows Declan's features as I step away. "Mel . . ." he says. "Don't walk out of my life."

My hand quivers as I pass my fingertips along my moist cheeks. "I'm not walking out of your life. We work together, Declan. I'll still be there come Monday."

"That's not what I mean!" he says, charging to his feet.

I almost say if we're meant to be, we'll find our way back to each other, but I don't. Chances are, being who he is and commanding the room the way he does, he'll move on to that perfect person I hoped to one day be for him.

I return to the hall where I dropped my purse and keys. I lift them from the floor, not bothering with my suitcase.

Declan circles my waist as I straighten, his head coming down to rest against my shoulder. "Don't do this," he whispers. "Please."

I start to cry all over again. I want to turn around and hold him. I want us to make love all night and wake tucked against him like I have so many times since he first kissed me. But I can't.

"Let me go, Declan. Give us both the space we need."

The words are hard to say. I don't want to imagine my life without his arms around me, and that's what I'm risking by walking away.

But I can no longer trust him to be the man I need.

I march forward when his arms fall away from my waist. My muscles tense despite how unusually light my feet feel. *Maybe he's right*, I tell myself as I reach the door. Maybe it's better not to believe in love.

Then I wouldn't be hurting so much.

CHAPTER 19

Declan

My eyes sweep across the evidence spread across my desk, my stomach shriveling so painfully, I have to look away. Seventeen children all under fourteen years of age, the biggest case of child abuse this office has ever seen, and it's up to me to figure out the next step.

Finn. Jesus Christ, all I can think about is my little brother right now. It's not just the images in front of me that make me want to puke. It's more that I'm actually *seeing* what was done to him.

I can't deal with this. Some things are just too evil to be real.

If it were up to me I'd drag the defendant out of jail and set him on fire in a public square. Problem is I can't do that. I represent the law. But it's the side of me that serves the public sector that wants to send this piece of shit straight to hell.

Babies, that's all some of them were. Innocent little kids taken by the wrong man. Just like my brother.

Three Assistant D.A.s sit in front of me, including Tess. Curran stands behind her and Detective Melo, the lead investigator, waits to her right. But my attention drifts to

Melissa who's sitting off to the side, beneath the framed picture Rosana drew of me. Her arms are crossed and her fair skin is a horrible shade of white. Like the rest of us, she's sick down to her gut.

Every gaze is anywhere but on the pictures covering my desk. It doesn't matter. They're ingrained in our minds and will likely haunt us for the rest of our damn lives.

"Tess, I want you to take this," I finally say.

Curran straightens, his balling fists ready to take a swing. The other two D.A.s, both new, sigh with relief and quickly pile out.

"No way," Curran mutters as the door shuts behind them.

Melo's eyes cut to me. "Will you excuse us?" I ask him.

He's barely to the door when Curran looms over the desk, ramming his face in mine. "You're not fucking giving her this case," he barks.

I shove away from my chair, the force slamming it into the shelf behind me and sending the contents crashing to the floor. "Do *not* question my authority," I bite out, our faces inches apart.

"She's eight months pregnant!" Curran fires back.

"And she's the best attorney I have for this case!" I straighten, motioning around. "Do you think any of us want to deal with this shit? *No.* But someone has to and Tess is the only one I have who's qualified."

The lines etched around his jaw deepen. If I was anyone else, in any another position, he'd have me by the throat. But just because he's my brother doesn't mean he gets his way. Not with all these kids on the line.

"Curran, it's okay," Tess tells him. I didn't realize she was holding onto his arm, my focus so fixed on him I didn't see her approach. But I see her now, just as I feel Melissa beside me.

I steal a glance. Her expression is riddled with worry. I don't know what I look like. All I know is the anger burning through me.

"It's a conflict of interest," he says. "I'm one of the cops who responded."

"You weren't the arresting officer," I begin.

"No," he agrees. "That was Sanders, who blew his fucking head off after gathering all this evidence." He shakes his head. "Twenty years on the job, he saw a lot of shit, but this was the call that pushed him to the breaking point. You think I want my wife a part of this?"

"You don't get a choice," I say. "That falls on me. And I'm choosing Tess because she's the best I have."

My tone is absolute. Curran knows I'm not budging and he's more pissed at me than I've ever seen him.

"Curran," Tess says, her voice soft. "Someone has to do this. Next to Declan, I have the most experience."

Her hand slips away to gather the stacks of photos. I don't miss how she keeps her eyes off the images. Curran's still fit to be tied, but as furious as he is with me, he's not blind to Tess. With a curse he begins to gather the pics that flew off the desk when he thundered toward me.

I lower my lids and release a heavy breath as I feel Mel's fingertips glide down my back. This is the first time she's touched me since the night she left my apartment. God *damn* I miss her. She's been at work every day, keeping a professional distance, all the while doing her job. She's not cold. She still smiles, although those smiles are forced. But it's the sadness that dulls her large brown eyes I can't get past. Probably because I'm going through it too, without her.

She stacks the last of the pictures and adds them to the ones Curran and Tess are shoving into the envelope. "Mel, when are you meeting with the victims' parents?"

She didn't tell me she was. I just know she will. These kids aren't the only ones hurting. "Wednesday night," she replies. "I set up a group counseling session with one of our top therapists."

"Will they all be there?" I ask.

"At least one parent or legal guardian will be there from

each family," she answers. "I called them individually to ensure their presence."

Those calls alone must have taken hours. Between work and looking after Miles . . . I have no idea how she does it. "What do you think about me and Tess being there?"

She pauses, knowing where I'm headed. "It's their first time meeting. I planned to attend to introduce myself as their liaison to this office. It might be too much to have the three of us there."

"What about Tess?"

Melissa nods slowly. Yeah. She knows where I'm headed. "I think they would appreciate her presence," she agrees.

I glance at my sister-in law, who, like Curran pointed out, is very pregnant. "Tess," I tell her. "If they can relate to you as a parent, it can help us plead this case out." My focus cuts to the envelope. "No way am I putting seventeen children on the stand."

"All right," she says, nodding. She rubs Curran's arm when he frowns. "We don't need seventeen counts of Indecent Assault to put this monster away for life," she explains. "Not with the multiple offenses he's charged with and the amount of evidence we have. If I can convince the families to plead this out to fewer counts, there won't be a trial and I can take him out of society."

Curran strokes a strand of her hair that escaped her bun. "And if you can't?"

"I'll make sure he never hurts a child again," she promises.

His stare softens as he continues to take her in, not that he's any less pissed at me.

He'll get over it. I meant what I said. Tess is the one for the job.

"We'll see you later," Tess says to me. She gathers the file in front of her and Curran grabs the rest. They walk out with Curran's arm resting against the small of her back, exactly how I used to hold Melissa.

"Mel, wait," I say when she tries to follow them out.

For a moment, she stares at the closed door. I don't think she'll turn around, but she does. "Tess will do right by those children."

It's not what I'm asking, but I think my face gives enough away.

I pull my chair back and take a seat. "How are you?"

"I'm okay," she replies.

God I hate this small-talk bullshit. It's all we've had lately. When neither of us says anything more, I'm sure she'll walk out.

She surprises me by taking a seat in front of me. "Is there a case you need to discuss? Some business you want me to handle?"

In other words, don't make this about us. It's hard not to. "How's your dad?"

"Okay. A little better now that he's off chemo."

"When does he start the next round?"

She sighs like she doesn't want to think about it. "Next month. He, um, told me you stopped by on Christmas on your way to see your family. Thank you for visiting. It means a lot to him."

"It's my pleasure. He's a good man."

"Yes, he is," she answers quietly.

I reach into my desk. "I have something for you," I say.

Her eyes round when I place a velvet jewelry box on my desk and slide it closer to her.

"You didn't have to do that," she says.

"Yes, I did. You work your ass off, you keep late hours, and you never say no to anyone."

Her attention stays on the box. "Most people who work here do the same."

"They don't mean what you mean to me," I tell her, my voice gruff.

Her lids squeeze shut. She's hurt, but she's not the only

one in pain. "Declan," she says, her voice splintering.

"Just open it," I tell her.

Melissa hesitates briefly, moving slowly, her fingers spreading wide to lift the lid. A soft smile forms as she removes the long silver necklace, the locket at the end swinging like a pendulum beneath her hands.

"It's beautiful," she says. She tilts her head when she realizes what it is, her fingers trembling as she pries it open.

Her breath catches, her voice quivering as she takes in the picture. "Are you trying to make me cry?"

"Your dad said it was your first ballet recital. You were almost eight, but you refused to have your picture taken without him."

In the photo, she's sitting on his lap, holding a little wand as she leans against him. I think she was supposed to be a fairy princess or something, but that's not what she remembers.

"I was terrible," she says. "I couldn't hear the music and struggled to keep up."

Shit. This was supposed to make her happy, not tear her up. "Your Dad told me you were the best one."

She laughs, her eyes brimming with tears. "Is this why you stopped by on Christmas?"

"It was one of the reasons," I admit.

She tilts her head.

"I missed you," I confess. "And wanted to see you."

She'd taken almost two weeks' vacation during the holidays to spend time with her father. She was out for a run when I stopped by. I couldn't stand to not see her on Christmas, but she was gone for a long time and my family was expecting me. With Miles as sick as he seemed, I think she needed an avenue to work out her stress. I don't tell her I drove around trying to find her. But that's exactly what I did.

"I have to go," she says. She places the necklace over her head, pausing to clutch the locket against her chest, her eyes shimmering. "Thank you for the beautiful gift, and for the memory."

I push away from the desk when she rises and lifts the box away. She wanted space, and I gave it to her. But enough is enough. I whip her around before she reaches the door, kissing her deeply.

Her body melts against mine, her mouth hot as my tongue slides in.

I used to rip into Curran for his lack of professional behavior around Tess, not understanding how the hell he couldn't control himself. But as my hands graze down Melissa's back to grip her ass, I get it. Damn it, I've been lost without her.

She doesn't fight me, her fingers gliding through my hair as our kiss turns frantic and my fingers knead her curves.

I'm briefly aware of the jewelry case falling on the floor, and of the knock at the door. But I can't stop and neither can she.

It's only when the door swings open that we break away.

My hands slide to her waist, but I refuse to let her go.

"Oh," Stephanie says. "Am I interrupting?"

She knows she is, and she's pissed about it. I've turned her down the last few times she's offered to come to my apartment and "help me with my cases" and warned her she needs to spend more time at her desk.

"What do you need, Stephanie?" I ask, not bothering to hide my annoyance.

She shoots Melissa one hell of a glare. "Detective Melo was looking for you."

"Detective Melo was just here," I grind out. "He knows where I am, and how to reach me. Don't ever barge in here again, and watch your attitude around Melissa."

"My apologies," she says with a fixed smile she doesn't mean. "Sorry for interrupting,"

Mel turns away as Stephanie walks out in a huff. Although I can't see her face, I know she's smiling. "I should go," she says.

"No," I tell her. "You should be with me."

I kiss her neck, making her shudder. "The governor is endorsing me for D.A. at the ball on Saturday," I whisper between flicks of my tongue. "I know you're going. I want you with me."

"As friends?" she stammers. She ignores what I'm doing, even though it's taking everything I have not to pull up her dress.

My hands wandering back to her ass. "No."

"People will think there's something between us," she says.

She gasps as I nibble the base of her throat. "Are you kidding?" I mutter. "They'll know the moment Stephanie opens her trap."

She laughs, angling around to kiss me like we haven't been apart. Shit. It's taking all I have not to slip my hand between her legs.

Our kiss grows more heated, leaving us panting as she pulls away. "I'll go with you," she says. "But I'm not making any promises."

"I'm not expecting anything," I tell her, lying to her face.

The limo hugs the curb. I adjust the tie to my black tux as the driver lowers the window separating the cabin from the front. "Would you like me to escort the young lady to the vehicle?" he asks.

"No. I'll do it," I inform him.

He nods. "The hotel is forty minutes from here, possibly longer due to traffic downtown. Any specific instructions, sir?" he asks.

"Privacy, at all costs," I tell him.

"Very well, sir."

He's one of those drivers who's escorted a lot of higher ups. He knows what I'm asking and is smart enough to keep quiet about what goes on in the rear of the limo.

He shuts the window closed and lowers the privacy screen. The lock clicks into place. Now, only I can unlock it. Not that I plan to. I finish adjusting my tie and pop the mirror closed.

I'm early, but that's how I planned it. I reach for my coat when Melissa sweeps down the concrete steps, her champagne cape fluttering open to reveal her strapless black ball gown that hugs her curves as if painted on. A row of long pearls dangle between her breasts.

I freeze in place, her dress reminiscent of the one she wore in that dream I had too many times about her, the one where she hovered over my ottoman on all fours. It's not exact, but it's close enough to make me hard.

The driver hurries to get the door. "Thank you," she says as she steps in.

She pauses when she sees me, her eyes flying open. She likes what she sees. Well, that makes two of us. "Um, hi," she says, edging in. "You look . . . nice."

I reach for her hand to help her inside and to ensure she sits beside me. The driver slams the door shut as my gaze locks on hers. "And you look stunning," I tell her.

I lift her gloved hand and kiss it. She's close enough that the skirt of her gown fans over my knee. I can feel her body heat just as she feels mine.

Her hair is pulled up, a pile of curls spilling from the top and delicately brushing her large pearl and diamond stud earrings. Her hair must have taken hours to style, but it's her face I can't stop looking at. Her lips are glossed a deep red and black eye shadow illuminates her large eyes. She knew I was coming for her and went all out. I just don't understand why she seems to hesitate to draw too near.

Maybe there's someone else in her life. After all, it's been over a month since she walked out on me. I doubt it, though. Not because she isn't irresistible. Hell, Melissa is sex in high heels. But she works too damn hard.

Either way, no man is going to come between us. Am I

being irrational and possessive? Damn right I am. I was the dumb prick who watched her walk away. But now that I have her all to myself, I'm ready to prove how much I need her.

My mouth finds her neck, just like it did the other day at the office, nibbling and sucking. "I was fucking stupid to let you go," I murmur against her skin.

"Declan . . ." she gasps, her body shaking against my chest as I press our bodies closer.

I backed off since that time in my office, mostly to keep her from cancelling our date. But each hour, each damn minute that I didn't hold her was too long.

It's not about sex, not anymore, not after everything that's happened between us. It's about me feeling close to her, and proving how much I've missed us.

My hand kneads her breast. "We have forty minutes," I whisper against her lips. "Longer with traffic." She jolts when I pinch her nipple. "And even longer after that if I ask the driver to circle the block." I yank her small purse out of her hand and toss it across the floor, then carefully remove her hearing aids and place them in the pocket of the arm rest.

"You said you weren't expecting anything," she moans as I return to play.

"I lied," I tell her, snatching her hand and cupping it over my thick erection.

"Jesus," she rasps, her eyes lustful as she begins to rub.

My tux cost a small fortune, and her dress probably did, too. But we peel off our expensive attire like rags until I'm naked except for my opened white shirt and she's down to her garter belt and heels. I stretch out along the wide seat, placing her knees on either side of my head, moaning as her head bobs up and down on my lap. Her sucks are hard, driving me crazy. Yet as much as my head is swimming with desire, I clutch her hips and pull her down, suckling her sweet skin.

She's whimpering as she goes deeper, the orgasm that follows making her thighs bat against my temples. I'm ready to come when the driver slams on the brakes. We fall forward and onto the floor, the loud honks of horns signaling some asshole cut him off. But it's as if nothing happened. Melissa and I don't stop. I flip her on all fours, pushing into her slowly as her body clenches around my length.

She covers her mouth, trying to muffle her screams as I thrust, my speed increasing with each lurch of my hips. My jaw clamps down. I'm trying to be quiet, too, but the way she's circling her ass and bearing down makes it impossible. We fall forward again as we finish, her dress in a pile on the floor and my tux—oh, who gives a shit where it is.

I push up on my arms and pull out, pressing her back against my chest as I fall onto my knees. She swivels around, wrenching her neck to stamp her mouth over mine.

Her kiss is long and sweet and she keeps her smile as she pulls away. "Hi," she says.

She expects me to tell her "hi" back, or say something cute. Instead I clasp her face gently, holding her focus so she can read my lips.

"I love you."

Her pause is dramatic, her brown eyes filling with shock as she takes me in. She didn't expect me to say what I did. And before her, I never would have. But she's my everything, even though no woman was supposed to be.

"I thought you didn't believe in love."

"There was a lot I didn't believe in before you," I admit.

I mean what I say. This whole time without her, it's as if I've been missing a part of my soul. If that's not love, I'll be damned if I know what it is.

My knuckles skim over the curve of her waist. "I've spent a long miserable month without you, and I'm done," I tell her. "I don't want to pretend there's nothing between us and I don't want to go forward without you."

She drops her chin. I'm not sure why until she lifts her face to meet mine. "You haven't been with anyone else?"

"No." I stroke her jaw with my thumb as a single tear escapes her eyes. I hate what I've done to her and need her to believe me. "You mean more to me than anything and anyone, even my fucking career."

I adjust our positions so we're kneeling in front of each other and take her hands in mine. Her hair is a mess, and her makeup is smeared, but I swear to Christ, I've never known anyone more beautiful.

"I know I fucked up," I say, watching her hang on my every word. "And I know that I hurt you. I'm sorry. God, I'm sorry." My lips sweep over hers, my body and soul begging her to believe me. "But when I say I love you, I mean it, and I only mean it for you."

"I love you, too," she says, her voice trembling. Her fingertips graze along my chest. "I just don't know where we go from here."

"From here we show the world," I say.

I snag onto her waist when we hit a bump and she loses her balance, kissing her again, and again after that. She meets my mouth with equal passion, our hands raking over our bare skin.

She clasps my wrist when my hand slips between her legs. "We need to get dressed," she stammers, her cheeks flushing a deep red.

"I'm not ready to," I say, brushing the tips of my fingers along her inner thigh.

She whimpers, her lashes fluttering. "Later," she says. "I promise."

Her lips crash on mine. It takes a hell of a lot of effort for us to break apart but we finally do. I lead her back to the rear seat, picking up our discarded clothes along the way and laughing as we sort through the pieces.

I yank on my briefs and pants, my stare passing along her face and those curves that heated beneath my touch.

She notices, flashing me a teasing grin as she slips her hearing aids back on. "Will you zip me up?" she asks, giving me her back and gathering her dress around her.

"Only because you're asking me," I say, trailing kisses

between her shoulder blades.

She moans. "You're really making it hard to stay dressed."

I finish pulling up the zipper. "Good. Remember that when we're back at my apartment tonight."

"Tonight?" she asks.

"Yes, tonight." She sounds surprised I want her with me, not that I blame her. I've been a total ass, but now that I have my shit together, I'm going to prove what she means to me.

"I still have your things at my place." I wrap my arms around her. "Say you'll stay with me."

"I'll stay," she says, so quietly I barely catch it.

I start to pull her in for another kiss when I realize where we are. "Shit. We're almost there."

Panic spreads across her features as she adjusts her breasts beneath her dress. "Oh, no." Her head jerks to the side. "Do you know where my panties are?"

"Nope. Haven't seen them since I ripped them off with my teeth."

"Declan!"

I scramble to the floor, searching for what I recall is a thong. I glance over my shoulder. "You sure you need underwear?"

"It's the governor's ball. I'm not walking in without panties." She reaches into her purse, passing me some mints after popping a few in her mouth. "I think we both need these," she says.

"Why's that?"

"Declan," she says, covering her face.

"Because you went down on me?"

"Don't—"

"While I was going down on you?"

She slaps my ass. "You're not helping," she tells me.

I can't help my grin or wink at the sight of her reddening cheeks. I find her lacy black thong beneath her wrap and pass it to her before rushing to pull the remainder of my clothes on.

We only have a few minutes more before we reach the hotel and we're still not fully clothed. It's a serious situation, but both of us can't stop smiling.

I'm adjusting my tie in the mirror as she wipes her smudged make-up away with a moist cloth from her purse. She fluffs her hair. "I don't think I can fix this. Can you help me take the pins out?"

I'll be the first to admit I don't know what the hell I'm doing. Melissa will be the second. "*Ouch*!" she says when I pull the first one.

I give her a quick kiss. "Sorry, like this?"

"No, no—never mind," she says. She throws her head back, laughing when I rip out another two hairs.

God, I've missed that smile.

She finishes pulling out the pins, combing through what remains of the curls with her fingers until they fall in a cascade around her shoulders. "Does this look all right?"

"When you say, 'all right', do you mean suggestive and wild, like we just had sex in the back of a limo?"

"Oh, God," she says, adjusting the curls.

I hold out a hand. "If so, we nailed it."

"Stop making me blush."

Her last few words trail as I nuzzle her neck. "I can't help myself," I murmur. "You get me hot."

"Baby," she groans, pulling away.

She barely has time to apply her lipstick when the driver pulls along the curb. A crowd of photographers and reporters rush forward, lining up against the velvet ropes.

Melissa turns to me. "They've been expecting you," she says.

The driver jogs around, scrambling to open the door. I step out amidst a light show of flashing cameras, reaching in to take Melissa's hand. She gathers her wrap around her and together we glide onto the red carpet.

I'm ready to show the press who this woman is to me. But when I try to slide my arm around her waist, she slips away. "We're on," she says.

She winks as a separate crowd of reporters swarm her. I watch her leave, smiling when the first of the media reps barks out a question and certain I'll never let her go.

CHAPTER 20

Melissa

It's hard to play the role of the consummate professional following some of the hottest sex I've ever had. Good Lord, we were like horny teens on prom night. But that's the effect this man has on me.

I wasn't expecting what happened to happen. That didn't mean I didn't welcome it or want more. I've been a mess without Declan. And now here he is, mere feet from me, speaking with a few congressmen and the D.A.s from the neighboring counties.

He winks at me as I step up to the podium. I return his smile, but do my best not to let it linger. I have to focus and do my job, not flirt with the sexy D.A. I'll spend all night with.

I take my place in front of the podium, signing as I speak. "Thanks to the generosity of Governor McAdams, we are establishing a Child Advocacy Center specifically for victims of violent crimes where they can receive therapy and be interviewed in a more comfortable atmosphere."

"What do you mean by comfortable?" the reporter in the front asks.

189

"The center will mimic a home," I explain, signing quickly. "No industrial furniture or anything that suggests an office will be incorporated. I've met with a designer who shares our vision. She's selected tranquil colors and comfortable furniture specifically designed to create a feeling of safety."

"Sounds expensive," another reporter says before I can finish.

"It is," I agree, having prepared for those comments. "Thankfully, most of it will be funded by existing grants to ensure that victims of crime receive the support often denied because of cost."

"Are you suggesting the state doesn't shell out enough to help victims?" a reporter in the back asks.

"It does under Governor McAdams's watch," I answer, smiling. "She's provided more assistance than any governor nationally to date." I tilt my head as if giving it some thought. "However, I do think you might have shelled out too much for that tie, Larry."

The crowd in front of me laughs, including Larry. Some of the press in attendance are notorious for bating speakers and bending them to their will. I learned very early in my career to establish a good relationship with reporters, even when their intention isn't always genuine. It's helped me in the long run and allowed me ample opportunity to sing the praises of those who help me and bring attention to the needs victims of violence lack.

The governor steps forward, beaming like always. She knows I'll always defend her and praise her work. It's the least I can do for someone as kind and dedicated as she is.

"Thank you, Melissa," she says.

I step to her right, signing as she endorses Declan and trying to keep my emotions in check. As hard as it is to know he's taking my father's place, I know he's earned the position and I'm so proud of him for stepping up.

"Acting District Attorney Declan O'Brien has not only

met the challenges placed on him head on, he has surpassed expectations, ensuring the safety of the Philadelphia community and beyond." I sign the last word to a round of enthusiastic applause. "In my political history, never have I seen an official accomplish as much as A.D.A. O'Brien has at such a young age. From acquiring record-breaking prison terms for dangerous felons, to winning cases most considered lost causes, to receiving international recognition for his obliteration of ruthless organized crime families that are decades old, A.D.A. O'Brien has demonstrated that he is most qualified for the position of District Attorney."

More applause, bringing more approving nods and smiles his way. I keep my excitement to a minimum, although by now my heart is bursting with pride.

"Many may question his youth," the governor continues. "But I assure you no one would question his degree of experience, high level of intelligence, or his dedication to the public sector. For these reasons and more, not only does he have my support as District Attorney, but I'm endorsing him for mayor at the end of his term."

My motions become a jumbled mess. I sign quickly, trying to catch up and recover. Mayor? She's backing him for *mayor*? The crowd of reporters whips his way, a fervor of murmurs and applause spreading along the crowd. Declan smiles in his regal way, meeting the governor's gaze and nodding his thanks.

"Governor McAdams," a reporter calls out. "Don't you think it's a bit premature to endorse someone as mayor this soon?'

"Not given A.D.A. O'Brien's extraordinary record and his aptitude for trying cases most attorneys would run from. He's not afraid to fight for those who are weak or intimidated by anyone, and he's most certainly not afraid to do the right thing." She looks across the room, meeting his gaze once more. "The nation needs more leaders like Declan O'Brien."

I wasn't expecting this kind of endorsement. It shouldn't

upset me, I mean, we haven't spoken much on a personal basis. But I'd hoped that he'd stay on as D.A. for two terms. Like my father had planned.

The staff needs him. And so do the victims.

"*Melissa.*" Kathleen, the governor's chief P.R. rep motions to me. I didn't realize I'd stopped signing and hurry to fix what I missed.

I smile as much as I can as I finish, my attention trailing to the governor as she steps down. "You were amazing as always, my dear," she says, linking my arm with hers.

"Thank you." I clear my throat, trying to sound relaxed. "I didn't realize you'd planned to endorse A.D.A O'Brien for mayor."

"I hadn't," she admits. "In fact, I didn't realize he'd planned to run this early in his political career until we met last week." She laughs. "I should have suspected, with his drive to succeed being what it is."

I barely catch her last few words. "You met last week?" I ask slowly.

"Yes, Tuesday, I believe. I apologize for not calling you, Melissa, but my schedule was booked solid." She leans close. "By the way, my best to your relationship. If you don't mind my telling you, I sensed a certain chemistry between you when we met all those months ago."

I try to play it off. "We're not exactly a couple," I say.

She turns around to face me, giving me an all-too knowing smile. "Aren't you?"

Her smile widens as my face heats. "Don't be embarrassed. It happens to the best of us."

"It?" I ask.

"Surrendering your heart when you least expect it," she explains.

I start to deny it. "Governor McAdams . . ."

The way she shakes her head cuts me off. "I'll be stepping down as governor by the time the campaign for mayor begins. With the state of our country being what it is,

I've debated who to endorse for months. Declan caught my attention during his last few trials and he's impressed me with his intelligence and refinement. But his age concerned me, although the other candidates neither possess his remarkable record nor his leadership skills." She glances at the slew of supporters surrounding Declan. "That changed when I learned of your relationship and I was reminded of the tremendous regard your father holds him in."

"Ma'am?" I ask.

Her smile softens. "Melissa, you and your father are two of the best people I know. If you both believe in him, I'd be a fool not to believe in him, too."

The bottom of my stomach crawls down to my toes. I want to push away the thoughts that warn me I've been used. My father, too. But Declan told her we were together, ignoring the weeks we've spent apart.

"Melissa, are you all right?" she asks.

"I'm fine," I manage, my body heating.

Declan told me I meant more than his career. Did he really mean I was good for it?

Kathleen hurries over. "Excuse me, Governor," she says, appearing rushed. "Senator Monroe is requesting a word with you."

"Of course." The governor lifts my hand, squeezing it lightly. "Shall we meet up later, Melissa?" She taps my ring finger with her thumb. "Or will we have more to celebrate soon?"

Jesus. What exactly did Declan say to win her vote? I force a smile, nodding like an imbecile. "I'm sure we'll catch up later," I tell her quickly.

I watch her walk away, unsure where to go. I'm supposed to meet with a reporter about my experience and accomplishments during my time in the office, and with a senator who's looking for input regarding the new legislation he's bringing before Congress. He's seeking millions to help victims of domestic violence re-enter the workforce and he's counting on me to support his campaign. I'm also supposed to meet up with Dad and Mae. But right now, all I can do is stand there.

The growing flutter surrounding Declan's endorsement overpowers me, not only because of all the sound the excitement emits, but because of everything I don't want to believe about it. As it is, I've been wrestling with Declan's actions over these last few days. He went from telling me he doesn't believe in love, to giving me that locket and kissing me in his office, *following* his meeting with Governor McAdams—a meeting he never bothered to mention!

We had sex on the drive here, and he told me loved me. But neither erase this past month apart nor give him the right to tell the governor we're a couple.

Unless he really is using me . . .

"Champagne, miss?" a server offers.

"Yes, thank you," I stammer.

I scan the crowd. Declan is surrounded by a group of big wigs, including the senator I'm supposed to meet with, a state supreme court justice, and Philadelphia's current mayor. They gather around him, shaking his hand, patting his back, and likely offering their endorsements as well. Declan was always rumored to be the next big thing. Now, he is.

He winks in my direction when he catches my eye. I whip around, taking a sip of my champagne, my hands shaking. *Please don't tell me you've been using me. God, please don't tell me you seduced me to become the next mayor.*

My gaze falls upon my father where he and Mae sit along the raised dining area. He smiles as he interacts with a few representatives and their spouses. The chemo left him outrageously thin and his skin gray and loose against his frame. Despite the early hour, he already seems weary.

I glance back at Declan. *Please don't tell me you used him, too.*

This entire time we were apart, when I all but died

without him, was it all a game to him? Did he manipulate me into leaving him, knowing I'd pine after him and rush back the moment he needed me again? I don't want to think this way. I don't. But right now, the pieces are falling into place and I hate where they land.

I don't realize how badly I'm trembling until the champagne sloshes against the sides of the glass and spills against my dress. I hand my glass to a passing waiter and bat at the beads of liquid on my dress.

"Hey, Mel!"

Curran snakes his way through the crowd, Tess tucked against him. He bends to kiss my cheek. "Great speech."

I smile, trying to compose myself. "Thank you."

He frowns. "Are you all right?"

"Yes, just a little overwhelmed because of the noise." I motion to them. "I apologize, I wasn't expecting you. Valencia mentioned you're close to your due date."

"I am," she says, appearing to tire. "And originally we weren't planning to attend."

"That's because we weren't invited," Curran says, laughing. "Declan called all of us this morning, saying he got us in and that we had to be here, except he wouldn't tell us why.'"

"He called all of you?" I ask.

My eyes widen when the entire O'Brien clan storms forward. Like at Thanksgiving, I'm pulled into bodies big and small.

"Hey, Mel," Finn calls, hauling me toward him and Sol.

"How you doing, girl?" Wren says, leaving Evan's arms just to hug me.

"Gawgeous. That's how you look," Molly insists. "Gawgeous."

Seamus, Killian, and Sofia embrace me next. Everyone's sweet, happy to see me, but instead of feeling a sense of relief from their show of warmth, I'm left more uneasy and confused.

Angus laughs, slinging his arm around me. "How about it, huh? Our brother and your man the future mayor." He lifts his glass toward Declan and yells, "To Philly's next mayor!"

The O'Briens hoot and holler, raising their glasses. I join them in their toast, although I can barely bring myself to smile. Angus referred to him as my man. Had Declan even told them we broke up?

Declan's grin widens at his family's tribute. He excuses himself and makes his way forward. I start to edge away, unsure whether I can pretend that everything is fine when my heart is breaking away in pieces.

I turn and run straight into Trevor Stone. Trevor *fucking* Stone.

"Hey, sexy," he says, snaking an arm around my waist and dragging me in for a kiss.

If I didn't jerk my chin at the last moment, his mouth would have landed on mine. As it was, he connected with my temple, the squeal created by the back noise making me shudder. I slide out of his hold, backing further away from the O'Briens. "Trevor . . . hi," I say, stumbling over my words.

"It's been a long time," he says, trailing me.

His stare drills into mine exactly like it did at the last governor's ball, hours before we ended it up in his hotel room with our clothes piled on the floor.

Good heavens, like I need this. "Yes, it has. How's your family?"

"Fine," he says. "My father sends his best."

His father can't even remember my name. But the way Trevor is eyeing me, he's not here to make small talk. He takes another step closer, playing with a strand of my hair. The sound creates more back noise against my hearing aid, the high-pitched squeak grating my delicate nerves.

I inch further back before I realize there's no place else to go. Not with the wall of people lined up behind me. "I like your hair like this," he says. "You look even more beautiful than the last time I saw you."

"And when was that?" Declan says, suddenly beside me.

It's then I notice how much quieter it is, probably due to the O'Briens gathered around us, their scowls in place and their mouths pressed tight.

Oh, God.

I edge between Declan and Trevor. But there's not a lot of space so I'm now standing inches from Trevor. "Declan, this is Trevor Stone. He's the State Representative for—"

"I know who he is," Declan says, his expression and tone as cold as ice.

Trevor frowns, his fingers skimming down my arm. "What's going on?" he asks, leaning in close.

Declan's focus follows Trevor's touch, his voice deadly. "What do you *think* is going on?"

Trevor's hand falls away. "You're here with *him*?" he asks me.

"We arrived together." Declan's hand lifts mine, drawing me to him, his frigid demeanor locked on Trevor. "And I guarantee we're leaving together."

I don't know who to be more furious with, Declan for acting so possessive or Trevor for assuming I came alone. For now, I choose Trevor. "It you'll excuse us, I don't want to cause a scene."

Trevor smiles. "What a shame," he says, honing solely on me as he steps away. "We had a great time."

Declan smiles with all the warmth of savage tiger. "That's in the past," he assures him. His fingertips graze down my side and to my hip. "I'm her future."

The band explodes with a very loud and obnoxious dance song, making it hard to make out the sounds around me. But I don't need to hear. I see enough. Trevor drifts away, maintaining eye contact with Declan.

Declan makes sure Trevor looks away first. "Tell me he's a friend of yours," he says, turning to look at me.

In other words, tell me you didn't sleep with him.

Perhaps he expects me to lie or tell him something to

stroke his ego. While Trevor's advances were unwelcomed, I refuse to lie. And a boost to his already soaring ego is the last thing Declan needs. "He's not a friend," I say, hoping he'll drop it.

Maybe he would if Wren didn't rush me. She punches my arm affectionately. "Holy shit, you banged a representative?"

"Ah," I say, because, yes, that's all I have.

"Not now, love," Evan says, leading her away.

She nudges Finn. "I told you she had a wild side," she tells him.

He nods. "I can see that."

They're trying to make light of it. I'm grateful and find myself smiling.

My lifting spirit is short-lived when I realize Declan isn't smiling. In fact, his expression about as calm as an advancing tornado.

I meet him with equal force. Wren rushes back, snagging my hand and leading me away. "Be right back, hotness," she tells Evan.

She takes me far from Declan and Trevor, escorting me toward the double doors that open into the lobby, but not before snagging a glass of champagne and handing it to me and taking one for herself.

"Where are we going?" I ask.

"The bathroom," she says.

"You have to go to the bathroom?" I ask like an idiot.

"No, *you* have to go to the bathroom and give Declan a minute to cool down. It's either that or have sex with him. It's what women do when their men go all alpha. Trust me, I know."

"Does, um, Evan frequently go alpha?"

She laughs. "Oh, yeah. But you won't hear me complain. When I met him, he was like a pent-up beast locked behind a cage of pinstripes and prestige."

"And now?"

She tosses me an impish glance over her shoulder. "Now the beast gets to come out and play."

"Oh. Okay . . ."

We hurry into the bathroom, falling onto the couch in the sitting area. My shoulders slump when the door swings shut and mercifully kills what's left of the noise.

Between the clamor of voices, the band determined to break the sound barrier, and Declan, forget my hearing, I'm overly stimulated in all the wrong ways possible.

"You okay?" she asks.

"No," I admit.

Wren crosses her legs, the sequined navy blue gown hugging her statuesque figure. Her hair is in a loose French braid, making her stunningly feminine, a strong contrast considering the comments that fly out of her mouth.

"All right. Maybe not," she agrees. She smiles softly. "But I think you will be."

I lean back on the couch, welcoming the quiet and the lack of drama. Except I know both will leave me the moment I leave the bathroom. "I wish I was certain of that."

She considers me a long moment. "So, you and the rep .."

"It was nothing," I assure her.

She quirks a brow. "Really? Didn't seem like nothing by the way he was feeling you up."

"He wasn't feeling me up." Much. He did, however, make it clear what he wanted.

"Feeling you up, groping, copping a feel. It's all the same thing," she says dismissively. "Anyway, how'd you hook up with a rep, especially that one? Wasn't he engaged to Miss Pennsylvania or something?"

I sigh. "Working where I work I meet a lot of high ranking officials. Most are older, or at least old enough to be married and settled. Trevor wasn't." I think about it. "I'd heard something about him dating Miss Pennsylvania, but I wasn't aware he was engaged." I pinch the bridge of my nose. "At least I hope not." God, the press would be all over it.

The more I think things through, the more I'm reminded Trevor wouldn't do that. Like most political players, he keeps his indiscretions private. Most likely, they'd ended their engagement before I came along.

"So you didn't sleep with him?" she asks.

I can't blame her for being confused. Trevor is almost as handsome and dashing as Declan.

Almost.

"We did share a night," I confess, grimacing when I realize that's not entirely true. "Okay, a few nights. But we never dated. It wasn't anything serious."

"Not like it is with you and my brother?" she asks.

"No, nothing like that," I add quietly. At least it's not for me. I'd missed Declan so much. Every free moment of time was occupied with thoughts of him, his smile, the way he listens to me as if only my opinion matters, and the way we made love.

Was I naïve to think he'd missed me, too?

I thought I was the only one lost without us, until he kissed me in the office. I returned his affections without hesitation, just like I allowed him to strip me of my clothes in the limo.

Wren shakes her head. "Holy Mother, I've never seen Declan like that."

"You mean angry enough to physically assault someone?" I shudder, remembering how he seemed seconds from taking a swing. "Neither have I."

She bats her hand. "Oh, no. I've seen him riled enough to throw down. Don't forget, he's a Philly boy. I meant jealous. He was ready to bust an artery when he saw Trevor trying to kiss you." She laughs. "Or bust Trevor's head open."

I cover my mouth. "He saw that?"

"Girl, we all did." She takes a swig of her champagne. "He was talking to us about the endorsement when his attention veered off. We didn't realize what was happening until we saw Trev making the moves on you and you walking away. Where were you going anyway? One minute you were right next to us, the next, you were halfway to the dance floor."

"I didn't want to intrude on your moment," I say.

She tilts her head like she doesn't completely believe me even though it's partly true. "You didn't know we broke up, did you?" I ask.

She lowers her empty glass onto her lap, no longer smiling. "When?"

"Thanksgiving night." I don't mean to say as much as I do. This is Declan's sister I'm speaking with, after all. But it's like I need to, having kept so much in. "When we went back to his apartment."

"Because he was being a prick?" she offers.

"After the way he behaved at dinner, I didn't want to spend the night," I explain. "I didn't expect us to break up, just thought we needed space. But we had a fight and he told me he never planned on things getting serious."

Wren plays with her glass, her attention on the rich stone tile lining the floor. I'm not sure she's listening until she looks up. "That's because he's never believed in love."

My gaze falls to my hands. "I know. He told me."

I lift my chin when she places her hand on my shoulder. "But I think he does when it comes to you."

My eyes well and I have to blink back tears. "He told me that, too," I whisper.

"So you both walked away during a time you needed each other most?" She lifts the glass of champagne out of my hand and switches it out with her empty, taking a long sip. "How did that work out for you?"

I believe she means, *How did that work out for you, dumbass*? "It didn't. At least not for me."

"Considering he's been a moody bastard for the past month, seems to me it didn't work out for him either. Should have known you two weren't together." She taps her nails on her glass, scrutinizing me closely. "I like you, Melissa," she finally says.

"I like you, too," I reply carefully, unsure where this is going.

"And because I like you, I'm going to tell you something you may not know, because you need to know it." She sighs. "Declan's the black sheep of the family."

"The black sheep?" I repeat.

She gives it some thought. "Okay. Maybe not the black sheep, more like the sheepdog watching out for the loud, fucked-up sheep grazing on the crazy grass and telling the cows in the neighboring pasture to fuck off."

"Hear me out," she says when I blink back at her. "Our father died when we were little, seriously little. As the oldest, Angus quit school, got his G.E.D, and went to work. He had to, the life insurance, pension, it wasn't enough, not with eight mouths to feed. Declan couldn't quit school. Not with his brains, not with his talent, shit, not with everything he's always wanted to be and do, even though as the second oldest kid, society kind of expected him to."

"Seamus, the third in line, took his place, knowing like the rest of us, Declan needed to keep going." She takes another sip of her champagne. "Declan didn't puss out. He studied, got the grades, got scholarships. He knew the best way to help us was by becoming that leader he was destined to be. He kept on us, making sure we did our homework, went to bed on time, and stayed safe. But when he went away to college, life fucking happened, and not all of us stayed safe."

Her voice splinters enough to tell me she's talking about their brother and maybe herself, as well. "Declan's the sheepdog," she says again. "Always watching out for us, even when he's not around to take in the crazy. Look at what he does for a living and how far he's come." She adjusts her position. "But he was always like that, always driven to be the most successful, the wealthiest, and the most powerful. Want to know why?"

I don't answer, but I don't think she expects me to.

"Because wealth and power afford you protection and the goods to protect those you most love."

I stop moving, understanding striking me like a slap.

Her voice quiets, growing sad. "He didn't plan on you. He didn't plan on anyone. But maybe he needed to."

And maybe he needed me.

I want to believe her, but after everything that happened out there, I'm not sure he needed me for the right reasons.

"Are you going to give him another chance?" she asks.

"I don't know," I admit.

"Why?"

Wren was counting on her insight of Declan to change my perspective. And it did, to a point. But there are too many facts I can't ignore, including his private meeting with the governor.

"I'm not sure I can trust him," I tell her, that sting in my eyes returning.

"It's hard to trust someone when you've been hurt. I get it. Believe me, I do. But Declan is nuts about you."

"Did he say that?"

"No, I can just tell. You're the wrench in his well thought out plan." She takes a big gulp. "Seriously, he made a pie-graph that outlined his life when he was like twelve. That plan didn't include a woman, but here you are all the same. And based on how he acted out there when another man put his hands on you, he wants you to stay. So stick around for the ride or get off. Either way, we can't stay in the fucking bathroom all night—oh, hey there, governor. How's it going?" Wren asks when she walks in with her security detail. "Voted for you last time."

The governor glances my way as we stand. "This is Wren O'Brien, Declan's sister," I say quickly, hoping she didn't hear Wren say "fucking." but realizing she likely did.

The governor greets her with a smile. "Ah, your future sister-in-law," she says, shaking Wren's hand.

She means to be kind. So does Wren. But their words only stab my wounded heart.

CHAPTER 21

Declan

"Declan, please calm down," Tess tells me.

I'm standing here like an imbecile waiting for Melissa to come out of that damn bathroom.

"I'm calm," I say. It's true, on the fucking outside.

She glances toward the ballroom where that ball-less piece of shit weasel Trevor is standing. He grins, nodding in my direction. I return his smile with all the warmth of a frozen tundra.

"Behave as the consummate professional I know you are," she insists.

"I'm behaving," I point out, keeping my grin. "He still has all his teeth, doesn't he?"

Curran nods. "He does. Not that he should," he reminds me. "Asshole's lucky you didn't break his Goddamn jaw."

"You're not helping," Tess sings.

"Babe, did you see him? He was all over her—nothing against Mel, Deck. She was trying to get away from him. You should have beat his ass then handed it back to him on a plate of hors d'oeuvres or some shit."

"Curran, *seriously*?" Tess snaps at him.

He holds out his hands. "I'm just saying, if any guy touches you like that in front of me, they'd be hauling him out on a stretcher."

She points to her bulging belly. "I think it's safe to say you have nothing to worry about."

I turn away when he pulls her to him, laughing as he nuzzles her neck. My feelings toward Melissa are fucking out of control. This jealousy crap is total bullshit. When Stone grabbed *my woman* and tried to kiss her in front of me—and my entire family! —I swear to Christ I could have ripped his spine out and busted it over his skull.

I pinch the bridge of my nose, trying to shake off the rage that all but blinded me when he touched her, stroked her—like he couldn't wait to rip off her panties. But when he wouldn't back off, even when she made it clear she didn't want him, that's when I snapped. If I was anyone else, and anywhere else, I would have made him bleed for it.

"Shit," I mutter, trying to stay quiet. This is my night to shine, to remind all the high-ranking officials who I am, and why there's no one better to lead this city. So why can't I just let this thing go?

Oh, I know why. Shit for brains Trevor touched Melissa like he owned her. If he somehow manipulated her, used her, or God help him, *hurt her,* I will end him.

My back stiffens when Mel and Wren slip out of the bathroom. Her expression falls when she sees me. What the hell? How am I the bad guy here? I kept calm and protected her from his wandering hands.

I march toward her in slow and steady strides. "I need a moment with Melissa," I tell Wren when I reach her.

Wren grins and pats my shoulder. "No problem. I'll be at the table looking after your club and saving Evan from all the money grubbing politicians who figured out who he is." Her face lights up when she sees him stepping out of the ballroom. "Hey, babe," she yells, hurrying toward him.

Melissa moves off to the side for privacy. I think she's

ready to iron things out, but when she lifts her chin, I can tell she's not happy.

Well, that makes two of us. "What the hell was that?" I ask her.

"Are you referring to your blatant and uncalled for display of possessiveness, the way you practically marked me as yours in front of Trevor, or what could have happened if the press caught sight of your interaction?" She narrows her eyes. "Grow up. You're the District Attorney for the state of Pennsylvania, not some jealous boyfriend."

Yeah. Not the kick to the balls I need. But this isn't about me and what I did. "What happened between you and Stone?"

If I didn't think she could get angrier, I was wrong. "You're seriously asking me this?"

"Yes. I am." She looks around, as if debating whether to answer. "Just tell me," I say.

She squares her stance. "I spent the night with him a few times," she admits.

"Was it consensual?"

She seems taken aback by my question. But I need to know, because if it wasn't—and he hurt her—I'm going to fuck up his world.

"Very," she says.

"*Very*?" I ask.

"We weren't intoxicated if that's what you're insinuating. We were both . . ." Her voice trails at the sight of my heating face. "We were both willing," she adds quickly.

Every muscle in my body tightens hard enough to yank me back to the ballroom and nail Trevor across the jaw. It's not that I'm not glad that he didn't hurt her. I am. But like I said, this jealousy shit is a vicious bastard. "You have to be *fucking* kidding me."

Her jaw pops open. "You're the one who wanted to know."

"No. I wanted you to tell me he's been pining after you and you rejected him every single time." No, I'm not an asshole or anything.

She raises her brows. "So you wanted me to lie?"

"No," I tell her flatly. "But how do you think I feel right now knowing he's touched you, the way only I should touch you?"

Her expression, so furious before, softens. "It's been several months since the last time I saw him, Declan. And I didn't go to bed with him that time."

"Oh, *that* time. That's great, babe."

She rams her hands on her hips. "It's been over a year since the last time Trevor and I slept together. But do you know what? It's only been a few weeks since we ran into someone *you* slept with."

I lean back on me heels, a hell of task considering how straight my spine is.

"What?" she demands. "I'm hearing impaired, not blind. Do you think I've missed the way those women have looked at you when they've seen us together? That hostess at that Japanese restaurant, the defense attorney you negotiated the Trammel case with—oh, and that bartender during happy hour. I'm surprised she didn't poison my drink. And don't get me started on all the women who *want* to sleep with you, including that airhead Stephanie who's ready to claw my eyes out every time I walk past her stupid pink cubicle."

"They don't mean anything to me," I bite out.

"Like me?"

I keep my voice as low as hers, but where she seems close to tears, I don't flinch, the truth behind my words keeping my voice even. "*You* mean everything to me."

Her expression caves, like what I say is more than she can take. I clasp her wrists gently, drawing her to me until my chest brushes against hers. "*Everything*," I repeat.

She lowers her lids. "Declan . . . Trevor didn't mean anything. I need you to know that, okay?"

His name alone riles me more than it should. I let out a breath, trying to keep it together, knowing I'm acting like a prick. "Did you know he was going to be here?"

"I didn't think about it," she says. "I should have, since he attends these functions, but my mind wasn't on him."

I rest my forehead against hers. "Who was it on?" I know it's me, because God knows she's all I ever think about. But I want to hear her say it.

"It was on you, it's always on you."

She says it like it pains her. I don't understand why she's so upset. Yeah, I get I'm behaving like a lunatic. But it's not like I lost my composure.

Like too many times before, she pulls away from me, as if she can't accept that I love her and need her more than anyone in this damn world.

My eyes lock on her. "It's always on me?" I question. "Like when we were in the limo when I went down on you?"

Her eyes close and she shudders, her face flushing in that way it does when I'm turning her on. I lift my finger and trail it against her jaw, stroking it lightly until she opens her eyes. "I like it when you blush," I rasp, speaking so quietly she has to read my lips. "You do it every time I'm on top of you and you're ready to come."

The feral look she pegs me with makes me lose my damn mind. Shit. It's all I can do not to get us a room right now, the need to take her blinding me to reason.

"Hey, Deck!" Curran calls.

With a great deal of effort, I glance over my shoulder and away from Melissa. He's standing close to the entrance of the ballroom with his arm around Tess.

"Come on, man," he says. He jerks his head toward the double doors. "Let's show our women how good we can dance."

His suggestion reminds me it's my night to shine, and I will. But I want Melissa to take her place in the spotlight with me.

I offer her my arm. "Will you dance with me? I want to show the world we're together."

She wavers, once more appearing close to tears. I don't understand her response. It's as if she's afraid to believe me.

I almost ask her what's wrong when she takes my arm and allows me to lead her forward. She seems stiff and hesitant. I'm wondering if she's having second thoughts about us. But she can't, not when my life hasn't been the same without her.

The governor steps out of the bathroom with her security detail, smiling when she spots us. She seemed happy when I saw her earlier and mentioned that Melissa and I were together. I wasn't looking for her approval, just happy to share something good with someone who knows us. Still, it was nice of her to give us her blessing.

I nod in her direction and slip my arm around Melissa, feeling oddly protective when we enter the ballroom and a crowd of reporters swarm us. I expected some buzz from the press and maybe a few questions when they saw us. I didn't expect all the flashing cameras.

"District Attorney O'Brien," a reporter calls. "Are you and Miss Fenske a couple?"

Oh, look, there's Stone, his cocky smile fading as I answer, "Absolutely, but don't tell anyone." I wink. "It's a secret."

The crowd laughs. We stop to pose for a few pictures. Damn, it's good to have Melissa back in my arms. She's breathtaking and poised and I'm so fucking proud of her. She took the podium as easily as the governor did, handling tough questions with grace and a winning demeanor that captivated her audience.

I keep her close against me as more photographers move forward. The gossip and entertainment columns will be all over the story, as well as the political circuits, but I don't care. This time without Mel has been among the worst in my life. I want us together, and I'm not afraid to show the public what she means to me.

"District Attorney O'Brien—Melissa, *Melissa!*" The

governor's assistant frantically waves, motioning us in the direction of more press.

We turn as one, my smile widening. As much as I believed I didn't need a woman, I was wrong. All this time I needed Melissa, a *strong* woman capable of holding her own and standing as my equal.

I lean in and kiss her cheek, stirring the media into a frenzy. More clicks of the camera. More flashes. More attention. We're getting more press than the governor. But although I enjoy coming out as a couple, I can feel Melissa is overwhelmed.

Her delicate senses are likely on edge. I hold out a hand, keeping my smile. "If you'll excuse us, I'd like to dance with this beautiful woman."

The crowd parts as we head to the dance floor. Stone glares as we pass. If there wasn't all this press, I'd flip him off. But there is, so a grin is more than enough.

We join my family already dancing. Wren and Evan are kissing like usual and Finnie's hands are just centimeters from Sol's ass. And look at that, Seamus is dancing with Senator Billings' daughter.

I play it safe and dance near Killian and Sofia, and Curran and Tess, pulling Melissa close. Killian and Sofia are still in that honeymoon phase, one I'm not sure they'll ever grow out of. Curran and Tess are ready for their next kid, but there's Curran, his hands even lower on Tess than Finnie's were on Sol's.

I motion to the way Curran curls around Tess and their unborn child. "I want that for us," I tell Melissa quietly,

Melissa turns to look at them, only to glance quickly away.

Shit. Too much too soon, I suppose. But I'm tired of denying how I feel or brushing it aside, like it will somehow go away.

That locket I gave her . . . as crazy as it sounds, it was almost a ring. More than once during my time in that jewelry store I found myself looking at engagement rings. *Me*, the same guy who was perfectly content to die alone.

My fingers skim over her back. I told her I didn't believe in forever. Now that I do, will she believe in it with me? It's too early to tell. This is our first night in too long. But as I gather her closer and kiss her bare shoulder, I can't think of a better start.

My lips trail to her cheek. I want to taste her lips. But I need to behave and watch my hands around the press.

"Have I told you how stunning you look?" I whisper, careful to not speak too close to her ear.

"Yes. Thank you."

Her voice shakes and it's not because of the way I'm touching her. Like I said, I'm watching my hands. Something's wrong. I angle my chin so I can see her. She turns, resting her cheek against my shoulder and shielding her face from mine. The rustle of fabric against her hearing aid should bother her in this position. Regardless, she stays where she is, attempting to hide.

My palms smooth down her back. "What's wrong, baby?"

She lets out a breath. "As soon as the song is over, I need to check on my dad."

Her father. Of course. No wonder she's so upset.

She holds me closer, like she's afraid to let me go. But I'm not going anywhere.

I stroke her spine. "I'll go with you," I promise. Hell, after all he's done for me and what his daughter means to me, it's the least I can do.

We spend the remainder of the night dividing our time between her father, my family, and some of the higher ups, my arm rarely leaving her waist. But when we return to the limo and the door shuts behind us, we're all over each other.

Her large breasts bounce in my face as she rides me. I snag one in my mouth to suck, my lap colliding against hers. She clutches my head, her circling hips slowing at the start of her orgasm. I flip her over, throwing her legs over my shoulders and pumping hard.

We're loud, intense, and unable to get enough. My hands grip the seat as I come. I'm not quite finished and already looking forward to the next round in my apartment.

I feather kisses along her throat. But when I reach her mouth, I freeze in place.

Tears stream down her cheeks in small, thin rivers.

I cup her face, carefully wiping her warm skin with my thumbs. "What's wrong? Did I hurt you?"

She shakes her head. "No."

"Are you sure?"

"Yes," she answers quietly.

I search her face. "What is it, baby?" I ask, hating the way she pulls away from me.

Her chest rises and falls like she's trying not to break down. "I just really love you, Declan," she whispers.

It's what she says. And I believe her. But the more I take her in, the more she seems to regret it.

My ringing cell phone wakes me from a sound sleep. I reach for where it's perched on my nightstand, trying not to disturb Mel tucked against me.

We've only been asleep for a few hours, but my movements stir her awake. She lifts her head from my chest. "What's wrong, love?" she asks.

I look at who's calling. "It's Curran," I say, my voice hoarse with exhaustion. It's not quite nine, and we were up all night, but I can't help my smile. "I bet Tess is in labor."

"Hey, man," I say, answering the phone. "Am I an uncle again?"

"Declan, it's me," Tess says, her voice unusually morose. "I have some bad news."

I push up in bed, suddenly awake. "Are you okay—is Curran all right?"

"We're fine." Her voice breaks. "It's Rosana, the victim in the Iker Escobar case. She's dead, Declan. Iker killed her."

CHAPTER 22

Melissa

Declan leans back in his office chair, rubbing his jaw as if it will somehow remove the ire cloaking him like death itself.

"Tell me what happened," he says.

Chief Lee and Detective Melo exchange glances from where they're seated in front of Declan. Like me, they sense his anger. But they're doing a better job of masking their fury. Declan . . . my God. If I didn't know him, I wouldn't dare approach him right now.

"Escobar was being transferred to a different jail because of threats against him by the other inmates," the chief answers. "Based on your reputation and your unwillingness to plea bargain, he knew he was headed to prison. He and three other transfers overpowered the guards and escaped. The other three headed south and away from the city."

"But not Escobar," Declan finishes for him.

The chief doesn't speak. Not right away. When he does, it takes all I have not to cry. "No. He went to the victim's house and killed her."

"How'd he do it?" Declan asks, his stare drilling a hole into the picture Rosana drew of him.

"He choked her with his bare hands," Chief Lee answers. He's been in law enforcement for decades, witnessing the evil people are capable of firsthand. But behind his jaded stare, I see it. The sadness we all feel when someone this young and innocent dies.

Brenda, my victim services worker on call can't take it. She breaks down, sobbing into her hands, her cries the only sound in the room.

I put my arm around her. I want to cry with her. But if I start, I won't stop.

Rosana, a sweet kid with an even sweeter smile and a gift for art, who had a horrible life that no one deserved, *died* in a way no one deserves. Life is so unbearably cruel.

"Come on," I whisper to Brenda, helping her to her feet.

Declan and the chief need to form a plan, and for that they need quiet. They can't have quiet with Brenda here. She's in full-blown hysterics. As much as I empathize with what she's feeling, an emotional breakdown won't help anyone.

"Do we have *any* idea where Escobar is?" Declan asks.

I pause at the door to hear the chief's answer. "No. The neighbors heard the victim screaming and called 9-1-1. Three people saw him flee the apartment, including the responding officers. One of badges ran after him but lost him a few blocks away. They're combing the area now. The other badge ran into the apartment, but the victim was already dead."

I step out and close the door quietly behind me, guiding Brenda down the hall and past the row of cubicles. A few of the on-call staff came in when they heard what happened. They watch us in silence, their expressions somber.

It's only Valencia who speaks. "I'm sorry, Melissa."

"I am, too, Valencia."

Law enforcement personnel, attorneys, and even the clerical staff employed here, often become cynical and numb to the brutality we're frequently exposed to. It's survival and what it often takes to do the job. But the cases like this one trigger our emotions and remind us how human we remain.

I lead Brenda to my office, motioning her to sit in one of the chairs. I sit beside her and wait for her to calm.

"I can't keep doing this," she finally says.

"Brenda, this is a tough job," I begin.

"No," she says, cutting me off. "A tough job is getting up at three in the morning to haul garbage like my father did. A tough job is driving a tow truck like my brother does. A tough job is working as a teacher in the inner city school system like my mother has for the last twenty-nine years. *This* is hell!"

I lean back, letting her yell because she needs to. "I quit this unit," she says. "I'm sorry, Melissa. You'll have my official transfer request on your desk tomorrow."

I don't ask her to reconsider or to think things through. Bottom line, she can't do the job. Eight months on my staff and she's already burnt out. "That's not necessary. I'll just take your resignation."

She blinks back at me with red, swollen eyes. "Can't I just transfer to another unit?"

"Not without my recommendation."

"And you won't give me one?" she asks.

She didn't even know Rosana and lost all semblance of control. "No," I reply quietly. "This isn't where you belong." I'm not trying to be insensitive or mean. I'm being honest. Someone this fragile can't work here. Victims of crime deserve better.

Tears stream down her face. She knows I won't change my mind. But before she considers cursing me out, I hope she remembers the riveting speech she gave me during the interview process about how passionate she is about victims' rights and how social work was all she had ever wanted to do.

"Just go home," I tell her when she doesn't move. "Leave your phone and your keys and I'll take care of the rest."

She doesn't argue, but she does release a few more tears. She places the cell phone and keys on my desk. "The pass code is 1-2-1-4," she manages.

I don't bother to thank her, I simply watch as she slips out the door and shuts it lightly behind her.

I rub my tired eyes the moment she's gone. It's Sunday morning. The weekend is almost over, and we have an entire week ahead of us. But there's no time to rest.

Rosana is dead.

That lovely girl is dead.

There's a knock on the door. "Come in," I say, trying not to lose it.

Valencia opens the door. "How are you?" she asks.

I shake my head because that's all I can do then.

She leans back and looks down the hall. "Brenda quit?"

"Pretty much," I answer.

"Fine by me. She was baggage anyway." She walks in and sits in the chair Brenda had occupied. "If I have to comfort my victim services rep, no way in hell should she be within ten feet of this office."

"I agree." I adjust my position and cross my legs, knowing I need to get back to business. "Did the patrols have any luck finding Vilma, Rosana's mother?"

"Yup. Just got the call." She huffs. "She was cleaning someone's house for extra money. When the local cops showed looking for her, she knew her daughter was dead."

"Oh, God," I say.

"I know," she mutters, likely picturing how it all played out. "She's at Temple University Hospital. She was admitted after she lost her shit. I know you're going to reach out to her, but don't plan on her sticking around. She'll be on the first plane back to Honduras the second she's discharged."

"I know, I think so, too." I can't erase Rosana's face from my mind and I'm struggling not to picture the last few moments of her life. She must have been terrified.

I hug my body, fighting not to cry as I speak. "Vilma told me she came to this country to make a better life for her and her daughter, and this is what she gets."

"I know," Valencia says. "Was Rosana her only kid?"

"To my knowledge," I answer softly. "You know, for all Vilma wasn't a perfect mother, she loved Rosana. I can't even imagine what she's going through."

"I can't think about it," she confesses. "And I don't even have kids."

Detective Melo pokes his head in. "Melissa, the press is ready. Declan wants to see you before he meets with them."

Valencia and I stand and hurry down the hall, trailing detective Melo. "Are you going to meet with the press, too?" she asks me.

"No. This is all on Declan," I respond. "I have to call the principal at Rosana's school and make sure they have counselors in place to support the students." My voice cracks. I'm ready to break down. Somehow, I manage to keep it together. "She was well liked. She'll be greatly missed."

"Yeah. She will." She gives my arm a squeeze when we reach Declan's office. I try to offer a smile, but it doesn't quite come.

She and Detective Melo watch me walk in, but neither follow, recognizing we need a moment. I'm not sure what to expect. I only know it won't be anything good.

Declan waits for me alone. He stands with his arms crossed in front of the picture Rosana made him, his anger as tangible as a punch to the stomach. I close the door behind me and carefully move toward him.

"She was just a kid," he tells me quietly.

I come up behind him and wrap my arms around his waist, the only tear I'll allow dripping onto his shoulder. "She was supposed to be an artist," he rasps. "She was supposed to get her chance and grow up and be happy. She was supposed to *fucking live*."

"I know."

It's the only thing I can say.

"She was just a kid," he repeats, staring back at the picture.

There's a rap at the door. "Declan?" the chief calls from

the hall. "The press is waiting."

I drop my hands and step away. Declan reaches for his suit jacket and shrugs it on, his expression so lethal I can barely stand to look at him. God, wasn't it just last night he met with the press to accept his endorsement?

Now he faces them to discuss a little girl whose life ended too soon.

He passes me, pausing with his hand over the door knob. "Where will you be later?"

"Wherever you need me to be," I reply.

"All right," he says. He doesn't tell me where he wants me, maybe he doesn't know. He simply walks out of the room, shutting the door behind him.

I start to clean up his desk for something to do. I can't bring myself to leave. When I don't do more than stack a few files, I return to my office to gather my purse and coat.

I step onto the elevator, ready to head to the parking deck when I change my mind and hit the button to the next level. I'm wearing the clothes I'd left at Declan's apartment all those weeks ago: jeans, a black turtleneck sweater, and ankle-length boots. I didn't have time to run back to my place and change, and while it's not appropriate attire for a press conference, this time I'm not the one in the spotlight.

My feet move fast when the doors part and I step out onto the fourth floor. The conference room is just down the hall, but already I can hear the clicks from the cameras and the questions being thrown Declan's way. I slip into the room packed wall to wall with people. Thankfully Valencia is standing near the door. She scoots over, making room for me along the back wall. "Thank you," I whisper.

"There's a state alert for four fugitives at large," Declan says. "Law enforcement will be working around the clock to ensure they're brought in as quickly as possible."

"District Attorney O'Brien," a female reporter calls out. "Who in your office will be handling the charges against Iker Escobar—the suspect accused of murdering Rosana Secco provided he's apprehended?"

"I will," he bites out. "I swear to you, I won't stop until Iker Escobar is caught and he gets everything he deserves."

I straighten as the team of reporter jumps to their feet. "Did you know Declan was taking over?" Valencia asks me.

"No," I say, struggling to hear. "I had no idea."

Another reporter shouts a question I barely make out. "How do you expect to try a murder case as the head of the Sexual Assault and Child Abuse Unit?" he challenges.

"I'm no longer leading SACU," Declan grinds out. "You're looking at the new Head of Homicide."

My stomach bottoms out. In the span of three days Declan managed to get everything he wanted.

Including me.

CHAPTER 23

Declan

"Come here, beautiful," Melissa says. She lifts Clodagh from Curran's arms, even though it's clear he doesn't want to give up his sweet baby girl.

"My turn after," Seamus says, rousing Wren and everyone else sucker punching each other to hold the baby.

"Back off," Curran snaps. "You already had a turn." He does a double take when he sees Angus standing in the corner eating a sandwich. "What are you doing here, Angus? You were supposed to pick up the food for tomorrow after you dropped Ma and Fiona back at the house, not stop and get lunch for yourself."

"They said it wouldn't be ready until twelve."

"It's one now, asshole."

Angus looks at the clock. "Oh, yeah. It is. I'm going, I'm going," he adds when Curran glares at him. He wipes his mouth with the back of his hand and heads over to Tess to kiss her cheek. "Congratulations," he tells her. "So glad she looks like you and not numb-nuts over here."

"Nice, Angus," Tess says.

Mel tucks Clodagh against her, her large eyes meeting

her little face.

Damn, what a week. All this shit with Rosana, then Miles being admitted in the hospital after he collapsed at home. I wasn't sure how much more either of us could handle. But Tess going into labor and having the baby was the break we needed. God, this kid is gorgeous.

And so is Melissa and the way she cuddles her against her.

I kiss my little niece's head then turn to grin at Curran. "You had another girl," I tell him, smirking.

His smile fades. "I know. What the fuck am I going to do? I already want to point a gun at every male who looks at Fiona." He edges away and climbs into bed with Tess. "You were supposed to give me a boy," he tells her, stroking her chin. "We discussed this."

Tess smiles, despite her heavy lids giving away how tired she is. "I'll try harder next time, cop."

Curran slips his arm around her, tucking her against him. "Twenty-nine hours of labor. Can you believe that shit?" he asks.

"It was only five once labor actually started," Tess clarifies, her head falling against Curran's shoulder.

"Not for me. I've been up like thirty-four hours."

"Curran, you went to sleep almost immediately after I received the epidural, after Clodagh had her first feed, and then again when she had her second. Trust me when I say you haven't been awake that long."

He kisses her head. "But I was with you in spirit, angel face," he tells her.

Melissa rocks Clodagh gently. I can already picture her holding our baby and am fully invested in making it happen. But I can't be sure she's completely on board.

I don't know. I think we're together. Except ever since the governor's ball last Saturday, I don't think we're as solid as we need to be. Maybe after all that time apart, I moved too fast. But that time apart nearly broke me, and from what she told me, it nearly broke her, too.

I've tried talking to her about us and what she's feeling. But each time she shuts down, telling me she's worried about her Dad and that she needs to be there for him. Maybe that's what it is. That, and what happened to Rosana. But we haven't spent a night together since the ball so there has to be more to it. Hell, we didn't even drive here together. And if it wasn't for Curran calling her himself, I can't be sure she'd be here at all.

"I think she's ready to eat again," Melissa says, inching back over to Tess.

Tess lifts up from Curran and starts to unsnap the front of her gown.

"Whoa—wait—what the fuck?" my brothers all yell at once.

Tess's hands fall away and she sighs. "Can we at least *try* and watch the language?"

"It's not like Clodagh can understand us," Finn points out.

"That's what you said about Fiona," Tess mutters, reaching for another snap. "And look at all the words that have flown out of her mouth."

Curran whips around when he realizes she's one button away from freeing her breasts. "Everyone out except Wren and Mel. No one gets to see my wife's goods but me."

Evan stands, motioning to the door. "Gentlemen," he says.

Seamus looks around, appearing confused. "Is he talking to us?"

"Yes, dumbass," Wren says, lifting up on her toes to give Evan a quick kiss.

I step closer to Melissa. "Here, I'll take her," I say, reaching for the baby. I frown at Curran when he glowers. "I'm the godfather. That means I get a turn."

"Give him a moment," Tess says, rubbing Curran's arm. "He's the only one who hasn't held her."

"Fine," Curran says. "But I get to pass her to you."

"Come here, Clodagh," I say, tucking my hand beneath her small head.

Melissa passes her carefully into my arms, her expression shattering as she looks up at me. "What's wrong?" I mouth.

She shakes her head and edges away from me.

Here's the thing, I should be enjoying this moment. Clodagh is the second baby born into our immediate family, and the first already has us wrapped around her tiny fingers. But I can't. Not when Mel feels so far away.

"Congratulations," she says to Tess and Curran. "She's as beautiful as Fiona and her mama."

They exchange warm hugs and kisses, but the moment Clodagh is back in her daddy's arms, Mel is almost to the door.

"Congrats," I tell Curran, stopping only to give Tess a quick kiss. "I'll see you tomorrow at the house."

They try to smile, but Curran's eyes cut to the small hall leading out.

Melissa is already gone, not bothering to wait or say goodbye to me. I hurry out, passing Sofia and Sol, who'd left to pick up lunch for Curran and Tess.

"Excuse me," I tell them, moving fast.

I'm expecting to run down the corridor and chase Melissa down. I sigh with relief when I find her waiting just outside the room. But as I approach, her eyes glaze with tears, slowing my steps.

"What's going on?" I ask her.

She angles her head toward the set of windows at the far end of the hall. "I need to see my dad. They moved him to the oncology unit on the other side of the hospital."

"All right. I'll go with you." I march forward to place my arm around her shoulders. Instead of welcoming my embrace, she steps out of reach.

I let out a breath. "Mel, what are you doing, love?"

If I didn't think she could appear more broken, her

reaction to me calling her "love" proves me wrong. She curls inward, trying not to break down. What the hell?

She glances up, realizing my family is standing just a few feet away. "I need to talk to you, privately," she says.

"Fine," I say.

I follow her to a small seating area just around the corner. The space is nothing more than a small cubby, unlike the larger waiting rooms at the end of each hall. Two chairs and a table, just enough for two people to speak quietly. I have a view of the main hallway and of the staff and visitors rushing past. But it affords a pocket of peace away from the hustle of the busy hospital.

I want to say this bit of space is what Mel needs. Yet as I take in her emotionally battered exterior, I know she needs a lot more than that.

She remains standing, her hand gliding over the back of the chair beside her.

I move closer, grazing my thumb along her cheek. "Tell me what's wrong," I say.

She swallows hard. "I'm taking a leave of absence so I can take care of my dad when he's discharged. Julia Wall will serve in my position while I'm gone."

I lower my hand slowly. She doesn't think Miles has much time left. "Take as much time as you need," I tell her. "Come back when you're ready."

At first she doesn't speak. She doesn't even look at me. When she finally glances up, what she says knocks me on my ass. "I may not be coming back."

"You're quitting?" That can't be right. Her work means everything to her.

"I'm going to need a fresh start if . . . ." She crosses her arms and averts her gaze. "My dad isn't doing well," she adds, quietly.

The noise around us fades eerily away and it's as if we're the only ones left in the world. "I know he's not, baby. But what do you mean you need 'a fresh start'?"

She takes her time, gathering her words, each moment that passes making me think the worst. I'll be honest, she doesn't disappoint.

"Sylvia Albright, the head of Victim Services for the nation, has been trying to recruit me for the past year." Her voice splinters. "If my dad doesn't make it, I'm going to take her up on the offer and move to D.C."

The air stills. I'm not sure I can move. "What about us?"

She doesn't answer, but her eyes pooling with tears inform me there is no "us".

Anger builds deep inside me, pulling me out of my shock. "You're not even going to discuss this with me, are you? After all we've been through, I don't even get a say?"

A tear falls, streaking down her cheek as she lifts her chin. "You want a say when you didn't even discuss leaving SACU with me, or bother telling me you appointed yourself Head of Homicide."

The truth hits me at once, and motherfucker, I don't like what it shows me. "Is this the reason you haven't stayed with me all week? Why you've barely spoken to me?" All this time, despite my concerns, I've been giving her the benefit of the doubt—giving her space and not pushing her because I was sure she was sick over her father and grieving for Rosana.

Forget shock. I'm beyond pissed. "If this is what you're so angry about, you should have told me."

"I'm not angry, Declan," she fires back. "I'm disappointed. You turned your back on all those victims you were supposed to help."

She's acting like I lied and somehow betrayed her, fueling the rage already singeing my chest. I inch closer. "No. I didn't," I snap. "I'm looking out for Rosana and guaranteeing she gets justice."

In the silence that follows, three other people pass by with flowers and a giant "It's a Girl" balloon trailing behind them, similar to the one Finnie and Sol bought for Clodagh.

Mel doesn't say anything. She's done talking, but I'm

not. "If you think this is about me getting what I want or purposely keeping things from you, you're wrong."

"No. I'm not," she tells me, straightening to her full height. "If I hadn't shown up at that press conference, I would have found out about your self-appointed promotion second hand."

"That's not true."

She tugs on the hem of the thick sweater she's wearing over her jeans, but it's not a nervous gesture. She's fired up and fighting to stay calm. "I wish I could believe you, but I can't."

"*Why?*" I don't realize how loud I'm getting until a volunteer carrying a tray slows her pace as she passes me.

Melissa shakes her head. "Because regardless of what you claim, you *did* get everything you wanted, including leading Homicide."

"I did it for Rosana," I repeat because that's the Goddamn truth. A truth she doesn't accept. No, not the way she squares her stance. "Call me an arrogant son of a bitch, but no way was I giving this case to another D.A., not after what that pathetic excuse for a man did to that little girl, and not when Zabrinski—the only guy with enough experience to handle this clusterfuck—was all but begging me to retire."

"You should have warned me, Declan," she says. "Included me in your decision, allowed me some input, given me chance to tell you what I thought. But you didn't. You just did what you wanted regardless of how I felt."

"I'm sorry, and you're right. I should have discussed it with you. But I was blind with rage over what happened to Rosana. You saw me when I found out, and what it did to me. All I cared about was seeing the man who hurt her pay." I rub my jaw when she doesn't say anything. Maybe she's disappointed in me. And maybe she has a right. But right now, watching her turn her back on me, on *us*, she's not alone.

"Why are you leaving?" I ask. My voice is so low, I'm

not sure she hears me.

"My dad's not doing well," she repeats. "The doctors told me if he can't get through this next round of chemo and dissolve what remains of the cancer, he won't survive."

"I'm not asking you why you're taking a leave." I inch as close as I can without touching her. "I'm asking you why you're leaving me."

She steps away. "I can't talk to you about this."

"Why?" She starts to turn. I reach for her hands, holding them lightly and keeping her in place. "Mel, *please*. Just tell me why."

Her eyes swim with tears. "I can't trust you, Declan. I wanted to and I needed to, my God, I *really* needed to." She breaks down. "But you've proved to me too many times that I can't."

Her words are like slaps across my face. "Were you going to tell me about your meeting with the governor?" she asks. "You know the one, where you just happened to mention you wanted to be the next mayor? Or how about when you told her we were together, when I didn't even know what we were myself?"

Hurt and fury burn through my veins. But it's what she thinks that I can't get past. "You think I used you."

Tears drip down her face and her hands slip from my grasp. "No. I think you used *us*. Me *and* my father."

What remains of my patience abandons me, leaving only rage. "You *can't* be serious. You can't possibly mean what you're telling me."

Her expression turns cold. "Come on, Declan. You accomplished everything you set out to do. You're being sworn in as D.A. and there's no one else big enough to challenge you for mayor, not after my father *and* the governor backed you, as well as all her sheep you cozied up to at the ball."

My breath is coming so fast, I don't even know how I'm able to speak. But I do. She needs to hear what I have to say.

"I earned that D.A. spot and you know it. So does your father which is why he backed me. It's what he wanted before there was *ever* anything between us."

"So this thing between us was real?"

The way she asks proves she no longer believes it. After telling her I love her, nothing she could have said would have crushed me more. "You think I dragged you to bed, told you how I *feel*, to secure this spot and get ahead?"

"What do you expect me to think?" she asks, her expression bruising like I'm the one hurting her. "The governor was thrilled to death to hear we were together, so much so that the moment you approached her at the ball and told her all about us, any reservations she had about endorsing you for mayor were pushed aside. She told me that if Dad and I believed in you, she had to believe in you, too."

Her chest heaves in an out, her emotions barely under control. But I'm so pissed, so *fucking dumbfounded*, I can barely move.

"Did you have fun parading me in front of all those reporters, pretending like we've been together forever?" she asks. "Acting as if you never pushed me away and broke my heart?"

"You're the one who walked away from me that night in my apartment. *You left me.*"

"After *you* told me you didn't believe in love." She cries into her hands, but then shoves them away. "Did you honestly expect me to stick around after that? How could I have hope for us when you didn't have any at all?"

"You need to stop," I bite out. "You need to stop this shit right now."

She points at me. "But then suddenly you were there again, right? Conveniently in time for the governor's ball, practically telling me you couldn't live without me—"

"Because I can't!" I close the remaining distance between us. "Yet you're standing here—accusing me of things that aren't real—telling me you're leaving and not coming back."

A row of people hurry past us, but I barely notice them, my attention fixed on Melissa as she continues to cry. Her tears, her pain, I can't fucking take it. As livid as I am, her misery is my undoing, forcing my own hurt to the surface. "You have to believe me," I tell her. "You have to trust me." My hands clasp her arms, my voice barely audible. "When I say I love you, I've never meant anything more."

Agony marches across her features. "Declan, I can't believe in you anymore."

I freeze in place, bowled over by her admission. She whirls away, a sob breaking through her throat. She disappears around the corner, I start to race after her, but Wren's voice halts me in place.

"Declan, *Declan*!"

My head whips back to where she's standing in the hall leading to the maternity ward. I rush forward only to have the chief cut in front of her. "We got him, Declan."

I barely hear him, watching as Curran steps out of Tess's room and speaks to a few cops in uniform. "What?"

"Iker Escobar, he's been apprehended and en route to county." He frowns when I don't move. "The press is already assembled outside the courthouse. We need you back at the office."

I drag my hand over my face, my head still reeling from my encounter with Mel. This isn't happening. Not now. I have to go after her.

"Declan," the chief says. "I need you to do your job."

CHAPTER 24

Declan

I sit at my new desk, in my new office, in the same fucking chair Miles sat in for years. My new secretary asked me if she should order a new one. But getting rid of it, I don't know, as bizarre as it sounds, it's like getting rid of Miles.

He's taken another turn for the worse. Evan has come forward with new technology his company developed to try and help, and he's using his clout to push through the red tape and allow Miles a trial run. I'm not sure if it's too little too late. But if it is, I want to hang onto any part of Miles that remains and do the best job I can as long as I sit in this chair.

I met with the press about Iker Escobar's apprehension like a good D.A., said all the right things, and left the podium to rousing applause. The court dates are set and my prep for this case is going smoothly. But nothing feels right. Rosana is still gone. I can't bring her back.

Just like I can't bring back Melissa.

I walked into Mel's office the day after all the shit went down. She was already long gone, nothing of her left in that office except maybe the lingering scent of her perfume.

Her replacement was getting comfortable at her desk like

she planned to stay. "Hi, D.A. O'Brien," the leggy blonde said to me. Julia, I think that's her name. "I'm looking forward to working with you."

That made one of us.

I've called Mel several times and each time I'm sent through to her voicemail. She hasn't returned my calls or texts. The only good thing I can say is that she hasn't blocked me, yet. But she's made it clear she doesn't want to talk to me. I tried stopping by her place a few times, but she's never there when I swing by. As sick as Miles is, I can't show up there if it's going to lead to us fighting again.

You might say I've given up. That doesn't mean I've forgotten her, and it as sure as hell doesn't mean I've stopped loving her. Nothing is the same without her. Nothing. Just like it was the last time we were apart.

I hit the speaker when my office phone rings. "Yes?"

"District Attorney O'Brien, there's a young man here to see you claiming to be your brother."

A familiar laugh echoes through the speaker. "I'm not claiming, I just am, lady. Although you should let him know which one. Can I borrow that a sec? Thanks." Finn's voice amplifies and there's some rustling. I can almost picture him lifting the phone out of poor Tasha's hand, his grin probably the only thing keeping her from screaming for help. "Hey, Deck. It's your little brother—the good-looking one, the one with the ginger hair you wish you had and a set of abs his woman can't stop touching." He pauses. "You know, Finn."

Despite my mood, I can't help my chuckle. "Give Tasha back her phone and come in, Finnie."

I lean back in my chair, resting my hands behind my head. Finn opens the door and steps in. He looks around. "Nice," he says.

I don't have to tell him to take a seat, he just does, plopping down in front of me. "What are you doing here?" I ask.

"Oh, Aileen let me in," he says, motioning to the closed

door. "You know, the receptionist out front."

"I know who she is." I frown, letting my hands drop. "How does she know who you are?" Hell, even the people who work here can't get past Aileen without the proper I.D.

"She knows me on account of all those times I've stopped in to see Melissa." He shrugs. "She told me Melissa is out on leave. I figured since I was already here, I'd see you, instead."

"You come here to see Melissa?" I ask. He nods. "Since when?"

"Since I got in trouble that last time. She's nice. Sometimes, though, I just call and check in."

Why did I not know this? "You've been calling my girlfriend?"

"Don't you mean ex?" he asks. He rolls his eyes. "Yeah, you fucked that one up, didn't you?"

"Shut up," I tell him, flatly. "You don't know a damn thing."

"I know she's easy to talk to. I know you were happier when you were with her, and I sure as shit know you cared about her."

Care. Yeah. That's putting it mildly.

My face warms and I'm ready to tell Finn he can't put this all on me. That I'm not the only one to blame. But I don't know anymore. Not with how I'm feeling.

I rub my face. "When was the last time you talked to her?" I ask. "And how did you start calling her to begin with?" The trouble Finn was in made him a defendant, not a victim. But Mel didn't treat him that way. It shouldn't surprise me, being who she is. But it does.

Finn looks at me closely, like he's trying to get a fix on me. "It's been a while since we talked, and long before Thanksgiving, you know, the first time you fucked up." He grins at my narrowing stare. "When I first got in trouble, she told me if I ever needed to talk, to call her and she'd be there for me." He shrugs. "So I did and she was."

When I don't respond, he shakes his head. "Shit, Declan. You finally meet someone actually worth spending time with, and just like that you let her go." He huffs. "Dumbass."

"It wasn't just like that," I say, my temper rising.

"Wasn't it?" He leans forward. "You know what Wren recently said about you?"

I slump in my seat. "No, but I can't wait to hear it."

"That you're the shepherd in the family."

"The shepherd?" I ask.

"You know," he says. "The guy with the big stick."

"I know what a shepherd is," I say. "But what the fuck does that mean?"

He glances down at the industrial strength carpet. "No, that can't be right."

"Good, because it sounds—"

He perks up. "You're the sheepdog," he says, pointing. "That was it, which makes total sense cause you're acting like a little bitch."

"What the hell, Finn?"

"Hear me out." He holds his hands out, like what he has to say is important but he can't remember exactly what it is. "We're the flock, the seven of us with Ma. Yeah, that's it. So we're in the field, eating grass, playing with the cows, and jumping over fences and some shit, you hear what I'm saying?"

"I hear it," I admit. "I just don't know what the fuck you're talking about."

He ignores me, speaking fast like he's onto something. "But it's like, all this time you've been biting our heels, barking out orders, keeping us in line and being a dog, you forgot to look at the rest of the pasture."

"The pasture?" I ask slowly.

"Yeah. And it turns out there's like this whole farm."

"With a barn full of crazy?" I offer.

He brushes the comment aside. "No, with like other pastures. And in one of those other pastures there's another sheepdog, looking out for the flocks of ducks.”

I just blink back at him.

“Melissa,” he says, like I’m the stupid one. “Melissa is the other sheepdog. The one who looked after you, took care of you, even though she was still looking after the chickens, ducks, and goats.” He leans in. “She was the sheepdog you needed, the one you shared your bed with, the one you introduced your flock to, the one who showed you how good the rest of the pasture is and everything you weren’t seeing on that farm.” He makes a face. “Believe it or not, it sounded good when Wren said it.”

“Are you trying to tell me Melissa showed me everything I missed out on? That where I looked out for everyone, I didn’t look out for myself as I should have—in the way that mattered most?”

“Close enough.” He smirks. “Oh, and that maybe you should have puppies.”

He’s trying to tell me I shouldn’t let her get away.

And he’s right.

CHAPTER 25

Melissa

I run down the street and cut a hard right onto my block, my lungs burning as the frigid January air passes in and out with each harsh breath. I hate running. I really do. Except I no longer do it to eat what I want. In fact, there are days where I have no appetite at all. But I *have* to run. It's the only weapon I have against the stress plaguing my life.

"The will is in the vault," Dad told me this morning, his body so weak he could barely speak the words.

"I'm not having this discussion with you," I replied. I gathered his blanket and tucked it around him, hoping he would fall asleep so we wouldn't have to have this talk.

"Melissa, please listen," he said. "I'm not sure we'll have another moment."

He had a bad morning, a worse night, and a really bad week.

My feet brush the pavement, moving faster as I recall the conversation. He's leaving me everything, but asked me to put money aside for Mae to ensure she'll have a comfortable retirement.

"I couldn't give her everything she wanted from me. But

I can give her this," he said.

Tears streak down my face, freezing against my cheeks. "I'll do whatever you want, Daddy," I told him. It was as much as I could say.

One week. In one week he's scheduled for an experimental procedure to remove what's left of the tumors. If he survives and recovers from the surgery, the doctors think he'll be okay, his body ravaged, but okay.

But I'm not sure he has a week left . . .

I practically fall onto my front stoop, my breath so labored anguish fills my chest. But I'll recover by the time I step into my kitchen. I'm healthy, unlike my poor father.

"Don't cry, Melissa," he said. "If it's my time, I'll go willingly."

"And if it's not?" I asked. "Will you fight and stay with me?"

"I'll always fight for you," he promised.

I sniff as I lower myself into deep lunge, trying not to lose it. It's bad enough I sobbed in front of my elderly neighbor the other day when she asked how I was doing. But it's hard trying to stay strong. Every thought wanders back to my father and how frail he appeared beneath those heavy blankets, and how sad Mae appeared when she saw us.

Mae, poor sweet Mae. Her heart is breaking. I can see it and feel it every time she's at my father's side.

As lovely and supportive as she's been, she'll return to England if my father doesn't make it. "It's not home without him," she confessed.

I know what she means.

My father, my only family, and the one constant in my life, may no longer be around in a few days' time. I don't think I've ever felt so alone.

I switch legs, stretching my tight muscles. This morning started out with me clicking the television on while still in bed, only for Declan to be the first face I saw. There he was, bigger than life as always, but this time on my flat-screen.

"Governor McAdams swore in Acting District Attorney Declan O'Brien today," the reporter said. "Officially making him the youngest D.A. in Pennsylvania's history."

His mother held the bible beneath his hand as he recited the oath while an army of O'Briens lined the back wall, the pride they emanated appearing to drift into my living room.

Curran stood directly behind him, holding Fiona who couldn't stop waving at the audience. Baby Clodagh was there, too, wearing a sweet lavender dress and fast asleep in her mama's arms.

When Curran called me to say she'd been born and invited me to the hospital to meet her, I couldn't say no and thought I'd be okay. At first, I was, despite everything going on with Dad. This beautiful baby was a reminder of what a miracle life is.

Everything changed when Declan lifted her into his strong embrace. It was the first time I saw him hold a baby. He was a natural and it warmed my heart. But it was hard to witness what we'd never share and I had to look away.

Damn it, I hated the way we broke up and how everything transpired. The whole thing was a mess, but I can't put it all on him, just like I can't stop thinking about our time together. Every night when I slip beneath the cool sheets, I remember how warm his skin felt against mine. Mostly though, I think of the times we spent laughing and speaking softly.

I pull down the zipper on my running jacket, trying to cool off. I wonder if Declan knows what it took for me to trust him and how lost I am without him. I also wonder if he thought of me when he took his oath. I would have given anything to be there and celebrate the moment with him regardless of how I continue to struggle with whether our relationship was real.

Real or not, it doesn't stop me from loving him.

I finish my pathetic attempt at stretching and climb the steps, punching the security code quickly and slipping inside.

The door shuts behind me as I come to an abrupt halt and my gaze locks on Declan.

He's sitting at the top of my steps. It's only been a few days, but seeing him is like taking a full breath after almost drowning. The relief he brings is startling, flooding me with too many emotions to count, and even more than I can bear.

My hand smooths over the railing. He must have been waiting a while. His long wool coat is folded beside him and the sleeves of his dark blue sweater are pushed above his muscular forearms. The sweater, cashmere I think, clings to his broad chest, the color accentuating his light eyes and hair while dark jeans cover his long legs.

And here I am in running attire and my hair dangling around my face.

Still, it takes all I have not to bolt up the stairs and throw myself in his arms.

"Hi," he says.

"Hi," I answer, just barely getting the word out.

I've entertained a thousand times what I would do if I saw him again. I knew we'd eventually meet at some political affair, a fundraiser, *something*. But here, like this? No. Someone like him, so proud and capable of having anyone he wanted wouldn't come back, not after everything I said to him.

My legs feel like lead as I climb. I force myself forward, despite how his presence seems to cement me in place. I stop suddenly when I realize that on each step is a paperback novel with a shirtless man gracing the cover.

I lift my chin to meet Declan's face. "I thought about bringing you roses," he says. "But I figured you'd prefer Scots in loincloths to posies and petals."

The corners of my mouth curve upward. I lift *My Highlander, My Hotness,* tilting it so Declan can see the cover. "Dem Scots don't wear anything beneath their kilts."

He makes a face. "Thanks for the visual."

Despite everything I'm going through and everything

between us, I can't stop my grin. I lift the next book and examine the cover. "Classic Fabio," I tell him.

"Yeah . . . that one was on clearance shoved between a few packs of edible underwear. The lady at the store said it's a collector's item." He pauses. "That's bullshit, right?"

I try not to laugh, but it's hard. "Are you calling the woman who sells these babies *and* cherry-flavored panties a liar?"

"How did you know they were cherry-flavored?" he asks, smirking.

It's only because I know him the way that I do that I'm able to say what I say next. "You made Wren buy these, didn't you?"

"Oh. Hell yeah," he answers. "I wouldn't be caught dead buying this shit." He points to the one on top of my pile. "By the way, she wants to borrow *Lord of My Loins* when you're done. She said it reminds her of Evan." He holds up a hand and grimaces. "I don't want to know."

This time, I do laugh. But as I tuck each paperback against me, and close the distance between us, my humor fades and every emotion I've experienced in his absence hits me all at once. God, I've missed him.

He stands with his coat folded over his arm as I reach the step beneath where he's seated. "Here, let me help you," he offers.

I pass him the stack of books. "Thank you," I tell him quietly.

I reach for the key in my pocket, wrestling with what to do as I unlock the door. He's hurt me so badly and I'm scared to trust him. But he's trying, and if I'm being honest, I don't want him to leave.

I also don't want to walk away from him like I did in the hospital, afraid to look back and even more scared when he didn't follow.

"Would you like to come in?" I ask.

"Yes."

I lower my lids at the familiar rasp to his voice. What I'd give to have him hold me, and mean it, and . . . damn it. I push the door open, allowing him through before following and locking the door behind us.

He steps in, past the foyer and into the kitchen. I kick off my shoes and remove my socks, placing both in the washing machine as Declan sets my books down along my granite counter.

He walks around the island and stands in front of my couch, the same couch we made love on so many times. "Would you like some water?" I ask, averting my focus.

"No, thank you," he says. "I'm good."

"All right." I pull a water bottle out of the fridge, twisting off the cap as I return to the living room. "Please have a seat. I'll be right back, I just want to freshen up."

I head into my bedroom, stripping down to my black sports bra and capri running pants as I step into my bathroom. The hair tie is barely holding my messy strands in place. I leave it in just long enough to wash my face and hands then pull it out to give my hair a quick brush.

In all the ways Declan could have found me, he had to see me at my absolute worst. I'm not even wearing make-up, and here he is looking as perfect as always.

Regardless, I don't swipe my lashes with mascara or add a little gloss to my lips. He's already seen me and I don't want to keep him waiting.

I grind to a halt when I find Declan leaning against the doorway to my bedroom.

"Hey," he says. "I probably shouldn't be in here, but we've been apart for so long, I didn't want to wait anymore." He sighs. "I fucking miss you, Melissa."

My gaze falls to my clasped hands. "I wish I could believe you, Declan."

His voice deepens. "I wish you could, too." He pushes off the frame and walks forward, lowering himself onto the edge of my bed. "Will you sit with me, please?"

I nod, carefully settling beside him. At first, neither of us speaks or moves.

He's so close, his body heat radiates against mine. Not so long ago, we wouldn't hesitate to touch each other. Knowing so makes this moment all the more painful.

I swallow hard when he takes my hand in his. "I went to see your dad tonight after work. He told me you were here, and about the surgery next week."

His hand stays over mine, covering it completely and reminding me of better times. "I was sure you'd be with him," he says when I don't respond.

"I have been," I assure him, though I don't confess that I've rarely left his side. "I came back to sort through my bills and then went for a run." We're making small talk, which I'd normally hate. Right now it just feels good to hear his voice despite the subject.

"How are you doing?" he asks.

"Not great," I answer honestly. My fingertip passes over the hook to my hearing aid, more because I'm nervous than a need to adjust it. But the feel of it beneath my touch, and the squeal I create from the contact, remind me of my imperfections, something I could do without in Declan's presence.

I remove both, and place them beside me. The sudden loss of sound grants me a little peace despite how exposed it leaves me.

"Tell me what you're thinking," he says when I look up, permitting me to read his lips.

My thoughts revert to all the insecurities I possess. I'm not certain why. Perhaps it's because Declan has a way of stripping me bare and unmasking my vulnerability without ever touching me.

I take a breath and let those thoughts release.

That I wish my father could live and that I could be that perfect person you needed. That I can't find my smile without you and what remained of my heart stayed with you the day I walked away. It's everything I'm thinking. It's also everything I can't tell him.

So I tell him what I've been feeling since I left my dad this morning in Mae's care. Mae, who's suffering right along with him because, like me, there's very little she can do to ease his pain. "I'm thinking that my father gave up everything for me, even love." My voice shakes. I'm ready to cry, knowing what I say is true.

He wraps his arm around me, pulling me close. "You're wrong," he tells me. "He sacrificed what he thought was necessary to be a good father. In turn you made him proud and gave him more happiness than any man could hope for." His fingers skim along my waist. "You say he gave up love for you. What you don't understand is he found it the day he met you."

His lips pass along my jaw. "Declan," I whisper.

He pulls back, making certain I can read his lips. "I'm not trying to seduce you," he says. "That's not what I'm here for. But I have to tell you, it's killing me to see you in pain." I brush a tear away. "Melissa, please don't cry."

I drop my hand away. "I can't help it. It's so hard to see you and not . . ." I don't finish my thought.

He smooths his hand across my belly. "And not what?" he asks, his voice lowering. "Tell me what you want to say. I need to hear you say it."

"And not be with you," I reply.

His hand sweeps through my hair to hold my face. "No, tell me how you *feel*. So I know you still feel it."

Tell him I love him, he means. But it hurts too much to say. I squeeze my eyes shut, allowing more tears to scatter along my cheeks.

When I don't respond, I wait for him to pull away and steel myself for what will be our final goodbye. He's upset. After our fight at the hospital and now this, he must be. So when I open my eyes and his features hold nothing but tenderness, I'm not prepared. Nor am I prepared for his words.

"I'm not staying on as D.A., and I'm not running for mayor. If you leave for D.C., I'm leaving with you."

"What? *Why*?" I scan his face. "Declan . . . this is everything you've ever wanted."

The muscles tense along his jaw. "Because last night when I was sworn in as District Attorney—when I took the first major step in getting everything I've worked for, and fought for, and dreamed of, it meant absolutely nothing. None of it—the job, my career, my fucking life—means anything without you." His hand strokes my face, his touch so gentle I barely feel the caress. "I need you, Melissa," he says, his gaze drilling into mine. "For all the good and all the bad. I need you with me for all of it."

His words drill down to my soul. I try to pull away, too afraid to believe what he says. Declan won't let me, keeping his arm fastened around my waist.

He lifts my hand and places it over his chest. "If you don't believe me, feel me. Feel my heart. It hasn't been the same since you left me."

Beneath my palm, the strong steady beats increase in speed, matching mine as they race ahead.

"I'm tired of being apart," he tells me. "Tired of being something when I'm *nothing* without you."

I pull my hand away. "Declan, I'm never going to be everything you need."

He shakes his head slowly. "You already are, Melissa."

I break down, and it's that ugly, awful cry that women hate. Declan doesn't care, bending forward and kissing my lips. "I know you're afraid you'll lose your family if you lose your dad," he says. "But as long as you want me, I swear to Christ you'll never be alone."

When his mouth again meets mine, the walls I so carefully solidified come down in one mighty crash. I reach for Declan's sweater, pulling it off. My pants follow as he yanks them down. I barely finish peeling off my sports bra when he pushes his hard length inside me.

My spine bows back and I bite back a blissful scream.

"I love you," he gasps, thrusting hard. "I'll love you forever . .."

EPILOGUE

Melissa

The wrap securing our newborn infant keeps her close to my skin. But as the hearing screener continues to fiddle with her portable laptop, I feel the need to clutch my baby closer and protect her from what I'm certain the screener will say. Allanah is content against my skin, having had her fill of milk. Declan sits beside me, his thumb smoothing over my hand as he patiently waits for the test to finish.

I'm not so patient. I'm scared.

I release his hand and sign, *I think there's something wrong.*

I'm not familiar with the device the screener is using. I only know it's measuring our daughter's ability to hear and it's taking too long to get the results. This machine, as high tech as it's supposed to be, is incapable of predicting how other children will treat her if she's hearing impaired. It won't help her through her struggles when she tries to learn to speak with her hands. Nor will it shield her from the looks cast her way. It won't protect her from harsh words or explain to her why people can't seem to understand her.

It will only tell us one thing, and although I've prepared

myself for the possibility that she may not hear within normal limits, my fear remains.

Declan doesn't seem worried. He shifts his position in the hospital bed, angling closer. There's not much room, but as always, he knows when I need him close. *We don't know that yet,* he signs. *But if there is, I promise we'll get through it.*

His motions aren't smooth. He's still learning ASL. But I understand him and sense his devotion behind every gesture.

There's no flicker of doubt in his expression, nor does he show any fear. That's good. One of us needs to be strong and I'm not feeling very strong at the moment. Did I survive my childhood? Yes. I did. That doesn't mean I want my child to face the same struggles I did.

"I'm sorry, Mayor and Mrs. O'Brien," the screener says. "I have to adjust the probes. I don't think they're in the right spot based on these readings."

She repositions the circular devices on our baby girl's head. I kiss her cheek when she fusses and whimpers. "It's okay, sweetie," I whisper.

The screener smiles when Allanah settles against me. "That's right, peanut," she says. "Just cuddle with your mama."

Declan looks to where Curran and Tess sit by the window. "Curran, it's late. We'll catch up with you guys tomorrow, all right?"

Curran exchanges glances with Tess. The entire family arrived to meet Allanah, but they're the only ones who remain.

"Okay," Curran says. He adjusts Fiona and Clodagh where they're fast asleep over his shoulders, and stands. "Call us if you need anything. Otherwise, we'll see you at your place tomorrow."

Like Dad and Mae, and the rest of the O'Briens, they hesitate to leave. I love them for it, I do. But as soon as the hearing screener announced who she was, it's like all our worries clouded the room and thickened the air with tension.

They piled out quietly at Declan's request for privacy. Curran and Tess stayed when I insisted she finish feeding Curran, Jr. Initially, I stayed positive and hoped for the best. But now . . .

I barely notice them, too worried about our little one.

"It's going to be all right, love," Declan tells me softly.

What if it's not? I sign, trying to keep our conversation private.

He smiles gently. *Your dad raised you on his own, barely knowing anything about children. Our baby has you, she has me, and so much more we'll be able to give her. No matter what, she's going to be okay and so will we.*

I don't want her to endure what I did, I admit.

He considers me, as if finding his words. *I hate what you went through and that some people were too ignorant to see past your hearing impairment*, he motions. *But I love who you are and who you became. You're the strongest person I know and the best part of my life.*

I smile, my husband's sweet words warming my heart like no one else can.

The hearing screener glances down at Allanah and carefully removes the probes. "Okay. We're all done, passed in both ears."

I fall completely still. "There's nothing wrong?"

"Not at all," the woman assures me. "She's perfect."

Declan doesn't miss a beat, leaning in close and kissing my lips. "She's perfect," he repeats. "Just like her mama."

This book contains excerpts from *Once Kissed*, *Let Me* and *Crave Me* from the O'Brien Family novels by Cecy Robson, in addition to excerpts from *Inseverable* and *Eternal* from the Carolina Beach Romance series. The excerpts have been set for this edition only and may not reflect the final content of the final novels.

Once Kissed

An O'Brien Family Novel

Cecy Robson

CHAPTER 1

Curran

"Are you fucking kidding me?" I nail my brother with my best cop face. Any perp would freeze, curse, or take off running. Declan doesn't so much as blink. It shouldn't surprise me. He's never been the type to run from a fight, even before he earned his title as assistant DA.

"Curran, quit your bitching. It's a cake assignment," he says. "Look at it as a break until you're back on the job."

"You sayin' I can't do the job?"

Declan's jaw tightens hard enough to stiffen every muscle in his face. Either I pissed him off or I'm on to something. "I'm saying it wouldn't hurt to have more time before you're back on the streets," he answers, keeping his voice low. "What happened to your partner Joey isn't something you just get over."

"Who's saying I'm over it? I know I fucked up." *And so does everyone on the force,* I don't add. "That doesn't mean I'm washed up or can't do my job."

Declan's already stiff posture tenses even more. "I never said you were washed up, or that you can't—"

"Might as well have."

"Curran, don't you get it? It's not a punishment."

"Don't *you* get it? While you're sitting here behind a desk, I got dealers and gangbangers offing people left and right—and you're asking me to play bodyguard to your librarian."

Declan leans back in his high-back office chair, clearly annoyed, but also worried. "She's not a librarian, Curran. She's an intern in her last year of law school who's helping me with research in the Montenegro case."

"Like I said, librarian."

"Jesus. Just help me out, will ya?" he snaps, rubbing his forehead hard.

Ya? Okay, now he's pissed. Behind that new suit, clean-shaven face, and hundred-dollar haircut, my brother's Philly through and through. One more smart-ass comment from me and the "youz" are going to drop like water ice and his fist will swing my way.

With a groan, Declan pushes away from his desk and stands to face the window. Useless gesture, if you ask me. His view is a brick wall. But I suppose it's either that or pace, and his closet-sized office isn't big enough to take more than a few steps.

The thing is, I can read faces. He knows as much, and doesn't want me to read his now. "Curran. This is my chance to move up," he says. "Zabrinski, head of Homicide, is retiring in a few months. I've paid my dues, worked the shit cases, and won trials seasoned DAs thought I should plead out." He looks at me then. "If I can put Montenegro away, it would upset organized crime from here to Jersey."

"And seal your position in Homicide," I finish for him.

"Yeah. It would."

I cross my arms. "So why the hell do I have to babysit your librarian? If anything, I should be watching your back. You painted a bull's-eye on your forehead by taking this case. Vincent Montenegro isn't just a mob boss. He's a legend only a dumbass would cross." I roll my eyes at his glare. "Calm your shit—you know what, I mean."

"Don't you think I know that? It's the reason I don't want anyone else helping me with this case. No other names. No one but me for the mob to target."

"And no one else to steal your glory," I add, which earns me yet another glare. "Declan, I know you want the promotion, just like I know you want the street cred. But don't be stupid and get yourself killed in the process. Let me watch your back. The librarian can get another badge to shadow her."

"I already have someone watching me."

I straighten. "One of the boys in blue?"

"Actually a few. They alternate nights. When I'm at the office, or courtside, the detectives and sheriffs here have my back. Contessa will be—"

"*Contessa?* Is that even a real name?" Declan coughs into his fist in a lame attempt to muffle his laugh. "Damn. If it doesn't mean 'I have a stick rammed up my ass,' I don't know what does."

My remark only makes my big bro laugh harder. "She's . . . intense, and at times rigid, I'll give you that."

"Like I said, stick up the ass."

"She's a hard worker and a nice young lady, I assure you."

I assure you, I repeat in my head. Okay, the Philly boy has officially left the building.

"Curran, just take the assignment. From what we hear, Montenegro isn't going to go to prison without making a lot of noise. The badges assigned to this case have the smarts to watch my back and theirs."

"But no one's guarding the poor homely intern's back. I get it."

A sly grin edges across his face. "I never said she was homely, bro."

Contessa

"Why *her*?"

"No idea. I have more experience. So does Tyler, and Emily's been here longer."

"We've all been here longer," Emily adds, jumping in.

They're all talking about me—not just the other interns, but every law clerk here. I get that the Montenegro case is one most attorneys would kill to say they were a part of—one that will make history and open doors to a successful career in law, and one that provides an opportunity to work with Declan O'Brien, the gorgeous assistant DA who's on his way to becoming a legend. I get it, I really do—and I'm thrilled that I was selected to be a part of it. What I don't understand is why they have to be so mean-spirited. I would never treat someone this way.

"Do you think she knows someone?" Brett mutters.

"Probably," Sarah offers. "It would explain why she thinks she's better than us."

I don't think that, I want to say. But I don't say it. After all the times I've passed on lunch and happy hour with them, they wouldn't believe me anyway. I have my reasons. Yet those reasons are too personal to share, especially with people who think so little of me.

The comments continue as if I'm not sitting close enough to hear. I'd like to say their remarks have no effect on me, but they do. They kick at the pride I feel being the law clerk selected to help Declan. According to DA Miles Fenske, Declan and I will be the only non-investigators on the case. All those nights of staying in, studying, and working hard are finally paying off. My path to independence is close—I can see it. No, I can *taste* it. All I have to do is get through the next few months.

And probably a lot more jabs thrown my way.

"Well, looks like U Penn steals it from us again," Janice chimes in.

I cringe, wishing the comments would simply roll off my back. But I never could ignore insults. They've always hurt. Yet unlike in high school and college where I could hurry away, pretending to bury my face in a book, there's nowhere to run. So I focus on finishing the deposition I'm working on and do my best to ignore their harsh words.

"What makes her so special, anyway?" Brielle adds.

"Not her clothes, that's for sure," Burton mumbles, causing the others to burst out laughing.

Their comments are bad enough, but their laughter is more than I can take. This time, I don't stay quiet. "You don't have to behave this way," I say aloud, keeping my back to them. "I'm sure there will be other opportunities—"

"Other opportunities?" Burton mocks. "Oh, yeah, because cases as epic as this one come along all the time."

I used to stick up for him. I suppose it's too much to expect the same in return. "I'm not saying that it's not a good case to have—"

"Then what are you saying?" he demands.

I force myself to continue typing, even as I speak. "I'm only saying you don't have to be so rude."

"And you don't have to be such a bitch," he barks back.

I whip around, stunned. The huddled group disperses to the rows of desks occupying the center of the law library. No one bothers to glance my way, not even Burton. It's as if I don't even matter, and he never called me what he did.

If I report him, it'll come down to my word against his. That much is clear given how they're all now back at their stations, pretending as if the past several minutes never occurred.

My voice quivers from anger, and from the humiliation heating my body. "I didn't realize you thought so highly of me, Burton. I'll make a note of it in case it happens again." It's my way of warning him that I'm documenting this incident in case his behavior continues, but of course, he doesn't care.

He lifts his head from his work and smiles. "I'm sorry, Contessa. Did you say something?"

Angry tears burn my eyes. *You asshole.*

His smile vanishes. Not because of me, or because he realizes he's being a monstrous prick, but because of who he sees approaching.

The door to the library opens and DA Fenske walks in, his status and presence drawing everyone's attention, and rescuing me in more ways than one. "Hello, sir," we all say at once, because that's the type of respect this man evokes.

"Good afternoon, everyone," he says, smiling. "Contessa, may I see you a moment? It's with regard to the Montenegro case."

"Yes, sir. Right away." I reach for my iPad and purse, trying to collect myself.

DA Fenske opens the door to allow me through and I rush forward. I smile when he joins me in the hall, thankful to be leaving the law library. "I truly appreciate this opportunity, sir," I say. "I've already begun to prepare the deposition and have requested the case files from the records department."

"Excellent, Contessa." He nods to several staff members as we proceed down the hall. Some are renowned attorneys, some hold modest clerical positions. Yet Miles Fenske greets everyone by name while managing to stay on task. "I'm sure you'll be a tremendous asset to Declan. However, as you may know, Montenegro's reputation is one of extreme violence. While we think he'll ignore you given your minor role in the case, we'd like to assign you after-hours police supervision."

I trip in my alligator loafers. DA Fenske manages to steady me, although the action clearly causes him pain. He releases me slowly, pressing a hand to his side.

My attention travels from his hand to his face. "Sir, I'm so sorry. Are you all right?"

He lowers his hand and continues forward, forcing a smile. "I'm fine," he says. "Just an old football injury acting up."

Based on his hunched posture and strained expression, I don't believe him, but I don't dare press. We cut right, past the Homicide Division and down the row of cubicles, as I carefully gather my words.

"Sir, my apologies, but did you say I would be assigned a police escort?"

DA Fenske adjusts the button to his suit jacket, graciously appearing to miss my grimace. "Correct," he answers. "While we believe Declan will be Montenegro's sole focus, Declan feels it would be in your best interest to have protection in case Montenegro becomes aware of your presence and misinterprets your role."

I clutch my iPad tightly against my chest, not wanting to believe this is happening. Don't I have enough people watching my every move? "And if I refuse, sir?"

DA Fenske stops a few feet from Declan's closed office door to consider me. Although I tried to keep my tone casual, I couldn't stop my voice from shaking. "Then another law clerk will take your place."

Unlike my voice, his is firm, making it clear this matter isn't up for negotiation.

Another collar wound around my neck, another leash pulled taut. I want to cry. Yet I know I can't. So instead of fighting, or crying, or pleading, I quietly obey. Just like I've done a thousand times before. "Very well, sir. I'll accept the conditions of my assignment."

Miles Fenske takes a moment to consider me. He's not blind, he knows something is wrong. Thankfully, he releases me from his scrutiny and knocks on the door. "Declan, it's Miles and Contessa. May we come in?"

"Ah, Miles. Yes, please come in," Declan calls from behind the door.

I adjust my tiny black-framed glasses and take a breath before stepping forward. For all my nervousness, the heavens seem to part as the godlike Declan O'Brien greets me with a dashing smile. He and the hulking male sitting directly in front of him rise from their seats and—

No . . . not . . . *No!*

The police officer in full uniform turns his six-foot-plus frame my way, his light blue shirt tight against a dense mass of muscle, his blond hair shaved close to his scalp, and his light blue eyes staring straight at me. But it's not his physique, those eyes, or even that humungous gun strapped to his hip that cement me where I stand. It's his face.

The same face that had dipped between my spread legs all those years ago.

Holy. Shit.

"Hello, Contessa," Declan says, keeping his smile. He was so busy greeting DA Fenske that he didn't catch my stupefied response.

I jerk my head and pull the strands of my blond hair forward before nodding Declan's way. "Hello, Assistant DA O'Brien."

He chuckles. "I told you, just call me Declan." He motions to the police officer. "This is my brother, Curran. He'll be watching you."

Brother? Cold sweat pours down my spine. *Murder me, Jesus. I beg you.*

My hands clutch my iPad, hard enough to crush my minute breasts. I bow my head, hoping to shadow my features. "Ma'am," he says.

Declan motions us to sit and immediately begins discussing his progress on the Montenegro case with Miles. I open my iPad and type feverishly. Or at least, I try. Curran is looking at me. Right at me.

I adjust my position to angle away from him. *Damn it.* Why *him*? Why *here*? The one time I let loose—the one time I slept with a man I barely knew—the frat boy I avoided, the loudmouth I did my best to ignore—of all people, *he's* assigned to guard me?

I pinch the bridge of my nose. This is the same man I tied to bed with my argyle socks!

I stare hard at my iPad, feeling the heat rise to my cheeks as I envision my future and reputation imploding around me.

"Montenegro's second was arrested this afternoon," Declan adds. "And we have a lead on his third."

"Do you think either will talk?" Miles asks him.

Declan widens his grin. "They will once they know how much we have on them."

Both men laugh. I shift my weight and steal a glimpse Curran's way. The prosecutors may be talking mob bosses and arraignments, but his attention is all on me.

"Contessa, make a note that I'd like the records clerk to bring everything they have on Gus Mancini, starting from his first arrest."

My fingers sweep across the screen. "Yes, sir. Right away, sir."

"Do I know you?" Curran asks, his deep voice cutting through the other men's chatter and tensing every ridge in my spine.

My fingers pause their erratic typing. "No," I answer quickly.

The old wooden chair creaks as he leans back. "I could swear I've seen you before. You hang out a Lou's Barbecue or Romeo's Pizzeria?"

"N-no, not at all."

"What about Frank's Bar? Or—I know, O'Malley's Tavern?"

"No," I mutter, doing my best to shield my face.

"Curran, do you mind?" Declan asks.

"Oh—sorry. I thought I knew Contessa here from one of my stomping grounds."

"I assure you, I've never been to those places," I stammer.

My nervousness and direct eye contact totally give me away.

Curran straightens as stunned recognition spreads along his features. *"Argyles?"* he asks.

READ ON FOR AN EXCERPT FROM

Let Me

An O'Brien Family

Novel

Cecy Robson

CHAPTER 1

Finn

I see the strike coming at me a split second before it connects with my skull. My head snaps back from the force, the crowds' hollers resonating like a muffled cry in the distance. It was a good punch—lightning quick with enough impact to knock most guys on their asses. But I'm not most guys.

You hit me, I'm only going to hit you harder.

My right hand shoots up, blocking and smacking away the kick gunning for my ribs. I pivot out of the way, again, and again, and again, avoiding Easton's arms and legs as they come at me. He's fast, strong, with a six inch reach advantage. But he's too eager to take me out and not pacing himself like he should. Already he's breathing hard and it's just the start of the second round.

I take my time to figure him out, planning each move, searching for that opening I need. Do I take a few bashes because of it? Sure. It's part of the job. But believe it or not, it's part of the job I look forward to.

Those punches and kicks remind me that I still *feel*, that I'm still human. And that for now, I'm still alive.

"Oh!" some drunk behind me yells when my uppercut finds Easton's chin.

He staggers back, swiping the blood oozing from his lip, yet he keeps his grin. He's trying to make like it was a lucky shot. That it won't happen again.

Like me, Easton needs to win this match. And if he does, he'll move up to the top ten, making him a contender for the UFC Lightweight title.

Talent aside, the guy's a raging asshole, and so are the idiots in his training camp. They've been trash-talking since the moment I agreed to this match. I didn't really care and laughed most of it off until they got personal and took it a step too far.

Again he nails me in the head. It's not as hard as it was last time which tells me he's getting tired. Does it hurt? I guess.

But let's say I'm a guy who's used to pain.

Easton grins. He thinks I'm afraid of him. He thinks he has me where he wants me. But fear is an emotion I don't allow myself to entertain. Fear gets you hurt and rips you apart till you think there's nothing left.

I dodge out of reach. He scowls and takes another swing. This one gets close enough to my jaw to create a breeze that whips across my skin.

"Finn," my brother Killian barks from the side. "Take him out *now*."

He's worried about me. So is my family. But now's not the time to think about them. I keep my hands up as I edge away, letting Easton think I'm backing down, that I'm tired and need to catch my breath.

I sidestep when he lunges forward, avoiding his next swing and use the momentum to drop my head and nail him in the temple with a roundhouse kick.

Like I said, Easton's fast.

Too bad for him I'm a little bit faster.

The kick is my signature move, as natural for me as the next breath. He goes down like I planned. But in the Octagon you don't stop just because your opponent collapses like timber. You charge forward. You show him what you're made of. And you prove just how tough you really are.

That muffled screaming, isn't so muffled anymore. The crowd loses their shit as I pounce, my blows nailing Easton in the face until the ref's arms hook beneath mine as he hauls me off. I back away, my fists up because I already know I won.

I should do a back flip or some crazy shit to incite the crowd. This is it. My time has come to own it. But the good things aren't as great as they can be. Not with the memories that haunt me. And not with the anger they stir.

Killian rushes in as the medic wipes down my face. I'm bleeding from the punch Easton caught me with at the beginning of the round. I didn't think it was that bad, but the way the ringside medic is pressing the towel against my head clues me in the gash isn't closing like it should.

"I'm going to have to stitch you up, Fury," he mumbles.

"I figured," I tell him.

Kill pats my back. "Good job," he says.

Maybe he believes it, but I don't miss the concern in his voice. He thinks I took too many unnecessary hits. I can't really argue, seeing how it's true.

He doesn't understand that I don't feel those strikes the way I should. Hell, I don't think I've felt anything the way I should in a long time. Not like I used to. I try to tell myself that maybe that' a good thing. That numbness is better than pain. But I'm not so convinced anymore, and neither is my family. I try to shrug it off like I'm fine. Except given the way they've been eyeing me, I'm not fooling anyone.

I'm scaring everyone around me. And it sucks. Not only because I don't want them scared, but mostly because I don't know how to stop it.

"The referee has called a stop to this match at two-minutes and forty-nine seconds into the second round," the announcer begins. "The winner by TKO, Finn 'The Fury' O'Brien."

The crowd screams and pumps their fists in the air when

my hand is raised. I take the few seconds I need to thank my sponsors, my camp, and my brother, because that's what I'm supposed to do despite the fog clouding my senses. I wish that disconnect had something to do with all the hits I took, but deep down I know that it doesn't.

I'm back in the locker room before I know it getting stitched up, too many people talking at once. God, I barely hear their questions or my responses. But they're there and somehow I make it through.

"I'm worried about you, Finnie," Kill says when everyone piles out.

"Don't. I'm not drinking tonight. I'm headed home," I assure him.

"That's not what I mean," he says. He's sitting in a fold out chair, his arms resting against his muscular legs. "I think you need to talk to someone."

I stretch out my arms. By now they're so tight, they pull against the bones. "I am. I'm talking to you."

I don't have to see him to know he's shaking his head, or that he's looking sad, disappointed, and maybe something else, too. "I'm not who you should be speaking to," he says. "Not for what's going on in your head."

"You're enough," I say, even though I know it's no longer true.

"Finn," he begins.

I don't wait for him to finish, leaving the changing area and heading toward the showers. "Go find Sofia and Wren," I call over my shoulder as I strip out my shirt. "See if they're up for some dinner."

I don't remember peeling the rest of my clothes off. That numbness I've been feeling too much lately claiming me like a mist until it fully engulfs me. Fuck. It's like I've stopped living even though for the most part I think I'm still alive.

I lean against the tile with my arms spread, allowing the water to beat against my back. It's too hot. I should turn it down, but I don't bother. Eventually, like everything else, the sensation fades.

I'm not sure how long I'm in that position. A few seconds? A few minutes? But then Easton and his trainer Yefim are suddenly there. "You got lucky, O'Brien," Yefim calls out, taunting me with his thick eastern European accent.

Shit. Like all the trash talk before the fight wasn't enough.

"Did you hear me, you pussy?" he fires back when I don't answer. "Did you hear me, you goddamn coward?"

Coward? Fuck you. It's what I think, but not what I say, focusing instead on the streams of water that gather along my feet before they swirl into the drain.

It doesn't help. The rage that's building, the one I only manage to barely keep in? It stirs in my gut like a heavy pot filled with hate, sin, and all the curses my Ma would still beat my ass for saying.

"What're you doing?" Yefim asks.

His voice is closer, he's drawing near. It doesn't matter that I'm standing here naked. He wants to be next to me. I shudder, that feeling I keep buried drilling its way up.

"I know about you," Yefim says, not bothering to keep his voice low. "But everyone knows, don't they? Even if you don't want them to."

My body shakes a little more, but it's not from the cooling water. It's from his words and all that anger they trigger. *Don't do it. Don't go there.*

"You like to keep it a secret. Don't you, pussy?"

Yefim laughs when I keep my trap shut. He thinks I'm backing down, just like Easton did before his face met the mat. "He's crying," he calls out to Easton. "What? Not so tough now?"

That's where he's dead wrong. Every muscle I've conditioned serves a purpose—to take down those who fuck with me. And right now, Yefim is seriously fucking with me.

"You like to pretend that it's girls you like, don't you?" he says. "But that's not true, is it? Oh, no, that's not true at all . . ."

I raise my chin, knowing that someone's not leaving without bleeding, and I've bled enough tonight.

Yefim kicks at my calf. "What? Nothing to say? Can't speak without your boyfriend here?"

"Boyfriend?" Easton asks, laughing. "No fucking way."

"Yes. Way," Yefim insists. "Didn't you know this little pussy takes it up the ass—"

I punch him so hard, I feel his teeth crack against my knuckles. For someone with decades of boxing experience he never saw me coming. But I see Easton flying at me out of the corner of my eye. I toss him over my shoulder, slamming him hard onto the ceramic tile floor. Like in the octagon, I throw myself on top of him, my fists colliding against his skin.

Voices rush forward, telling me to stop. A woman screams, but I don't stop fighting off the bodies trying to grab me, breaking through the arms wrenching me back. I need to hit him—I need to feel my fists meeting his face—I need to feel *something*.

God damn it. I need to feel alive.

I don't want the pain.

I don't want the terror.

But once more, it's all I feel.

Crave Me

An O'Brien Family Novel

Cecy Robson

CHAPTER 1

Wren

I drop the keys in Mr. Esposito's hand and smile. He stares at them in his open palm like a precious gift, because to someone like him who's worked hard all his life, it very much is.

"Thank you, Wren," he says, meeting my smile. "I never thought I'd own a new car. Let alone be able to give one to my son as a gift."

"You deserve it, Mr. Esposito," I tell him, shaking his hand. "And so does your son for getting into Drexel. Tell Antonio, hi for me—Oh, and be sure to have someone take his picture when you hand him the keys." I motion to my office behind me. "I want to add it to my memory wall."

"I will." He presses his lips tight as if considering what to say. "Your father would be proud of you," he tells me. His soft brown eyes take in the massive dealership, fixing on the sales board displaying my current rank at number one. "Very proud."

I hold onto my smile as he walks toward the brand new candy apple red F-150 hugging the curb, ignoring the brutal January wind that sweeps in when the doors to the lot zip open. Mr. Esposito pauses when he opens the driver's side door. I had the boys in the back place a bow on dash like I do for all my customers. I think it's a nice touch, and a way to thank them for their business. Mr. Esposito tosses me a grin over his shoulder. Maybe it's the wind slapping against his face, or maybe it's because he's just that touched, but I catch his eyes glistening with tears.

Slowly he slips inside and grips the wheel, his widening smile lifting his deeply worn features.

The moment he pulls away, my smile vanishes. "Your father would be proud of you," he'd said. He meant it as a compliment. Mr. Esposito has always been nice like that. But instead of giving me the warm fuzzies, that familiar pang tugs at my insides.

My heels click against the bleached white tile as I cross the showroom. The phones ringing off the hook have me turning toward the finance department. It's been a nasty winter with all the snow we've been hit with, but I can't say it's been bad for business. One of the secretaries waves to me as she hurries to answer the phone. I wave back, not that she seems to notice. She starts writing as she takes the first call. Yeah, it's going to be a busy week. But busy means work, and that's something I've always been good at.

My eyes narrow when they fix on Oscar looming over Penny. Penny is smart, and an overall good person. She's young, and hasn't been here long, but she's trying, and I know she has it in her to succeed. Too bad Oscar is stomping on her success, luring customers away from her every chance he gets.

"You snooze, you lose," he tells her, pegging her with one of his more sleazy grins.

Penny was making headway with the guy who walked in, until Oscar shoved his way between them and baited him away, making Penny look like she didn't know what she was talking about. If I hadn't been busy with Mr. Esposito, I would have stepped in. Nothing gets me more than men who target those they think are weak.

"Wren!" Suze calls from behind the counter. "You have a call."

"Okay. Send it through to my office," I yell. I rush across the last few feet of the showroom, but not before I make sure Oscar steps far away from Penny.

The phone rings one, twice, before I slam the door behind me with my foot and reach across my desk and put the call on speaker. "Erin O'Brien," I say.

There's a brief pause before I hear, "Hi, Wren."

Shit. My stomach twists the way it always does when I hear his voice. "What do you want, Bryant?" I ask, digging out my cell phone from my desk drawer.

"I miss you," he says.

"Do you miss hitting me, too?" I fire back.

I'm talking tough. It's what I do. Too bad I don't feel so tough right now. Not when it comes to Bryant. A familiar sense of dread sends a chill down my spine, reminding me what happened the last time I pissed him off. I hit the record icon on my cell phone, hoping to catch him saying something I can use against him. But the damn thing beeps, and for all Bryant is an asshole, he's not stupid.

"Are you recording me, pretty girl?" He laughs when I don't answer. "Now, why would you do a thing like that?"

"Because I don't trust you, because you hit me—oh, and because you're an asshole."

"I don't know what you're talking about," he says, keeping his voice easy. "I'm just returning your call. You keep calling me so—"

"That's a lie," I say, my face heating with anger. He knows I'm recording him and trying to switch things around. "Don't call me again. I want nothing to do with you."

I hang up the phone. It's been months since I last saw him, months since he last put his hands on me. But just when I think I'm rid of him, he reminds me he's still there.

I could call the police. The problem is, he is the police. .

Evan

My Jaguar skids, again, again, and again, fighting to keep pace with the other drivers insane enough to travel the Blue Route in this weather. Chunks of wet snow smack against my windshield. My wipers squeak against the glass as they race to keep my line of sight clear when another vehicle cuts me off, pelting my windshield with more ice. My current struggle with life and death does not evidently discourage Ashleigh from barking messages over my Blue Tooth.

"Yodel called again, Evan. They want you to reconsider."

"No," I reply, cutting my steering wheel toward the left when my car veers right. "We're representing Mellon, their biggest competitor. It's a conflict of interest to supply both companies with the same technology."

I mutter a curse when the minivan in front of me slams on their brakes and I narrowly miss ramming the bumper. And I suppose, because we're in Philadelphia, the City of Brotherly love, the woman rolls down the window, permitting snow into her vehicle just to wave an irate middle finger at me.

"Rich Bitch loser," she cries out.

I rub my face. Bloody hell, why am I here again? Before I can finish the thought, Ashleigh reminds me.

"Evan, we're at risk for financial collapse. The company needs the revenue."

"Not at the expense of our ethics," I counter.

True, my company is at risk. But it's due to poor business practices, such as the ones Ashleigh suggests I entertain. I understand she learned these tactics from my predecessor, but he was a conniving snake—which is why he's currently serving time for embezzlement and I had to leave London to rebuild my father's dying empire.

"What about your eleven a.m. with the V.P. of County General?"

"Have Anne and Clifton start straight away. I emailed them the presentation last night—"

"Do you really think they're qualified?" she interrupts.

I open my mouth to insist that they are and to remind her I'm her superior, not the other way around. But I'm not oblivious to what she tells me. Anne and Clifton are fairly new and not at the level I'd prefer them to be. Nevertheless, they're learning fast under my tutelage and the only ones from the original staff I trust.

"Evan," she presses.

"Ashleigh, Anne and Clifton will handle it. That's my final word." I disconnect, swearing as I take the ramp and practically slide down sideways.

Another proud Pennsylvanian sticks his head out the window. "Get a real car, fucker," he hollers.

I rub my face again, tired and frustrated. I didn't arrive home until three this morning. It wouldn't have taken as long had I been driving a vehicle capable of enduring this ungodly weather.

I glance up, releasing a tense breath when the sign for the Ford dealership I researched comes into view. Saving iCronos will take me time. Time I can't spare driving a Jaguar on roads better maneuvered via dogsled.

My car slows to a stop in front of the massive dealership. The combination of the vehicle I'm driving, along with the expensive suit and coat I'm wearing, command attention. The moment I step inside, a young woman with dark spiky hair hurries over. "Good morning, sir. I'm Penny," she says. "Welcome to Ford Nation. Are you interested in acquiring a new vehicle?"

She seems young, but eager, a respectable attribute. Yet no sooner does she finish speaking than a man about my age steps in front of her, adjusting the jacket of his gray suit. "I got this, P," he tells her. "Get us some coffee, will you?" He holds out his hand. "Hello. I'm Oscar Nelson. Welcome to Ford Nation."

My frown bounces from his hand to the young woman whose face is now bright red with humiliation and possibly more. "Are you his assistant?" I ask her.

"No," she answers. "I'm a car sales representative—"

Oscar speaks over her, but it's the sound of quickly approaching footsteps that causes me to turn. A woman with a pinstripe jacket and matching skirt hurries forward, the quick motions of her long legs causing the edge of her skirt to brush above her knees and swing her hips seductively. Long hair flutters like streams of ebony smoke, revealing a staggeringly beautiful face better suited for my wildest fantasies.

I spent the first five years following the completion of my doctorate in either a lab or boardroom packed with men in alternating stages of balding, and these last nine months trapped in a building working a minimum of eighteen hour days. I haven't had the opportunity or time to meet women. But if I'd known she was out here, I'd have spared a moment.

Good . . . God.

I don't realize I'm staring until she stops directly in front of us and juts out her chin. "Problem?" she asks Oscar.

Oscar straightens to his full height. "No. I was just showing Mr. . . ." He motions to me. "My apologies, what's your name, sir?"

"Jonah," I say, returning my attention to the stunning young woman. I offer her my hand. "Evan Jonah."

Full pink lips lift into a dazzling smile that resonates in her deep blue eyes and lights her creamy white skin.

"I'm Erin O'Brien, but I go by Wren," she says. She shakes my hand with a firm grip, releasing me to guide the smaller woman forward. "How can Penny and I help you today, sir?"

"I'm afraid my vehicle isn't equipped for this weather and I am seeking a better alternative, possibly a truck or SUV," I reply, doing all in my power to keep my focus on her face.

"Then you've come to the right place. Penny, will you

show Mr. Jonah—"

"Evan," I interrupt, mentally kicking myself for morphing into a fourteen year old boy the moment my eyes locked on this woman.

"Okay, Evan," she says. "Penny, please show Evan the latest members of the Ford family."

"Of course, this way, sir," Penny answers with a grin.

I reluctantly follow behind Penny. But as we reach a black Explorer my gaze trails back to Wren. She and Oscar have moved away from the showroom and closer to the rear offices. Yet it does little to muffle their exchange.

"What the fuck was that?" Oscar snaps.

My spine stiffens. I storm forward, ready to demand he apologize for using such foul language in the presence of a lady.

"You being a raging asshole," Wren replies.

I'll admit, her response gives me pause. And she doesn't stop there. "Look, I know you have to compensate for your less than average-sized dick. But that doesn't give you the right to mistreat Penny or pounce on every client she approaches. That's bullshit and you know it."

"Um, perhaps a truck will be more to your needs," Penny says, motioning to the opposite side of the dealership and away from the heated conversation.

I don't typically involve myself in affairs that don't concern me, nor do I interact with women who speak in such a manner. But it's not simply Wren's colorful vocabulary that captivates me, it's her strength and desire to defend her small friend.

"Where the fuck did you hear that?" Oscar responds. "I don't have a small dick."

Of all his possible retorts, this is the one he chooses?

"Suze," Wren calls over her shoulder in the direction of the finance counter. "What was it you said about that night you went out with Oscar?"

The woman behind the counter scowls and holds up her

pinky. Wren smirks. "Looks to me like you should have called her back." She pats his shoulder. "My condolences to your man parts."

She starts to walk away, stopping when she realizes I witnessed their encounter. Instead of making a quick escape or pretending I didn't hear them, she walks toward me with her head raised. "Sorry about that, Mr. Jonah—"

"Evan," I clarify as she reaches me.

Her smile stirs one of my own. "Evan," she repeats, lifting a hand toward her friend. "I see Penny is taking good care of you."

"Um, maybe you can take over," Penny says. She edges away, aware how taken I am with Wren.

Wren tilts her head. "I don't want to step all over your pitch," she says.

"You're not," she responds. "I'll take the next one. Honest."

Wren waits for Penny to leave before turning to face me. She considers me a moment, but then motions back to the Explorer. "This is the latest model in Ford luxury," she begins. "Comfortable, secure, capable of meeting all your commuting needs, and packed with plenty of toys."

I follow her as she leads me around the vehicle. The ease of her speech and relaxed posture demonstrate a confident woman who knows her job well. I question her about the vehicle's basics first: mileage, warranty, and safety features, before testing her intelligence further. She doesn't disappoint, explaining everything in detail down to the engine's construction, adding to my growing attraction.

"Would you like to take her for a ride?" she asks. She punches my arm affectionately, the motion only briefly luring my attention away from her delicate features. "This way you can see how smoothly she handles the road and ask, 'Wren, how did I ever survive without a Ford?'"

"I'd like that," I answer, my deep voice quieting. This woman who appears more elite model than sales representative knows exactly what she's doing. "Very much."

"Good," she says, pointing at me. "You'll wonder how you ever got along without her."

As I watch her walk away, I start to wonder that myself.

Inseverable

A Carolina Beach Novel

Cecy Robson

PROLOGUE

Callahan

Three days.

That's all I have left until this shit ends.

Three days shouldn't feel like forever, not compared to the eight years I've bled to the Army. Thing is, good men have been killed in less time. In as quick as a blink, a squeeze of a trigger, or a small breath right before a grenade blows is all the time it takes to shove someone right out of life and well into death.

That's what makes three days as long as it is. Three days is plenty of time to die.

My eyes tear when the wind picks up and shoots grime through the small hole of my lookout point. This blown out piece of cinderblock is only big enough to allow me a view of the street below, but not so small I don't get smacked in the face with more filth. The tarp flaps above me as I spit out another layer of the dirt-sand mix spackling my teeth. Christ Almighty, I need a swig of the water resting near my elbow. But my thirst, like everything else has to wait.

I have a job to do.

I adjust my hips against the cracked cement of my bed,

bathroom, and home all rolled into one, thankful that the agonizing ache stretching over the lower half of my body has settled into a now familiar numbness.

Out of all the points I'd scouted, and all the accumulated years spent in this position, I should be used to it. And in a strange way, it should almost be home. Yet nothing ever has been home.

But in three days, maybe something finally will be . . .

I shove my thoughts away and breathe as my fellow Rangers stalk along the street. It's then I see them, a mother and daughter walking straight toward my team. Less than one city block separates them from the men counting on me to keep them alive.

The hell? How did they get past the other sniper unreported? Rogers is new on watch. But the quick paces these two are taking should have clued him in that something's up. I train my scope on their faces; their expressions are blank, unreadable. 'Cept that's not what keeps my attention.

The little girl can't be more than five. So why the fuck isn't her mother holding her hand? I lift my radio and bark a warning, dropping it beside me as I lock my scope dead center on the woman's head.

The radio crackles and Modreski chimes in, yelling at his team to hold their positions. He asks me what my plan is, knowing if something's caused the short-hairs on my neck to rise, he and the boys damn well need to listen. But I don't hear him, with a breath and a squeeze of the trigger, I leave a kid without a mother.

Just beneath the sleeve of her *abayah*—the dress completely covering her body—I see it, a detonator that would trigger the explosives likely strapped to her chest. A few Rangers I know—Simons and Boreman, rush forward. I start to mutter a curse, pissed at her for making me shoot her in front of her kid. But the curse lodges in my throat when I see the kid isn't looking at her mother lying next to her dead.

She's watching my advancing team as she lifts the detonator clasped tight in her hand.

CHAPTER 1

Trinity

"Trin! You coming?" Hale calls.

Even over the steady hum of the ocean, his deep voice cuts through the small opening of our lifeguard station.

"I need five more seconds," I yell back, my thick southern accent drawing out each of my words.

"That's what you said nine minutes ago," he complains.

"But I didn't mean it last time," I holler back.

I grin because even though I can't see or hear him, I know he's chuckling, no matter how much he's trying to hold it in. I hurry and finish writing the schedule on the white board and cap the dry erase marker, before tossing it in the small cup holder to join the rest.

No sooner do I reach for my beach bag and throw the sandy thing over my shoulder than the office phone rings.

Most people would run away, ignoring it, after all by now it's seven thirty and way after closing. But I've always been one of those goody-goody responsible types—you know the ones the teachers assign as classroom monitor and who always turned in her library books a day early? What can I say, I'm all about a good time.

I lift the receiver before it finishes ringing. "Magenta Groves Beach Resort, lifeguard station seven, this is Trinity speaking. How may I help you?"

"Trin. Screw the whiteboard and get in the damn car!" Hale yells through the receiver. I whip around as his voice echoes behind me, as well as through the phone. He hops up the steps as he disconnects, laughing like that was the best prank ever.

"Why did you do that?" I ask.

"Because I knew you'd stop to answer the phone, even though the rest of us have been waiting on you."

I pretend to scowl, but don't quite manage. Me and

scowling don't go hand and hand. Life's too short to wrap your mind around everything that's wrong with it. So I grin, because that's something I can do and do well.

"You think you're so smart. Don't you?" I ask, placing the phone back on the charger.

"You forgot good-looking," he says. "But I'll let it slide on account of I'm modest, too."

I laugh, but don't argue—at least about the good-looking part. We've only been back at Kiawah for a week, but already Hale's wavy blond hair has bleached significantly and his skin tone deepened to a light bronze. His steps are slow and purposeful as he crosses the small space separating us and stops in front of me.

"Let's go, Trin," he says, hauling me along. "You've done enough for the day."

I readjust my bag over my shoulder, and follow him out of the office, the usual bounce to my walk kicking in despite my heavy bag.

"Here. I'll take that," Hale offers, reaching for my bag.

I step just out of reach, knowing he has his own stuff to carry. "I've got it, big guy," I tell him.

"You sure?" he slams the door behind us. I stare out to the beach where a young couple is chasing after their little toddler as Hale fumbles with the lock.

"I'm sure," I reply, my attention staying on the young family. "Hey, Hale, you know how I always mind my own business."

"Nope," he says, leading me forward.

"Well, this time I can't," I continue, ignoring his comment. "For your own good, I have to tell you that this maybe your last chance to do something about Becca. The summer hasn't quite started, but it won't be long before it's gone."

"Yeah. I know," he mumbles.

"And?" I ask, turning back to him.

He tugs on my long ponytail. Unlike Becca, my best

friend in the world, I'm neither tall, blonde nor leggy. My hair is as black as midnight in winter, and I'm just barely five feet three. And where her eyes are light and striking mine are a dull brown. But I do have something my bae doesn't have. Freckles. Y'all feel free to envy me at any time.

"Well?" I press. "You going to do something about that girl or aren't you?"

He shoves his key into the pocket of his long red lifeguard shorts and glides the sunglasses perched on top of his head back onto his face. "I guess we'll just have to wait and see," he tells me.

His smirk widens into that grin of his—the one capable of sizzling panties like coals over a fire. I shake my head. "Boy, between that smile of yours and that face it's a wonder Becca's not running to you rather than away."

He flings his arm around my shoulders as our feet dig through the sand. "Now, sugar, I'm sure I don't know what you mean," he says, keeping his grin in a way that tells me he's lying.

"Come on. You can have anyone you want. And if it's Becca, you need to act fast before those girls slapping each other just to lie their beach blankets near your post lead you astray and down a long dark path of sin, sex, and STDs."

"Is that so?" he asks.

"I'm just watching out for you," I say, stepping with him onto the gray weathered steps leading to the lot. "It's the kind of friend I am. You know, the kind who likes to pretend you're still a virgin and not the man whore you've become."

He laughs hard enough to shake us both as we reach the edge of the pier. Ahead of us in the sandy lot, Sean, Mason, and Becca look up from where they've been waiting for us.

Mason's dark skin glistens with sweat, likely from having dragged all the heavy equipment we weren't using back into the shed. But he's got the muscle and the stocky build for it. Poor Sean has the endurance to swim a few miles and back, but his long-limbed body is better suited for reaching things the rest of us can't, and his personality is best for those who don't mind the occasional dip in the gutter and can appreciate his not-always brilliant remarks.

But of course it's Becca Hale hones in on.

I can't blame him. Becca is leaning against the Jeep, poised like Miss America and as alluring as Miss Universe.

"What the fuck's taking y'all so long?" she yells.

But that mouth of hers makes her all Becca, so does that smile that pulls Hale closer.

"You know how she gets," Hale hollers, hooking his thumb my way. "Had to get the floors waxed, the office dusted, and mend that sea gull's broken wing before setting it free."

"You did all that shit?" Sean asks, moving forward. "Man, and here I was thinking you were just working on the schedule."

Mason who tends to be the most serious among us just shakes his head and laughs, because that's what we all do around Sean.

Becca backs away toward the driver's side, keeping her grin as she points to our boys. "Alex Pettyfer, Nathan Owens, Channing Tatum, y'all got the back," she tells them. She grabs my bag and tosses it onto the floor of the passenger side. "You, get to ride with me, cutie."

I almost ask to switch with Alex Pettyfer, aka Hale. But I've known Becca long enough to know something's up. So I hop in the front, barely snapping my seatbelt in place before she shifts in gear and tears out of the lot.

We catch the road leading out of the resort. Mason tugs on my hair just like Hale had, just to say "hi". Like most men I meet, he thinks I'm cute. As in a kid sister or a BFF cute. Not cute as in, "hey how about you let me rip off your thong with my teeth?" You know what I mean? The kind of "cute" that really matters.

I've pretty much resolved myself to BFF status, even though I wish I could be more.

Hale, whether because of what I said, or because he realizes time is running out for him to make a move, leans in between the seats, his attention fixed on Becca. Unlike me, that's not sand filling out the cups in her swimsuit.

"Hey, Becks, how about we catch dinner Tuesday after work? Maybe even a movie?"

Becca's wild hair—highlighted in alternating shades of blonde and blonder—slaps around her gorgeous features as she grins. "I don't know. The boss may not like me dating a co-worker." She looks at me then. "Isn't that right, Boss?"

I crack up. All my lifeguards can do whatever they want during their time off. But these four in particular? These four that have been my friends since before any of us learned to read, swim, or cuss. I know they're a good bunch. I know they have my back. For all we joke, the minute their toes dig into that smooth white sand, it's on.

I perch my legs up and over the dash and cross my arms behind my head. "As your fearless leader, I hereby let that be your call, ma'am."

Okay. Maybe I'm not so fearless. And "leader" is a pretty loose title considering all I do is run a few drills each day and make sure everyone has a shift.

"I'll think about it," is all Becca tells him.

Hale is a good guy. Good enough to slink back and give her space. Like all my male besties, he's had a crush on Becca since he hit puberty and his male parts saluted her in celebration. Capable of stirring erections with a single glance was Becca's super power. Mine is the ability to make people snort drinks through their noses at my jokes. I adjust my head beneath my hand after another glance at my beautiful friend. We all have our gifts, and if mine includes making others smile, I can't complain.

Her grin widens as she takes the road that leads to Your Mother's Coconuts, better known to the locals as "Your Mother's". Once off the resort we're no longer lifeguards expected to abide by the rules. We're just fresh college grads ready to run amuck, do some skinny-dipping, and partake in all the fun our young selves demand.

In less than a minute, Becca is screeching to a halt at the far end of the half-filled lot. It is a quarter to eight on a Friday and our work week is done. With a hoot and a few hollers, our buddies jump out the back, rousing the other lifeguards who beat us here to do the same.

"Where the hell have y'all been?" the new girl calls out. "I'm thirsty."

Sean holds his hands out. "Then what're you newbies waiting for? Order up the first round."

"Us?" she asks, looking at her friend. "*We* have to pay?"

"Damn straight, yeah," Sean says like it's obvious. "Everyone knows virgins always buy the first round. Ain't that right, boys?"

The rest of my team, even those loitering on the outside deck, start chanting "virgins, virgins, virgins," pumping their fists in the air.

"Aw, hell," her friend says. "Come on. Let's go get our cherries popped."

They walk in, but we don't follow. Becca's made no move to slip out so I know she means to talk. I smile softly. "What's up?"

She looks to the ocean, where the waves sweep in to bathe the sand with all its salty heaven. But I doubt she really sees it, even though like me, Kiawah is a part of her. She crinkles her nose and then takes my hand. "Last summer," she says.

"Yeah, last one," I answer quietly, knowing how she feels because I'm feeling it, too. I squeeze her hand, my tone mirroring all the emotions fluttering inside me. "Time to grow up, right?"

"I wish we didn't have to," she mumbles, keeping her stare on the sea as if trying to gather some strength from it. "You still serious about applying to the Peace Corps?"

I was hoping we didn't have to have this conversation any time soon, but I've kept things from her long enough. "I applied over winter break, Becks."

Her mouth slowly falls open. "I told you to wait—to not do something drastic just because of what those doucheheads did to you."

The "douchebeads" she's referring to are Hunter, my ex-boyfriend, and Blakeney, my ex-friend. They once held my heart, until I caught them in bed and they ripped it from my chest.

Her words chip away at me. Not because I'm not over Hunter, or Blakeney. I am. I'm just not over their betrayal. I could never hurt anyone I claimed to love or called a friend. But they didn't feel the same.

I try to smile, knowing Becca needs my reassurance. But I can't quite manage this time. "You know I've always talked about going and serving. Ever since I was little."

"So you're telling me, if he'd stayed faithful and been a real man instead of a little bitch—if you'd agreed to marry him like he kept talking about—that you still would have signed up to join the Corps? Come on, Trin. Finding him fucking Blakeney was like a pen being slapped in your hand, forcing you to sign on that dotted line."

"No, it wasn't," I insist.

I don't want tonight to be about the bad things of the past. Not with the five of us together after too many months apart. But here we are, focusing on things I've tried hard to forget. "Becks, as much as I thought I loved Hunter, and as much as I believed that he wanted to marry me, I realize now we never would have worked out. I'm going into the Peace Corps, exactly like I've always planned. But knowing who he is—who he *really* is—he wouldn't have waited for me, and he sure as anything wouldn't have joined up just to be with me."

Even through her sunglasses, I can tell Becca's eyes are narrowing. "He's still a douche head, and so is she."

"I won't argue with you about that," I tell her. My head falls against the seat rest. Do you want to know something about Becca? She's sweeter than maple syrup and about as kind as people get. Until you hurt someone she loves. I'm among the lucky few she loves. But it's because she loves me, that she reacts the way she does.

She pushes her sunglasses up to her head, pegging me with enough disappointment to make me ache. "When do you leave?" she asks.

"September. But I won't know my placement for another few weeks." I answer so softly, I'm not sure if she hears, but her tensing posture assures me she does. "Daddy used his connections at the UN and arranged it so I'd have time to take my boards and have one last summer here with all of you."

"So from Princeton to the Peace Corps. From rich kid, to just another volunteer. "She sighs in that way she does when she's trying not to cry. "Nice," she says, not that she means it.

My attention falls to our hands and to how hard she's holding me. "It's the right thing to do, Becks," I tell her.

"Helping people *is* the right thing to do. Signing up for twenty-five months with no way out, that's above and beyond." She shakes her head. "Hunter and Blakeney are assholes for what they did to you."

They are. But she needs to know that's not why I applied. "Becks, it's time to grow up and move forward, and to do the things we've always planned."

"What if I don't want to?" Her voice splinters and tears glisten her eyes. "What if none of us do? I don't want life to go on without the five of us together—you, me, Sean, Mason, and Hale—especially you, Trin."

Like me, she wishes she could stop time, and that somehow things could be different. But somethings can't be helped, and this is one of them.

Her parents and mine had offered to send us backpacking across Europe, but we chose to come back here. Back home to spend one last summer doing what we loved, and to pretend to be forever young, forever free of life's demands, forever friends. As I look to my pseudo sister, I swallow hard and hope that the latter stays true.

Tears trickle down her cheeks, causing my eyes to sting. But Becks doesn't need me crying with her. Right now, she needs my strength, and maybe a little of my humor.

"*Trin, Becks*!" Sean hollers from the deck. "What the hell? We've got shots waiting and horny women who can't wait to have a piece of me."

"Sorry!" I yell, hopping out of the jeep. "Becca dared me to spell my name across her belly with my tongue and I couldn't refuse."

Instead of taking it for the joke it is, Sean freezes. "No, shit," he says.

Becca doubles over, practically falling out of the driver's side seat. I hurry around to steady her and lead her forward. Sean continues to stare at us, his eyes clouded with whatever dirty thoughts are swimming through his mind as we stumble into Your Mother's.

My laughter fades as I look to where the rustic blue double doors open up to the rear deck. But I'm not staring at Hale as he points to his raised shot glass filled to the rim, or at Mason who's smiling politely at the women admiring his muscles. And my, I barely notice Sean shooting past us.

I'm too busy gaping at the smoking hot bartender with the Army Ranger tat inked to an arm as thick as my thigh.

Holy Baby Jesus in a manger sleeping on a bed of hay.

"Hmm," Becca says in a purr. She leans in close to whisper in my ear. "Who do we have here?"

Brown strands of wavy hair spill around his strong features and startling light eyes, and a thin beard lines a jaw I could probably pound horseshoes on. If I knew anything about horseshoes. Or horses. Or, pardon me, what was my name again?

Not to be rude, or inappropriate—I do have morals, after all—but that tight blue shirt stretching across his broad chest is one pec flex shy of ripping in half. Or me ripping it in half when I straddle him.

"You want to straddle him?" Becca asks, a delighted gleam fixing on her face.

I look at her, realizing I spoke out loud. "No?"

She busts out laughing. This time, she's the one dragging me forward. "Come on, Trin. Time to have fun."

We stroll toward the hot guy. Or as I call him, 'my future baby daddy' because for the first time in too long I'm looking—we're talking full-out gawking—at a man. He has my attention and whether he means to or not he's not letting go.

I smile his way, not because of what he looks like, but because I can't seem to help myself. I think maybe Becca smiles at him, too. But "sex in a tight T-shirt" isn't impressed by her charm, and he sure isn't captivated by mine. He scowls—as in *scowls*—which of course earns him a wink from me.

Hey, sticks and stones, or whatever, I'm going to get this guy to smile. Even if it's clear he doesn't want to smile at me.

Eternal

A Carolina Beach Novel

Cecy Robson

CHAPTER ONE

Landon

The wind picks up, brushing the gritty sand along the shore in that graceful way it only seems to do during winter. Kiawah is always bustin' at the seams in the summer, drawing tourists from as close as North Carolina to as far as Sweden.

I take a long pull of my beer and dig my feet further into the sand. This time of year there are two a kinds of people: the locals and lonely. I was always the former and only mildly entertained the latter. That changed when I caught my wife blowing her manager with the same wild enthusiasm she blew me.

"God damn it," I mutter.

I'm not sure which part was more disturbing. Her blowing him in the kitchen, the same place we'd fucked earlier that morning, or her finishing him off while I stood there like an idiot.

I'm going to go with her finishing him off.

I can still picture her rising from her kneeling position, the front of the four hundred dollar blouse she insisted on buying flapping open and exposing her bare breasts with each step she took.

"It didn't mean anything, Landon," she told me, wiping

her mouth with the back of her hand.

Maybe. But his teeth meant something to him. I could tell by the way he kept batting at his face, looking for them when the police finally pulled me off him.

The pathetic way he looked bordered on comical. Shit, the whole damn thing was comical. I might have even laughed if my heart wasn't busy joining his teeth on the floor.

Bernadette wasn't a perfect person. I knew that long before I put a ring on her finger. But I'm not either so I thought we'd be perfect together. She needed someone to help her, to take care of her, and I was willing to do it. Hell, I was willing to do anything for her.

Up until that moment when I found her on her knees.

Call me a fool in love.

But don't make me look like one.

I push my half-drunk bottle into the sand, reminding myself it's been a year, and it's time to move on. Sounds great in theory, but pride to a man is as important as working hard, decency, and family. That's how I was raised. That's how it should be. Bernadette, however brief, was family. She kicked at my pride almost as hard as I nailed Blaze (nice fucking name by the way) in the nuts. All that left me to do was work hard, and damn, didn't I give that shit my all?

The wind picks up, stirring swirls of yellow and sending them to ghost over the water. Mother Nature is doing her best to soothe me, reminding me of the peace and quiet I need and pulling my focus to the vast ocean and the cresting the waves that build and crash along the shore.

Peace, I repeat in my head.

"Quiet," I say out loud.

"Trin," I mumble when my phone vibrates in my back pocket.

I pull it out, sure enough it's my baby sister Trinity. The peace and quiet on Kiawah is no match for her. "Yeah?"

"Now, Landon," she says, her South Carolina accent as thick as mine. "Is that anyway to say hello?"

She doesn't wait for me to answer. "What if I was Miss Universe, calling to tell you I had the cure for diabetes, and whether or not I shared it with the world depended on how you answered the phone? Wouldn't you feel bad that all those people out there with diabetes wouldn't have a cure because you answered the phone with 'Yeah?' sounding broodier than shit, crankier than a leprechaun shoved up some poor unsuspecting bull's ass, and about as pleasant as the matador trying to coax him out—"

"What hell does that even mean, Trin?"

"It means you should go to Becca's New Year's Eve party tomorrow night," she explains like it's obvious.

"I'm busy," I tell her.

"Doing what? Besides drinking a beer and looking at an ocean that's not going anywhere?"

I pinch the bridge of my nose, muttering a curse when she plops down beside me.

Like me, she's barefoot. Most people wouldn't dare walk on the beach in the middle of winter. But ever since we were little, Trin and I have always loved the feel of sand sliding beneath our feet, even in the cold.

Her jeans are rolled up like mine and she's wearing a heavy coat like me. Hers is burgundy, mine is navy. I didn't bother with a hat. She did, a gray beanie tight enough to keep her long black hair away from her pixie face. Even after having my nephew, she's still thin, lacking the muscle that's keeping me warm.

She motions to my beer. "Landon, where are your manners? Aren't you going to offer me a drink? I am a lady after all." She huffs. "Your momma raised you better than that."

I pass her the bottle. She takes a sip and makes a face. "It's warm."

"I kept rolling it in my hands," I admit. "I suppose it's hard to keep it cold that way, even in forty-degree weather."

She nods like she understands. "How long have you been out here?"

I lie. "Not long."

"How long have you been out here?"

I smirk. "A while."

"How *long*, have you been out here?"

"I guess long enough."

I start to stand when her thin arms wrap around me, keeping me in place. "Landon, as your favorite and only sister on God's green earth, I owe it to tell you that dark, hairy, and cranky doesn't fit you." She rubs the scruff on my jaw like she's trying to swipe it off. "Lord, it's like an opossum crawled up your chest and spit out a litter of babies across your jaw."

I edge away. "Your husband has the same damn beard," I remind her.

"Oh, that's not true." She smiles and turns her attention toward the ocean, her stare getting that dream-like look it always gets when she thinks of Callahan. "My man's beard is all alpha and sexy." She makes a face. "Yours is, well, possumy." She holds out her hand. "And if that's not a word, it should be. At least when it comes to whatever the hell is on your face."

"Trin, if you're trying to use your charm to talk me into going to Becca's party, it's not working."

"Why? She was nice enough to invite you." She shrugs. "Besides, it's almost New Year's Eve. Time for a fresh start and a new beginning."

Her voice quiets at her last few words. She doesn't mention Bernadette. But after this year, I suppose I've mentioned her enough, and so has Trin.

If hate were a super-power, Trin's hate for Bernadette would have crushed the Fortress of Solitude and slapped Superman upside the head for being a little bitch. And Trin, she likes everyone.

My family is from money. It's not something I really think about, or obsess over it, it's just always been there. We were taught to take care of it, add to it, but most of all be generous with it, since we had so much. Maybe that's why it was easy for me to give as much as I did to Bernadette. I wanted to see her happy and maybe give her the life she always dreamed of. But where Trin and our Momma would drop a few grand setting up and auction to help raise money for the children's hospital, Bernadette would drop a few grand on herself.

My parents insisted on an air-tight pre-nup. It pissed me off at the time, especially since they didn't insist the same thing when Trin was marrying Callahan. But they saw Bernadette for who she was, not like me. Love makes you blind, but it doesn't make you deaf when the woman you thought you knew calls you a wife-beater to your face.

It should have been an easy divorce. Sign here, initial there, and walk away. Instead I dropped close to a hundred grand defending the abuse charges she filed against me.

"He's always been violent," she cried to the judge. "Look at what he did to my manager."

Her attorney was more than happy to present the pictures of her manager's busted up face and put the police officers who responded on the stand. Those fine members of law enforcement admitted they pulled me off Blaze (again, nice fucking name), but they were more than happy to mention Blaze's pants and drawers were down to his ankles when they found him.

"Landon," Trin says, her voice sad.

It's never a good sign when my sister grows quiet, and the way she wraps her arms around mine and leans her head against my shoulder. The last time she did that, our granddaddy Palmer had passed.

She knows I'm remembering, and she doesn't like it one bit.

It was bad enough Bernadette had accused me of hitting her, something I'd never do to any woman for any reason. But to try to make me out to look like a monster, and get all the gossip mags talking about Landon Summers, wealthy son of Owen and Silvia Summers, accused of threatening his wife's life, and soiling the Summers' name, it was more than I could take. She wasn't messing with me she was messing with my folks, two of the best, most generous people I know.

"She said I was hitting her," I say aloud, before giving it too much thought.

"I know," Trin says. She adjusts her hold. "But Landon, anyone who knows you didn't believe her."

"But there are a lot of people who don't know me, Trin."

She sighs. "I know that, too."

The waves start drawing closer, but it's not until a large one slaps hard against the shore that she speaks again. "Did she ever hit you?"

I don't bother telling her about all the shit Bernadette threw at me: her hair dryer, the damn crystal jewelry box, or all those dishes she smashed when she wasn't getting her way. But I don't need to. When Trin lifts her head, it's clear she knows enough. "Landon, why didn't you say anything?"

"I couldn't do that to her."

Trin scrambles to her feet, knocking over the beer, her face pink with rage. "But she did it to you—even when it wasn't true!"

"That doesn't make it right," I say. "To be accused of something like that, it's total horseshit."

"Horseshit she was more than happy to fling your way." Her breaths come quick. "She didn't even blink on that stand. You saw that, right? She wanted money and she didn't care what she had to do to get it."

Which was why I spent all that money on lawyer's fees. No way was I giving her more than she was entitled to after she pulled that.

"You should have said something," she says again.

"Anything I said would have made me look weaker than I already was." I shake my head. "Trin, when a man marries a woman who looks like Bernadette, he's supposed to keep her happy at all costs, and in every way possible. If she's fucking around on him, and other men find out, they don't care that you gave her a home, more money than she needed, or that you'd protect and look after her with your life. They assume you weren't man enough where it counted, and where it counts is in the fucking bedroom."

"You're not weak." It's what she tells me, but the way she says it, I think she understands as much as she can.

I tilt the bottle, letting what little beer that remains pour into the sand. "It sure didn't feel like that when I found her, and who I found her with."

The foam dissipates, like it never was. It reminds me too much of my marriage, making me mad, bitter, and probably sad too, despite that I'm tired of feeling all three.

I rise and brush the sand off my jeans. "One drink," she says.

I do a double take. "Now?"

She shakes her head, looking about as happy as I do. "No. Tomorrow night, at Becca's. One drink, a few hellos, and then you can leave." She inches up to me. "Please, Landon. Show me and everyone that's there you're okay." She smiles although the worry behind it dulls her soft brown eyes in the setting sun. "Even though you may not be."

I'm ready to tell her to go home and be with her husband and child, and that she's wasting her time. But Trin, she's trying, and the only person I've allowed in this whole year.

"It's just down the beach," she says like I already don't know. "C'mon, Landon. What could happen?"

What *could* happen? It's what I thought. The thing was, everything did.

Photo by Kate Gledhill of Kate Gledhill Photography

CECY ROBSON is a new adult and contemporary author of the Shattered Past series, the O'Brien Family novels and Carolina Beach novels, as well as the award-winning author of the Weird Girls urban fantasy romance series. A 2016 double nominated RITA® finalist for Once Pure and Once Kissed, Cecy is a recovering Jersey girl living in the South who enjoys carbs way too much, and exercise way too little. Gifted and cursed with an overactive imagination, you can typically find her on her laptop silencing the yappy characters in her head by telling their stories.

www.cecyrobson.com

Facebook.com/Cecy.Robson.Author

instagram.com/cecyrobsonauthor

twitter.com/cecyrobson

www.goodreads.com/CecyRobsonAuthor